Alison Hill is a new Scottish writer who studies history, myths and legends told around Scotland. When not looking after her grandchildren, she travels around Scotland with her dogs, collecting local information and stories about the areas she visits. She lives in Edinburgh.

To my brother in law, Michael, who took time out to read and critique my manuscript.

Alison Hill

SEAL LODGE OF KINTYRE

REVIEW COPY
Not For Resale

AUSTIN MACAULEY PUBLISHERS™
LONDON • CAMBRIDGE • NEW YORK • SHARJAH

A CIP catalogue record for this title is available from the British Library.

ISBN 9781788238021 (Paperback)
ISBN 9781788238038 (Hardback)
ISBN 9781788238045 (E-Book)
www.austinmacauley.com

First Published (2018)
Austin Macauley Publishers Ltd™
25 Canada Square
Canary Wharf
London
E14 5LQ

Acknowledgements

I would like to thank the people of Southend at the Mull of Kintyre. The Taylor sisters who ran Keil Hotel, that I based Seal lodge on, during the sixties. I stayed there twice as a child and have not forgotten the adventures we had there.

I would also like to thank Frances and Ian Hill who run Munaroy shop and tearoom, firstly for the fantastic slice of chocolate cake, but secondly for selling me a local book about Southend, with photographs of the Keil Hotel, as it used to be.

This story is completely fictional from my imagination, but my imagination would never have been inspired if I had never visited Southend.

Birlinn Colla Ciotach

Ho ree, ho ree ah, horan ah horan oh,
I see thy lone barque on the wild Mull of Oa,
O Colla, mo ghra, sacred theme of my woe,
Be ye daring and brave, for fierce is thy foe!

Be ye daring and brave, for fierce is thy foe,
Swift, smoothly she sails; the fair galley oh ho!
She cleaves the white spray o'er the mad racing foam,
She stems the huge wave; billows rave at her prow.

Duncan Johnston (1881–1947)

Prologue

In February 1623, Colla Ciotach's galley slid into a small, hidden harbour on the southern tip of Oronsay. Colla and his men had created the harbour there, as they had done on many of the islands in the Inner Hebrides. These ports had been a necessity in his pirate days when he raided Campbell strongholds on the islands, challenging their authority under the name of MacDonald. Colla was a giant of a man and was known for being ambidextrous, although he favoured his left hand when using his great claymore, it earnt him the nickname Colkitto, meaning crafty, left-handed Coll. The MacDonalds had been Lairds of the Isles for centuries, and Colla, in his younger days, felt wronged when the islands were signed over to the Duke of Argyll.

Colkitto was rightfully feared by many, and it was believed he could cleave a man in half with one swing of his claymore. Now at 53 years old, he was the official landlord of Colonsay. Colla paid a substantial rent to the Duke of Argyll so that he, his family and the other MacDonald residents could live there under his protection as Laird of Colonsay.

That protection had been challenged in 1618 by the last chieftain of the MacPhees, Malcolm MacDuffie, who laid claim to Colonsay on the basis that the MacPhees had lived there as land owners for centuries. His claim was denied and although the MacDonalds and the MacPhees seemed to get along quite well initially, a bitter feud grew between Malcolm MacDuffie and Colla Ciotach.

Over the last five years, Colkitto had been finding it difficult to maintain the peace between the two clans. As landlord, he was responsible for the maintenance of public peace on his island, but matters had finally come to a head. MacDuffie assaulted one of Colla's daughters in a drunken stupor and Colla decided that the red-headed MacPhee chieftain had insulted his family for the last time. Although Colla was a patient man by all accounts, he would stand for it no longer and he ordered Malcolm MacDuffie to be brought to him.

MacDuffie went on the run, managing to stay hidden, even though Colla and his men searched the length and breadth of Colonsay. The boats were carefully guarded so MacDuffie could not escape, but he had been seen crossing the strand to Oronsay in the early hours of the morning.

Whilst a small army of MacDonalds followed him across the strand, Colla and ten of his men, including his son, Gillespie, sailed his galley to the south of Oronsay in case MacDuffie had some means of escape from the island. When they arrived, they could see no sign of any other boat, so Colla and his men jumped off the galley, then searched the beaches at the southern end of the island.

The MacPhee chieftain hid under a pile of seaweed until the tide got low, then he took a chance and swam out to Eileen Nan Ron (Seal Island). He was spotted making his way across the water. Colla ordered his men to get into their small boats to search every inch of Eileen Non Ran coastline. They were about to give up as the currents were strong, so they thought he had drowned. Then suddenly, a seagull screeched and flew startled from a rock at the edge of the ocean.

Thomas McGilvray spotted him first, hanging onto the lip of the rock covered in seaweed. They hauled him from the water, dragging the last chieftain of the MacPhees back to Colonsay, where he was tied to a standing stone in Church Meadow and shot twice with a musket.

Colla Ciotach remained in charge of Colonsay for another few years, but his authority would be challenged again; his old adversaries, the Campbells, would once again hear the Highlander warrior cry from the legend that is Colkitto.

("Mercy, Thomas," cried MacPhee to Thomas McGilvray, who was first to see him.

"Mercy indeed," replied Thomas, "it's little mercy would be got from your red whiskers this time yesterday.")

Donald MacKinnon (1839–1914)

Chapter One

Kate MacPhee swung her car right onto the single lane road that led to the Skipness ferry. It was the last week in September and the trees were still green, just getting ready to turn. The ferry port itself was nothing more than a concrete driveway down to the water, with allocated car parking numbers painted on the road for easy boarding. It was just a small ferry that came from Arran to Skipness, maybe only 30 cars or so, compared to the much bigger Ardrossan ferry that went from the other side of the island to the mainland, which was more of a ship, with a restaurant, a bar and even a pet's room. This Skipness ferry to Arran did what it said on the ticket, took you across and no more. If you wanted to brave the elements, then you could climb up the narrow metal staircase from the car deck and stand on the wooden outdoor deck area and take in the view of the Mull of Kintyre and the Firth of Clyde. A beautiful and dramatic coastline, if not obscured by mist and fog, which were not unusual.

Kate loved standing on the deck in most weathers, but today, it was torrential rain, so she remained in her car with her little dog Gizmo snuggled in the seat next to her and reread the letter she had received. A handwritten letter was unusual these days, most people sent emails, and when she had found it in her mail box at her beautiful home near Carradale on the Mull peninsula, she was intrigued to say the least.

The letter was post marked Brighton, and as soon as she had opened it, a photograph tumbled out from the pages. She picked up the photo, which was an old black and white, and looked at the picture of an attractive young woman with huge dark eyes, dark hair piled on top of her head with a very serious looking expression. She was dressed in '50s style clothing and had her arm protectively around a small boy who was standing next to her. He too had similar dark features, but he was smiling happily up at the woman, whom Kate guessed to be his mother. Puzzled, Kate had read the letter.

Dear Kate

I can imagine the surprise on your face receiving this letter from your old friend Hamish, still reminiscing about our student days when we worked at the Granary Bar at the Hilton Hotel in Edinburgh. We had some great nights, especially during the jazz festival. Now I can hear your mind rattling and wondering why on earth I am writing to you.

Well, I managed to put my wild side to bed years ago, and I now have a GP practice in Brighton, along with a wife and two kids to boot. Yesterday, a man named Jamie MacDonald came to my surgery. I remembered him from my university days in Edinburgh, but he wanted to talk about you as he apparently had met you one night when we were working at the bar in Edinburgh. It was a night we were working together, so he guessed that I knew you quite well. You can imagine my embarrassment that one of my patients remembers my antics back in those days. The less said about that, the better!

He handed me this photo and said it was a picture of his father and grandmother. He had never met them and had not even known his real father was alive until a solicitor had contacted him a couple of weeks before. Apparently, his father had died, leaving him an old hotel named 'Seal Lodge' in Southend, right at the end of the peninsula of the Mull of Kintyre.

It is a ruin now and condemned to be pulled down. Along with the hotel, he was left a substantial amount of money with a request that the hotel be rebuilt and reopened.

By all accounts, Jamie is an architect and is very interested in the project. He read a magazine article about your books and the amount of historical research you have done in Scotland for your novels. He also saw that you reside on the Mull and wondered if I was still in touch with you, which I told him, sadly, I wasn't, though I could probably find your address through an old acquaintance and I would write to you on his behalf. He would like to know more about his father's family and has asked me to enclose this photo of his father as a boy. His father's name was Ewan MacDonald and his last known address was in Morningside in Edinburgh.

Jamie seems like a really nice guy and is very keen to find out as much as he can. He never knew his father, so it has all come as a huge shock to him. He is currently finalising a project he is doing here in Brighton and then has cleared his calendar for the next few months to travel up to Scotland to see if this project is viable. I hope you don't mind that I wrote, I am rather curious myself about the background to all this and also, I'm a little nosy, and I would like to know how you are faring. I saw the sad news about your husband's accident and want to say how sorry I am. Isn't it funny how life can sometimes go full circle and bring back old friends? I've enclosed my phone number if you want any more information. I said I would wait until I hear from you before I give Jamie any contact details.

Your long-lost friend,
Hamish.

Kate smiled to herself, she and Hamish had been close friends back then. They had been good days, working till three in the morning sometimes, especially during the festival, and then up for uni the next morning. She shuddered at the thought of doing it now. There had been five of them working, all good friends. Hamish was the comedian of the group, even though he was the smartest of all of them. The only one Kate had stayed in contact with was Cathy, who had been into sports in a big way. She had represented Scotland in the ladies rowing team in the Commonwealth games and then gone on to be a sports writer. She still lived in Edinburgh and Kate saw her every time she visited her flat there. Kate herself was a bit of a wild child, always planning adventures, and had many dreams of travelling the world. She had done a journalist degree, then took off travelling soon after graduating. She spent two years working her way around many different countries, it was a magical and adventurous time. She wrote many journals, as well as many letters, keeping in touch with all her friends. This was a time before internet, mobile phones and emails, so letters would take weeks to arrive. Eventually, as time drifted on, the letters became less frequent and Kate lost touch with many old friends, everyone getting caught up in their own busy lives.

Kate sighed, if only she had realised then how much it was important to stay in touch with people, it was something she would always regret. Her mind went back to what had brought her to the Mull eventually, it seemed like a long journey from the days of the Granary Bar in Edinburgh.

She had married an American, Tom, she had met him whilst travelling and lived in the States for a while. Whilst Tom was at work, she had taken to writing whilst waiting for a green card to enable her to get a job over there and soon had published her first novel. She couldn't believe her luck and could only assume that the publisher had liked her Scottish connection, which was why he took a chance.

Her book was a romantic thriller set in Scotland and it went on the bestseller list on both sides of the Atlantic. From then on, she never looked back. Six books later, she should have been living the dream, but Tom had been killed in his small plane whilst flying at Anaheim Airport in California. He had collided with a flock of seagulls on take-off, tried to land, but, unfortunately, one propeller was badly damaged, making his descent uneven and his wing hit the tarmac, flipping the small plane, which exploded as it hit the ground.

That had been three years ago, Kate had been devastated, of course, and after being consoled by her friends and her husband's family, she realised she no longer wanted to remain in California and returned home to Edinburgh. After a few days with her parents and her friends, she felt the need for solitude and decided to take a road trip. She needed to breathe and she was also looking for some inspiration for a new novel. She drove across to the west coast on the busy M8 and travelled over the Erskine Bridge to Dumbarton, then carried on up the side of Loch Lomond. Ben Lomond and the surrounding mountains loomed above her and she started to enjoy the drive.

Her plan was to keep on the A82 until she reached Tyndrum, then continue on to the haunting beauty of Rannoch Moor and the majestic mountains of Glencoe, but instead, on a whim, when Kate reached Tarbert, she turned off onto the A83 and headed to Loch Fyne, bringing her to Inveraray. She knew Inveraray was the Clan Campbell's stronghold through the centuries, and as she arrived at the town at the side of the loch, she saw the infamous grey towers of the Campbells' castle on the right. Kate decided to stay for the night in the town and managed to get a room at the George Hotel.

That afternoon, she took a walk and visited the monumental, turreted castle and its spectacular grounds. Kate didn't bother going in, as she had visited it many times as a child during family day trips in the past. Her father had often taken them out on historical journeys around Scotland's west coast. She felt dwarfed by the surrounding mountains and spotted the Campbells Watch Tower set high on the summit of Dun Na Cuaiche. Her father had told her there was a bell there and they would ring it when they spotted enemy clans running over the hills towards them. Her father had always been able to set her imagination on fire with his stories on these trips, though during these last few years, she had come to realise he had added a lot of his own embellishment.

Kate discovered, whilst she researched the area for one of her books, that the watch tower hadn't actually been built until 1748, after the clan's uprisings, and was used mainly for decorative purposes, as well as giving an amazing view of Loch Fyne. It was never manned by Campbell soldiers.

After her walk, Kate went down to the friendly hotel bar and was shown to a seat in front of one of the many roaring fires. She started chatting to some of the locals, who had told her that if she really wanted to explore Scotland, she should try the Mull of Kintyre.

The whole peninsula was etched in history with St Columba's arrival from Ireland back in 563, to many battles between the MacDonald and the Campbell Clans resulting in terrible betrayals and massacres. The views of the Inner Hebrides were supposedly spectacular with the Islands of Jura, Gigha and Islay all seen from the Kintyre coastline, as well as the beautiful Islands of Arran and Bute nestled in the Firth of Clyde on the other side of the peninsula.

Convinced of her route, Kate set off the next day and travelled up the side of Loch Fyne to the colourful town of Lochgilphead, where the road turned around the top of Loch Fyne then went south back down the other side of the loch. She continued down to the picturesque fishing town of Tarbert, still famous for its fishing and the wonderful Loch Fyne oysters.

She was now in the heart of the Kintyre peninsula and she followed the A83 by the sea coast. The views of the Hebrides made her stop many times for photographs, so it was early evening when she arrived at the Argyll Arms hotel in Bellochanthy, which was only six miles from Campbeltown. Luckily, it was winter in the highlands, so there was room at the hotel. Kate imagined it would be packed during the summer, as it was right on the white sandy beach. After a friendly welcome she felt exhausted after her drive, so she ordered some herb-crusted monkfish from the hotel menu and a large glass of pinot.

The next morning, Kate was up early and refreshed. She took a long walk along the beach, bumping into the hotel owner, David, with his two Dalmatians. It was freezing, with a strong head wind blowing off the Atlantic, but the owner was dressed in shorts and a light sweater. David laughed when Kate commented on his attire and told her he wore them all year around, he didn't feel the cold. He walked a little way along the beach with Kate while she told him that she was exploring the area. David suggested she drive over to Southend on the other side of the peninsula, where she could get to the Mull of Kintyre itself. He also recommended a café, the Muneroy Tearoom, the owner was famous in the region for her baking.

An hour later, she was in her car, following the signs until she finally arrived in Southend, where she found a small carpark at the end of the road by some caves. In the carpark was a plaque telling the story of the Dunaverty Massacre which happened in the first half of the 17th century. It was yet another story of the Campbells defeating the MacDonalds using treacherous methods. She turned and could see Dunaverty Rock about a mile away, where once Dunaverty Castle had stood, where the massacre of 300 men, women and children had taken place, earning the rock the name 'Blood Rock'.

Kate decided to go for a walk along Carskiey Beach to take in the view. It was a long, sandy beach and the cold wind was battering her from the sea, so much so, she had to turn out of the wind to catch her breath. Almost immediately, her eyes were drawn to the white ruin of a huge building set into the cliffs, and next to that, there seemed to be a much older ruin of some other building. As Kate looked at them, she decided that at some point, she would investigate further, this was probably the perfect setting for some sort of story, with the ruins, caves and Blood Rock.

There were seals watching her from just beyond where the waves broke, and the weather seemed to change every few minutes. One minute, a ray of golden sunshine would penetrate through white fluffy clouds, making the waters glisten and warming her face. Then a minute later, she found she was looking at black storm clouds, threatening to throw torrential rain at her, but they would disappear as fast as they had arrived. It was breathtakingly cold, but she loved every minute watching the crashing waves hit the shore. When Kate got back in the car, she felt totally invigorated, inspired and more alive than she had felt for months. This was what she had needed.

Deciding to explore further, Kate drove the road from Southend up to a perilous one-track lane that led six miles up Beinn Na Lice Mountain and eventually to the tip of the Mull of Kintyre. It was completely deserted apart from deer and some hardy-looking sheep, who refused to get out of the way of her car, despite honking her horn and yelling at them. They did things in their own time, it seemed. She thanked her lucky stars there had been no snow, or it would have been impossible to drive up there. Finally, she got as far as she could go in the car. The rest of the way would have to be on foot, the road was a good quality tarmac, but so steep it would be like descending a cliff, even though it was paved. It was completely deserted and Kate found herself wondering about the men who must have laid this tarmac on the side of this mountain, they must have been a hardy bunch.

She got out of the car, initially planning to walk down to the lighthouse, but the wind hit her like a mallet of ice, she couldn't see or breathe, and she was back inside her car within 40 seconds of being out there. Standing on the top of a mountain in winter, in Scotland, probably requires some extreme weather gear, which Kate did not possess. Her jeans felt frozen solid just in the few seconds she had been out of her car. She turned on the car heater and looked over to the coast of Ireland, as the Mull of Kintyre was the closest point to Ireland in the UK, only eight miles across. As she sat and warmed up, she spotted a huge bird fly over her car, circling high above the mountains. A Golden Eagle, unmistakable with its wing span, and the first time she had ever seen one in the wild. It was at that moment that Kate decided to stay. She was going to find a property on the Mull peninsula and make it her home, though she would also have to keep her flat in Edinburgh.

She drove straight from the mountain to the biggest town on the peninsula, Campbeltown, and went into the local estate agents. There were quite a few properties, but Kate fell in love with a striking converted chapel near to Carradale, which is an unusual little fishing town on the eastern side of the peninsula, overlooking the Firth of Clyde and the Island of Arran.

The converted chapel had been modernised, with polished wooden floors and huge arched windows that gave great views of Arran and the Firth of Clyde. There were three spacious bedrooms and a huge conservatory that looked out over the beach in front of the house. It was a no-brainer as far as Kate was concerned and before the end of the day, her offer on the property was accepted and she and Gizmo moved in three months later. Gizmo was her five-year-old Jackshit, acquiring that unfortunate name by being half Jack Russell and half Shih Tzu, the result was incredibly cute as far as dogs went, he was white with two black eyes and black ears like a panda.

Kate's parents had been a little concerned when Kate said she was moving down to Kintyre. It was the middle of nowhere as far as they were concerned, but her mind was made up and she and Gizmo settled into their new house very quickly. The days went by with her writing her books while Gizzy was chasing seabirds along the shore. If it wasn't for the midges during the summer months, life would be perfect. But these little blighters were relentless, and Kate looked like a bee keeper on her evening walks, donned in a bee keepers netted hat. She was soon accepted as one of the locals.

The people were honest and friendly, there was a useful library in Campbeltown, and she would go to Tarbert twice a week for fresh fish just off the boat. The fishermen brought their catch and sold it from a lock-up up behind the tourist information centre in Tarbert. It was a secret only known to the locals, so Kate was honoured when she was given local status and told about the place. She had never eaten so much seafood, even in all her years living in California, she had never quite tasted the sweetness of the ocean as she did in these fresh catches from these Scottish fishermen.

So now here she was, on the ferry to Arran, looking at the old photograph in her hand as she thought back to what had brought her here. It was a quiet life, but her days seemed to be filled. She knew she should really put herself out there and maybe start dating again, but she still wasn't ready and was totally comfortable where she was.

Hearing from Hamish had been a blast from the past, and she had phoned him immediately for a long overdue catch up. He had changed so much from the wild, single lady's man he had been back then. He was married, with two children and a cat. She had laughed at that, then even harder when he told her he had also lost his hair. Hamish sent her Jamie's email, Kate decided she would contact him herself, she loved a good mystery and it sounded like they were going to be neighbours anyway. Neighbours on Kintyre can be 30 miles apart.

She looked down at the photo of the beautiful woman with huge dark eyes and the little boy. He must have been about seven years old, dressed in a rough wool sweater and short trousers. She could tell they were related as the boy had the same dark, brooding eyes as what she assumed was his mother. She tucked the photo back inside the envelope.

The ferry horn sounded and the captain's voice came over the speaker, telling them they would be landing at Lochranza shortly. Kate waited until the ferry had docked before she switched her engine on and drove carefully up the ramp and into the small town.

The place was still full of tourists. Arran was a sought-after destination for hikers and cyclists even in mid-winter. The Arran Distillery was a popular place to visit up towards the hills turning left from the ferry terminal. Many tourists would go for a local whiskey tasting and a good hearty lunch. On a day like today, with the weather so poor, the place would be packed with even the most weather hardy opting to have an indoors day.

Kate turned right and was heading towards the south of the island to a tiny place called Pirnmill. She had probably driven through it many times but had not noticed. It wasn't much more than a group of stand alone cottages overlooking the Firth of Clyde.

She had done quite a bit of research on Seal Lodge, which had turned out to be the big white ruin she had seen from Carskiev beach at Southend. Kate had discovered there was a man living on Arran who had worked at the Lodge when the Riley sisters owned it 50-odd years ago. His name was Ronan MacDougall and he was the only local person she could find with any kind of association with the Lodge.

Kate had driven out to the Lodge the day before, although she had seen it many times when she came for her walks along the beach with Gizmo, she hadn't really paid it a lot of attention as it was sealed off from the public. It was a huge white building built into the cliffs, set behind an old graveyard that was the home to St Columba's chapel. The old ruin next to Seal Lodge was actually Keil House, which used to be a school for boys early in the 20th century.

The Lodge was some 200 yards from the road but she couldn't get close to the building as it was surrounded by a huge fence that was topped with barbed wire. It must have been spectacular in its day, but from what she could see, it was in complete shambles and it didn't look like it had a roof. Kate had made a few enquiries in Campbeltown about the hotel, chatting to local shopkeepers she had come to know over the last couple of years, but no one seemed to have much information. Kate was sure she could feel them become uncomfortable as soon as she mentioned the place, which was a little strange for the normally very friendly locals.

It had been built in the 1930s as a hotel by Captain Robert Riley, who had the architect James Austin Laird design this imposing art deco building. It was huge, five storeys high, with the outside painted white, it was an impressive sight from the coastline. Shortly after it was built in 1939, it was requisitioned by the Navy to be used as a

21

military hospital during the Second World War. Eventually after the war two sisters, took over Seal Lodge and ran it for 20 years as a hotel. They had worked as nurses in the hospital during the war, becoming very connected to the place. It was a popular place for the gentry to go fishing and shooting, and the Lodge became known for its fabulous cocktail parties. One of the sisters died suddenly and then the Lodge was sold. The new owners did not have it for long and it was sold another couple of times. There was a rumour of a terrible accident that occurred there, but no one seemed very forth coming about the facts. It was getting clear to Kate that it was a subject the locals did not want to talk about.

Eventually, it became a meeting place for the farmers on a weekend, many walking miles from their farms to have a heavy night out that lasted well into the wee small hours. Jamie's father had acquired the building in the early '90s with the intention of rebuilding; however, circumstances had left the building untouched and it had eventually fallen into disrepair.

The locals were in dispute about whether the building itself was an eyesore or a historical monument. Some local fishermen used the white building on the cliffs as a guide through the fog, as well as the lighthouse on the Mull of Kintyre.

Kate had not been able to find any other information about the hotel. Even her google searches had left her none the wiser. Feeling chilled, she popped into the Muneroy tearoom, which is connected to the general store in Southend. The welcoming smell of sweet, fresh baking hit her as she walked into the quaint little restaurant, which had an open fire burning in the grate. Kate was greeted by Lizzie, the owner and baker behind the delicious smells. She had got to know Lizzie well over the years, as she always stopped here after her walks. Kate was given a pot of hot coffee while Lizzie listed out all the freshly baked cakes that she had been up since 5:30 that morning baking. Unable to resist, Kate opted for the fresh cream butterscotch sponge, which was, without a doubt, the best cake she had ever eaten. The tearoom was decorated in teapots of all shapes and sizes, and from the huge list of cakes that Lizzie had reeled off, and the number of tables with reserved signs on them, Kate knew they were going to be busy later.

Kate had asked Lizzie if she knew much about the Lodge, and thankfully, this time, she wasn't met with cold dismissal. Lizzie sat down with her, happy to share all she knew. Lizzie had known the

Riley sisters and clearly had a real love for the old building. She also knew Ewan, Jamie's father, from the photograph Kate showed her, and was excited to find out that he had bought the place and given it to Jamie. The locals had all been wondering who now owned it. Lizzie was a child when the sisters ran the hotel, but she knew of a man who worked for the sisters back in the '50s and '60s. He had retired and lived on Arran now. She gave Kate his name and told her where he lived. "It would be awfie nice tae see that old place restored. We had some real hoots there back in the day," said Lizzie as she walked Kate to the door and waved her off.

Kate found Ronan's phone number and called him when she got home. He was delighted to hear from her and invited her over to hear all about the Lodge. So here she was, driving her four by four along the windy road around Arran's coastline, taking in the palm trees that seemed out of place on a Scottish island. Yet the warmth of the tropical Gulf Stream that flowed through the west coast of Scotland enabled the palm trees to flourish there. It took her 15 minutes from the ferry to reach Pirnmill.

She parked her car easily in the designated parking area next to the stony beach which was glistening with its colourful pebbles in the rain. She saw Ronan's cottage as he had described it. Set further back from the road than the rest, a small white building surrounded with pebbles from the beach, so she left Gizmo in the car, where he was happily curled up in his cosy bed, and walked up the lane to the house. The old man was waiting by the window and he gave her a wave then came to the door and swung it open.

Chapter Two

"What a day tae be visiting, come on in oot the rain, ye'll catch yer death!" said Ronan MacDougall, gesturing Kate to come inside. He was tall, towering over Kate and he had a full head of wild white hair and bright-blue Celtic eyes that shone through his glasses. Kate liked him on sight, he had a grandfather type of warmth about him and she found it hard to guess his age, probably somewhere in his 80s. Kate took his huge hand in greeting as she entered the house and Ronan helped her off with her coat, then hung it on a magnificent-looking, carved and polished wooden coat stand.

"Crivens, yer dripping wet already, come through tae the parlour, I have the kettle on," he said as she followed him through to a small, ornate room. It had floral wallpaper and a floral-covered settee with two matching chairs. There was a serving trolley covered in paper doylies with two teacups complete with matching saucers, a bowl of sugar and a jug of milk. There was also a three-tier cake stand with small sandwiches, shortbread and homemade tablet.

"My wife made the tablet and the shortbread," he said when he saw her look at the trolley.

"Is your wife here?" Kate asked, hoping the poor lady wasn't hiding in a back room somewhere.

"Ach, I told her tae gae oot. I didnae need her overhearing all these stories of the old Lodge again. I'd never hear the end of it, she says, I just blether nonsense half the time," Ronan replied, offering Kate the seat next to the trolley, before disappearing into the kitchen.

Kate felt at home already, he was so welcoming, and truth be told, she was a little bit hungry. He came back minutes later with teapot covered in a brightly knitted tea cosy. He poured the tea and handed her a cup.

"So, ye said on the phone that ye wanted tae ken aboot the Lodge. I spent over 20 good years there wi the Riley sisters when they had it. It wis a big old place and I kept it ticking over nicely fir them," he said, slowly lowering himself onto one of the floral chairs.

"Yes, I've been trying to help the new owner get some perspective on the place. It seems like it must have a lot of history connected to it, and I think it would help him to know what the place was about when it comes to rebuilding it," Kate replied.

"Rebuild it! I wudnae have thought I'd see that in my lifetime," said Ronan, surprised. "I've bin expecting them tae tear it doon these last few years. Naebody goes up there anymore, it's bin ransacked by thieves with all the copper wiring ripped oot, along with any metal fitting that were lying aroond. Of course, ye'll ken aboot the haunted hoose stories that fly aroond the place," he said with his eyes fixed intensely on Kate's face. "There's a lot of ghosts on that part of Kintyre."

"I think he is aware of the amount of work that will be needed, but ghosts haven't been mentioned as far as I'm aware. No one said the place was haunted when I asked around in Campbeltown," Kate replied, already intrigued.

"Aye, well they wudnae, they're all feart. There have been so many deaths on that side of the Mull spanning centuries. Brutal murders and betrayals involving many clans, ancestors of some of the folks who live on Kintyre. Nae one blethers aboot the past, it's all deep rooted in bitterness. Ye will be hard pressed tae find a Campbell living doon in these parts," Ronan told her.

Kate smiled, she had come across a lot of hostility towards the Campbells in many parts of Scotland during her research over the years. They had been held responsible for siding with the English armies and massacring many of the highland clans. Old stories don't fade in the highlands of Scotland, even hundreds of years later. Kate had once come across a small hotel just north of Oban that refused to allow guests with the name Campbell stay there.

"I saw ghosts many times whilst working at Seal Lodge," Ronan continued. "Clan armies strolling doon on the beach in the mists, bloody and battered, heading fir the caves. I've seen raggerty women and their bairns standing in the graveyard, staring up at the Lodge, as if we had nae right tae be there."

"You must have been scared," said Kate, intrigued by the story.

"Nae, I wasnae feart. The Lodge shudnae bin built there, strange things happened inside that hotel. The Riley sisters didnae seem tae pay attention and blamed the staff for their wild imaginations when they said the lights were flickering and the fires were lighting themselves in the grates. I told them that it wasnae the staff and that the place wis haunted, but they'd just say I wis havering and tae pack it up as I wis frightening the other staff. I didnae bother anymore. But I kent the sisters kent more than they let on. They were very careful where they allowed the guests tae gae. They kept them well away from the burnt oot ruin of Keil Hoose next door tae the hotel, and they didnae allow many with the name MacDonald tae stay there either. They didnae think I noticed, but I had a feeling they were protecting people frae the ghosts, and then one day, it all changed."

Kate's mind was already running wild with the stories Ronan was telling her. Everybody likes a good ghost story, or at least she did, and this one was a 'doosey'. "How do you mean, changed?" she asked.

"Well, let me see; it wis autumn in 1958 and I wis chopping logs for the fires oot at the wood shed at the side of the Lodge. Noo, I cannae be sure, but I saw, or at least I thought I saw, a lassie walk straight oot of the sea, holding the hand of a wee laddie aboot five years old. I thought I wis being daft, and I ken it sounds strange but there she wis. Her clothes were oot of date I can tell ye that, not that I'm one for lassie's fashion, but her skirt was way tae long tae not notice. She just walked straight towards me, heading fir the Lodge, wee laddie in tow. As she drew closer, I could see she was a bonnie lassie, long dark hair and deep set dark eyes, I wis caught in a wee spell of my own. She passed me and as she did, she turned and smiled. I will never forget that moment, she was a real beauty. I did notice her clothes were bone dry, so I thought my eyes had been playing tricks on me, she couldnae have come frae the sea, that wis daft thinking. She walked up and in tae the front doors of the Lodge, and I thought she was a guest, so I went back tae chopping the logs. That evening, wee Janette Riley introduced me tae the lass and her wee laddie. She wis called Isla MacDonald, and the wee laddie wis called Ewan. She wis Janette and Betty's niece frae the Outer Hebrides and she wis gonnae help oot at the Lodge. Well, that wis the first I'd heard of it, but I wisnae going to say anything."

"I'm guessing the wee boy Ewan is Jamie's father," said Kate.

"Aye, I heard Ewan had met a lassie frae the mainland shortly after his mammie had disappeared."

Kate smiled to herself, it always struck her funny how the locals called the rest of Scotland 'The Mainland' when the Kintyre peninsula wasn't exactly an island. "How do you mean, disappeared?" she asked.

"Nae, lassie, don't rush me, we havnae come tae that part of the tale yet," he scolded her gently before he carried on.

"Noo, for someone who wis supposed tae be helping, she wis gone an auffie lot of the time. She wasnae tae friendly either, kept herself tae herself, but as the years rolled on, she started tae warm tae me a bit. Janette and Betty adored the wee laddie and took over as the main carers for him. He wis a skinny wee streak o nothing into everything, but it brought a lot of fun tae the Lodge. Isla never ventured far, she never went in tae Campbeltown, even tae see Ewan's school. Betty always drove him there and either Janette or I would pick him up.

"I would see Isla walking oot every evening, doon tae the beach, but I would never see her come back, yet every morning, she wis always there helping dish oot the breakfast tae the guests. It wis the only time of day ye would see her as she never mixed wi the rest of the staff in the Lodge. One day, I ventured tae ask her what she did doon on the beach. She just looked at me with those big dark brown eyes of hers and said she liked the feel of the water on her feet. It reminded her of home. When I tried tae ask her aboot her home, she just smiled and said she missed it," said Ronan, picking up his cup and taking a deep gulp of his tea.

"Ah that's better, all this blethering is making me dry as a bone. Noo, where were we? Ah, yes, the wee laddie Ewan grew intae a handsome young laddie and wis soon getting noticed by the local lassies. As soon as he could, he managed tae persuade his aunt's (it's how he referred to the sisters) tae buy him a wee car and he wis oot most evenings. The sisters spoiled him, but he wis a decent, thoughtful soul and I kent he cared for them a great deal. He did his Highers in Campbeltoon, but then decided tae gae on tae Glasgow University. The night before he left, he and his mam walked doon tae the beach together. I was fixing the blinds up on one of the top floors of the Lodge and I could see them as they passed the graveyard. The ghosts were oot that night, but instead of staring at the Lodge, they turned and watched Isla and her laddie walk by. The mist was rolling in thick that evening and before long, they vanished deep into it. I thought I could hear singing and I opened the window. There wis a bonnie voice coming oot of the mists, a haunting melody full of both joy and sadness, I'll never forget it. The ghosts of the women and their bairns just stood as the mists swept over them. I watched and listened fir a wee while and then I felt I was trespassing on a moment in time that didnae belong tae me. I closed the window and turned away.

"The next morning, Ewan packed up his car and hugged the sisters and me cheerio. Isla wis nae where tae be seen. When I ventured tae ask where she wis, the sisters looked at each other strangely before telling me she had returned tae the Hebrides.

"A year later, Janette died suddenly and Betty sold on the Lodge. She left me a fair amount of money, saying she wis grateful for all I had done for them. I didnae expect it and I wis so touched as Betty kent I had a young family in Campbeltoon that I needed tae support. I stayed with the new owners only a few months. We didnae see eye to eye aboot things and they wudnae listen to my advice aboot the ghosts. I was tae set in my ways tae see the Lodge change so much and my wife wanted me at home more noo that the wains were getting older. My wife wis from Arran and wanted tae gae back there, so we sold oor hoose in Campbeltoon and we moved here tae Arran."

Kate let out a deep breath. Ronan McDougall could certainly tell a good story, that was for sure. Even if she didn't quite believe the bit about the ghosts, certainly the story of Ewan and his mother had been fascinating. She wondered what Jamie would think about all this.

"Thank you, Ronan, you have been really helpful with your background knowledge. It paints quite a picture, I'm sure Jamie will be fascinated," she said.

"Aye, well, if you're intending tae help rebuild that place, ye'll need tae ken about it all. The story has not yet ended," said Ronan, taking another slurp of tea. "There's a lot more tae it." Kate helped herself to another sandwich and piece of shortbread, then sat back to hear the rest of the tale.

"The sisters knew and understood the Mull, they were careful aboot where the residence should tread and encouraged them not tae visit the caves at night. But the new owners and the ones after them didnae ken what they were doing. The first couple that took over tried tae rebuild the tennis courts just behind the ruin of old Keil Hoose and St Columba's graveyard. They tried to add four more courts, which would have meant building ontae land they should have left untouched. I told them they should leave things alone but they didnae listen. Things went wrong frae the start, the ground started tae shift and great holes would appear in the courts and in the road leading tae the Lodge so that people cudnae drive up tae it. The coal cellar caught fire mysteriously and burned for days, filling the Lodge with smoke and nae one kent why. It took months for the burnt smell tae clear completely. I left them tae it then. They wudnae listen, there wis nae point in me being there and putting myself in harm's way. They didnae last long, there were tae many unexplained incidents and they just got fed up and sold up.

"Although I didnae see them for myself, I heard the next owners didnae fare any better. They were from overseas, Canada or America or somewhere like that. They wanted tae promote the Lodge as a golfing experience and more. Dunaverty and Machrihanish golf courses were both within easy reach. They had discovered the graves wi the skull and crossbones on them at St Columba's graveyard and decided tae have pirate themed parties and even hired actors tae play the parts. The parties were going tae involve a treasure hunt that led the guests aroond the graveyard, Keil Hoose ruin, the caves and on tae the beach at night."

"That doesn't seem very respectful, trapesing through the graveyard," said Kate.

"Aye, and the dead wudnae be happy. I could have told them it was a bad idea, but it wis tae late fir that. They decided they would have burning torches leading the way and lighting up the caves. Of course, it wis weather dependant as the winds could be fierce on the Mull. Some of the local staff were horrified at the idea and many refused tae work that night, even if it did mean their jobs.

"The night of the first treasure hunt came and the guests were on fine form, dressed as pirates and feeling the worse fir wear frae many drams of the local whiskey. They ventured oot on the hunt but not a soul noticed the thick mist coming in tae shore. The first man tae reach the Great Cave ran in tae collect his clue. Nae one kent what happened then, but there wis a blood-curdling scream and the man ran oot, all aflame, a human torch, burnt tae a crisp before the others could get tae him. By the time they had reached him, the mist had covered everything and they couldnae see their hands in front of their faces. People were screaming, terrified in the mist that had covered them all.

"That was the start of what proved tae be a night of horrors. Blinded by the mist and disoriented wi the whiskey, people found themselves falling down steep rocky chasms and getting injured on the sharp, jagged rocks. Some stumbled blindly on tae the beach and found themselves suddenly splashing in the sea. A woman drowned in two foot of water as she tumbled over rocks in tae a rock pool, knocking herself oot. The wise just stayed put, huddled, waiting for the deadly mist tae clear, frustrated they were so close tae comfort, yet unable tae move.

"The mist left just before dawn the next day, and as daylight came, it revealed the carnage of the night before. There were three deed in total, another man had fallen doon frae the caves, killing himself on the rocks below. The staff from the Lodge helped the frozen and badly injured guests make their way back up tae the Lodge. Ambulances were called, there wis a small investigation and the Lodge was shut. It couldnae have reopened again after that tragedy, the owners moved back tae where they came frae."

Kate was shocked. No one had mentioned this when she had been asking about the place in Campbeltown. If this was true, and she had no reason to think that Ronan was making it up, then Jamie would have to know. Surely, there must have been something about it in the local newspaper. Perhaps she could find a copy in the library. This Seal Lodge was beginning to take on a much larger character than she had first imagined.

"Ronan, thank you so much for your time. It's been absolutely fascinating and I'm sure Jamie would love to meet you when he comes here," said Kate, standing and collecting her bag.

"Aye, it would be good tae see Ewan's son. I have some great stories fir him about his pappie when he wis a wee lad. He wis a wee bugger at times," said Ronan, pulling himself unsteadily to his feet.

Kate let Ronan help her with her coat and promised him that she would keep in touch and let him know what was happening with the Lodge. She gave him a hug and kiss on the cheek, then stepped out of the cottage and made her way back to Gizmo, who was waiting patiently in the car. Ronan stood at the window to wave her off.

The rain was easing and the wind had dropped some, so she decided to drive onto Blackwaterfoot Beach, where she could let Gizmo out for a run around. By the time she got to the beach, the sun was bursting through with an unusual warmth for the end of September. It was always the case in this part of Scotland. It could be a torrential downpour one minute and bright and sunny the next. Kate walked along the beach, breathing in the fresh air and looking across to the Mull.

She wondered if she would be able to see Seal Lodge from here, but without her binoculars, she couldn't be sure. Her thoughts turned to Jamie and how he would feel when he would hear all the stories, especially about his father and grandmother. Kate decided the best thing to do was to put all she had learnt in an email, then it might not sound like it was coming from a complete mad woman. Ronan might be a storyteller, but it was hard not to believe him. She threw stones in the sea for Gizmo to chase and he ran around barking crazily. He never tried to catch the stones, so Kate never really understood why he loved this game so much.

They walked back to the car and Kate drove back to the ferry, but not before stopping at Arran butchers for some island steak and a couple of mutton pies, her one weakness. She excused it by telling herself it only happened a couple of times a year, so she and Gizmo wolfed down one of the hot pies, allowing the grease to run down her fingers.

Chapter Three

Two weeks later, Kate was half-heartedly working on her latest novel in her top-floor apartment in Edinburgh. Kate had emailed Jamie just after she had returned from Arran, telling him the complete story whilst it was still fresh in her mind. He had replied with a brief thank you and she hadn't heard from him since. He probably thought she was out of her mind when she thought about it. It was an extraordinary story and, no doubt, her email hadn't done it justice. She had wanted to go back to Seal Lodge and the local library to investigate further, if only to satisfy her own curiosity, but she had had a call from her property agent in Edinburgh telling her that her tenant had departed rather suddenly, defaulting on his rent and leaving her apartment in a bit of a state.

Kate hadn't been in Edinburgh for six months, so she was definitely overdue a visit to her parents. She arrived at her apartment, dreading what she may find, but it was not as bad as she had imagined it to be during her drive back to Edinburgh.

It had taken her a good five hours driving the scenic route until she eventually got onto Edinburgh city bypass and another ten minutes until she reached the Colinton junction. Her apartment was just through the little village of Colinton down at the River Leith, overlooking Spylaw park and the pretty Colinton church. They were new-built apartments, only two years old, but the location was perfect for Kate, who wanted to be close to the city centre but be able to see green from her window. It was handy for walking Gizmo in the mornings, the river walk alongside her apartment block went all the way out the city to Balerno. Her tenants had left the apartment untidy, covered in litter and beer cans, clearly from some sort of party. Thankfully, there had been no real damage and so she and her mum donned their rubber gloves and had the place spic and span in a couple of hours.

Kate's mum was a busy lady, full of energy, with so many charities and church duties that she never stopped. It drove her father mad as her mum was always out and their phone never stopped ringing. Kate loved spending time with her parents and felt guilty she had left it so long since her last visit.

Kate had been in Edinburgh for a week now and she told her mum she would stay for a couple of weeks this visit. She still had quite a few friends in the city she wanted to catch up with, and her publisher was also based there. Her mother was delighted to have Kate around for a bit longer than usual and was already getting Kate roped into helping her out at some of her visits to the elderly. Kate's mum loved showing off her famous author daughter.

Her latest novel was set in Aberdeenshire, and Kate had been going through the archives at the Scottish National Library, where she set up her laptop for the morning. Her inbox pinged to indicate a personal message and she saw it was from Jamie.

'Hello Kate,

My apologies for not getting back to you sooner. I was inundated with minor problems trying to get the golf clubhouse I've been working on finished and ready for its opening day. As usual, last-minute hitches seemed to cause major problems and I was working 24/7. You must think I'm terribly rude after all the trouble you took on my behalf.

I want to thank you for taking the time out to visit Ronan MacDougall. What a fascinating story, I was so jealous I was not there with you when he brought up the ghosts. I can't wait to meet the man. I'm actually up in Edinburgh just now, doing some research on my father. He lived in Morningside and, by all accounts, was an architect also. He was married and I have discovered I have two sisters, or half-sisters I suppose if we were to be absolutely correct.

We met at the official reading of the will. Like me, their mother has died also and neither of them knew about Seal Lodge or that our father owned it. He must have been quite wealthy, as he left them both a substantial inheritance, and they seemed really happy to discover they had a brother. They invited me to Edinburgh when I finished down in Brighton and are as enthusiastic as I am to find out more about our father and where he came from.

Carly is the oldest, she is married, with a young family, and has too many commitments to be able to come to the Lodge. However, Eden, who is quite the character, would love to come with me and help out. She was more than excited about your email when she read it and is determined to meet Ronan and squeeze every bit of information out of him she can. I'm currently staying with Eden in our father's old house in Morningside in Edinburgh.

We were planning to come down to the Mull next week and wondered if you would be available to meet up. I don't want to intrude on your time, but I would like to thank you personally for the trouble you took on my behalf. Perhaps you could call and we could arrange a date that is suitable for you.

Kind regards,
Jamie.'

Kate was surprised and delighted that he had responded in such a friendly manner. He was forgiven immediately for almost ignoring her last email. Now he was just down the road in Morningside, which was a short drive from Colinton. She reached for the phone and dialled the mobile number he had attached and within a couple of rings, it was answered with a deep "Hello".

"Jamie, this is Kate MacPhee, I've just received your email," she said, suddenly finding herself slightly nervous.

"Kate. Hi, I didn't expect you to get in touch so soon. It's so nice to actually speak to you," Jamie's voice was deep, warm and friendly.

"Yes, I wouldn't have if it wasn't for the fact that I'm currently staying at my Edinburgh apartment just down the road from you in Colinton. I couldn't believe it when you said you were in Morningside," said Kate.

"Really, that's fantastic. what a coincidence, can we meet up?" he asked.

"Well, yes, we can; to be honest, I'm fairly flexible. I've had a few business things to tie up here, but apart from that, I'm just working on my novel, but to be honest, it's slow going at the moment," Kate responded, hoping she didn't sound too keen.

"Well, what about this afternoon, I'm free and at a bit of a loss as I don't know many people in Edinburgh. I've been hanging out with Eden and her friends, who are slightly different to what I'm used to," said Jamie, laughing.

"This afternoon would be fine, where would you like to meet?" asked Kate.

There is a Starbucks up at Holy Corner, which is just a short walk up the hill from where I'm staying, shall we meet there at, say 2?" Jamie suggested.

"That's great, I know the place and I can park easily there also. I'll see you then," Kate said and hung up, heaving a big sigh. He had sounded lovely on the phone and she started to wonder what he looked like. She hadn't dated since her husband died, and to be honest, she kept so busy, she hadn't even thought about it. She had no idea why she felt so tingly at the prospect of meeting Jamie that afternoon and was already wondering what she should wear.

At two o'clock, Kate parked her car up by Napier University and started to walk towards Starbucks at Holy corner, so named as it had a church situated at each corner of the crossroads. She had opted for figure-hugging blue jeans and long tan boots with a small heel, a black long-sleeved tee-shirt with a short tan jacket. She wore a long necklace, which had felt strange as it had been a long time since she had bothered about jewellery. Kate had blonde shoulder-length hair and a pretty face, with eyes that seemed to change from ice blue to dark ocean blue depending on her mood. She didn't wear a lot of makeup, she had her mother's smooth skin, though she always wore mascara and a little bit of liner. There was no way she was going to admit that she had changed four times before leaving her flat and her bedroom floor was now covered in clothes. She kept telling herself how ridiculous she was being. She was a 36-year-old woman, not a teenager.

There were tables outside the coffee house and her eyes were immediately drawn to a tall dark-haired man sitting alone. He looked in her direction and smiled. "Kate, over here!" he waved at her and she started to relax straight away. As she approached, he stood and reached out, pulling her in for a typical continental welcome, kissing both her cheeks.

"You haven't changed a bit," Jamie said, pulling a chair out for her.

"You have me at a disadvantage," Kate replied. "I just don't remember meeting you."

Jamie laughed, "No, of course not. It was an incredibly busy bar that night, but it was hard to miss the beautiful blonde serving behind it."

Kate was horrified to find herself blushing and prayed he wouldn't notice.

"I'm sorry I'm making you blush," he laughed.

Damn it!

"So, what did you think of my email?" Kate asked, changing the subject.

"Let me get coffees first and then we can discuss it," he said, rising. "What can I get you?"

Two skinny lattes later, they were both seated and Jamie pulled out his iPad. "I think Ronan's story is both incredible and incredulous. I guess it all depends on whether you believe in ghost stories or not. Believe me, I have come across quite a few over the years whist redeveloping old buildings. Though I have to say, none quite as disturbing as this one."

Kate laughed, "He was quite the storyteller. I found myself getting sucked into and believing every word he said when I was there. It took a long walk on the beach to bring myself back to reality. But I felt you should know the story."

"I was intrigued, to say the least. My sister Eden has done some research on the area and it has quite a bloody history. More than 300 men, women and children were slaughtered at Dunaverty Castle by the Covenanter army in 1647, a stone's throw from the Lodge," Jamie told her.

"Yes, I saw the plaque on the carpark telling the whole bloody story, Kintyre has a huge amount of history linked to it," said Kate. "It seems that your clan, the MacDonalds, made quite a name for themselves on the peninsula."

"It's funny you should mention that as I have uncovered another story that links our name to the place. The MacDonald Clan were led by a man called Colla Ciotach, more widely known as the great 'Colkitto'," said Jamie.

"Colkitto? Where have I come across that name before?" said Kate, racking her brains, trying to remember.

"He was a legend in these parts and a thorn in the side to the Campbells for decades. He became the MacDonald landlord of the island of Colonsay but had many skirmishes against the Duke of Argyll and the Campbell stronghold, and was even an outlawed pirate at one time, just his name would strike fear in the hearts of the Campbell islanders. He was nearly 80 when he and his infamous son, Sir Alisdair MacDonald, were chased down the Kintyre peninsula with their men by the Marquis of Argyll, the Campbells and the Covenanter army led by David Leslie," explained Jamie.

"I've heard of Sir Alisdair MacDonald, he was Montrose's right-hand man in their fight against the Covenanters," said Kate.

Jamie nodded, "It was just after Montrose was defeated at Philliphaugh when Sir Alisdair and Colkitto arrived at Dunaverty Castle in Southend, they went on lock down in the castle. But Sir Alisdair had orders from the king to go to Ireland, so he commissioned his father on behalf of the King, to go to the Island of Islay and secure Dunyvaig Castle. Sir Alisdair then left Archibald MacDonald with 300 men, women and children to hold Dunaverty Castle against the Covenanters. Assuming the castle was impenetrable, Sir Alisdair MacDonald sailed with the rest of his men to Ireland. His father, Colkitto, sailed to Islay just before the Covenanters arrived.

"The Marquis of Argyll, David Leslie and their preacher, John Neave, were furious that Sir Alisdair and Colkitto had escaped them again. They laid siege on Dunaverty Castle, destroying the piping that fed the castle's water supply. The MacDonalds soon had to rely on rainfall, but it was not enough and so they asked for a parley. They requested a surrender on fair terms and the Marquis of Argyll promised them quarter, but as they came out the castle, they were all put to the sword and murdered."

Kate was impressed Jamie had done his homework. "I could use you to help research some of my books."

"I have to be honest, Eden has done most of this research. I'm just repeating what she told me. It is fascinating thought, the story itself changes many times depending on whose account you read," said Jamie.

"It's always the way with historians," said Kate. "I find that all the time in my work."

"Why the marquis decided to murder these people is still under dispute. Some say he was seeking revenge for having let Alisdair escape at Philliphaugh, but others say it was down to the preacher, a man called Reverend John Neave, a bloody preacher who had been commissioned by the marquis as his chaplain in Inveraray. He was a cruel man, renowned for medieval punishments and torture methods. When the marquis had agreed to quarter, the Preacher got in his ear. The Reverend John Neave likened the situation at Dunaverty Castle to a story in the Old Testament when Saul spared the Amalekite King after being told by God to kill him. Saul was cursed the rest of his life. The marquis was a religious man and was said to have been persuaded to commit many atrocities at the will of his preacher. So, he ordered his men to kill all the men, women and children who came from Dunaverty. General David Leslie was not so impressed with the murders, and it is recorded that he asked the Preacher after walking through the slaughter, ankle-deep in blood, 'Now, Mr John. Have you not gotten your fill of blood?'"

"I have heard a slightly different version of this story. I know at Kintyre, the locals say the prisoners from the castle were given a choice either to be put to the sword or they could leap off Dunaverty Rock to their deaths in the rocky sea below. Many chose the latter, so perhaps there was not quite so much blood," said Kate. "I read that on the information sign put up by the local council just by Keil Caves, telling the story of the Dunaverty Massacre."

"Apparently, according to records, there were two infants that managed to escape the slaughter because of the actions of a brave nurse. One of them was Ranald Og MacDonald, he was the son of Archibald MacDonald, who was in charge of the castle," said Jamie.

"I read that also, apparently, he was buried in St Columba's churchyard, though I haven't seen his grave," said Kate. "This Colkitto character sounds fascinating. I must find out more about him."

"He really does fire up your imagination. He was a legendary figure in Scotland at the time. He was known as 'Colla Ciotach' or 'Colkitto', meaning crafty or left-handed, but it was believed that he was ambidextrous and could use his sword with both hands. The legend says he was 6ft 6in tall but when I looked into it further, it was actually his son Sir Alisdair that had that reputation, as he was also known as a fierce warrior. But, by all accounts, Colkitto himself was still a giant of a man. There are so many stories surrounding him, he is almost a type of Robin Hood character, fighting for what he saw as justice, protecting his clan and his religion of course. Doesn't religion always come into it? He was a Catholic and hated by the Covenanters."

"You have really looked into this. I feel completely out of my league here. It's all fascinating," said Kate.

"I doubt we are anywhere close to your league!" a chirpy female voice broke into their conversation. Kate looked up and saw a slim, pretty young woman with the same deep brown eyes as Jamie. She had on a tight black leather jacket and jeans tucked into Doc Martin boots. Her hair was black, short and spikey with purple streaks, and she wore a silver ring through her bottom lip.

"This is Eden, my sister," said Jamie. "I hope you don't mind but I asked her to join us. She has been helping me research our father's life."

"It's lovely to meet you," said Kate, holding out her hand, which was swept away as Eden hugged her.

"I was so excited when I read your email to Jamie. I can't believe I'm actually meeting you, I love your books. And I can hardly wait to meet Ronan MacDougall," she said all at once.

"Well, thank you, and, yes, Ronan is quite a character," said Kate, laughing. "So, it's you that's done all this research into your father's family and the Kintyre history?"

"I overheard Jamie start to tell you about Colkitto, and I would like to finish the story if I may," said Eden, bouncing with enthusiasm.

"There would be no stopping her," said Jamie, laughing, and Eden scowled at him jokingly.

"Please do, I'm finding this all absolutely fascinating. I can hardly believe it's all virtually on my doorstep," replied Kate, enjoying the company of this new addition to their table.

Chapter Four

Jamie went and got Eden a coffee as she took her jacket off and made herself comfortable. Kate looked at the tattoo cascading down from Eden's neck to her left elbow. It was of some sort of mermaid swimming downwards, its tale wrapping itself around Eden's arm.

"Nice ink," said Kate.

"I've been obsessed with mermaids and the ocean all my life. My ex-boyfriend was a tattoo artist and came up with this idea for me. I love it," said Eden, holding out her arm for Kate to admire the details.

"So, you were going to tell me more about Colkitto?" said Kate, taking a sip of her coffee as Jamie returned to the table.

"Right, okay, so we know that Colla Ciotach was born as a Gael and a Catholic on an island in Antrim, Ireland, and was taken as an infant to the Isle of Colonsay, where he grew up as a MacDonald. In these days, surnames were not widely used and as far as I could find out, the name 'Ciotach' actually described the fact that he was left-handed or ambidextrous. There are so many legends dotted about Scotland about this man and many insinuate that he was a sneaky, treacherous character, but actually, he was more of a hero to his clan and to his faith," said Eden.

"I have to be honest, the name kind of rings a bell, but I just can't place it," said Kate. She could tell that Eden had seriously done her homework.

"Well, one of the most famous legends is that of his piper," said Eden, obviously enjoying herself. "The story goes that Colkitto had more than 2,000 men at his disposal and he sailed up the west coast of Kintyre amongst the Inner Hebrides, pillaging the properties of almost every Campbell who lived on the islands. I would like to point out that he didn't set out to kill them, just to inconvenience them greatly. In these days, it was not unusual for a neighbouring clan to attack and steal away your cattle and grain.

"Colkitto always had his piper with him. Pipers were an important part of any army and he had been given his piper by the

Chief of Clan Macintyre. Colkitto had helped him defeat the Covenanters in Glen Coe and the piper was given to him as a reward. The piper became a very close and loyal friend to Colkitto."

Kate listened with interest, Eden was a good storyteller but she couldn't help but wonder what this all had to do with the Lodge at Southend. Still, Kate liked nothing better than to hear the old tales of the exploits of the Highlanders, it was a great way to spend the afternoon. And her eyes kept meeting Jamie's as Eden went on.

"Colkitto and his army arrived at Duntrune Castle in Loch Crinan, and on a night raid, they surprised and defeated the Campbell defenders. Colkitto left only a few of his men and his piper at the castle, as he had a meeting with other Royalists fighting the same cause. The Campbells had waited for him to leave then retook the castle easily, killing all of Colkitto's men, except for the piper who, because of his status, was allowed to live and ordered to play for the amusement of his captors.

"The Campbells had sent many men and waited for Colkitto's inevitable return; finally, they spotted his galley coming around the Sounds of Jura. The piper asked if he may play his pipes to mark the occasion and they allowed him to play from the castle ramparts. He played a well-known pibroch, named 'The Pipers Warning to his Master'. Colkitto listened and noticed mistakes and missed notes, unheard of in such an accomplished piper, and so he recognised the warning, turned his galley around and headed out to open sea, raising his hand in a grateful salute to his piper.

"The Campbells, realising what the piper had done, took him before Lady Dunstaffnage, known as 'the black bitch', and she ordered his hands be cut off. She was another story, a real evil woman that one. Anyway, I diverse, the poor piper had his hands cut off and he bled out and died. And, of course, *Dah Daaaah!*" said Eden, building up to the end. "They say, to this day, that you can hear the pipes as the handless piper walks the ramparts of Duntrune Castle. Mind you if he is handless, I'm not sure how he is playing the pipes."

"Brilliant, another wonderful Scottish ghost story," said Kate, laughing. "You are as good a storyteller as Ronan MacDougall."

"Yes, but the story didn't end there. In 1888, whilst repairing the floor of Duntrune Castle, they found a skeleton in a shallow grave, and guess what?" said Eden.

"Erm, no hands?" replied Kate.

41

"Spot on, they buried him in a grave at Kilmartin's churchyard. Anyway, back to Colkitto. He carried on his pillaging through the islands, stealing cattle and burning down dwellings. His name struck fear in Argyll and so, the legend grew. He moved on from Argyll, causing general havoc in Inverness-shire, Perthshire and the Grampians. He eventually joined forces with Montrose and the Royalist armies. His son Alisdair MacDonald, also became known as 'Colkitto' and is certainly more famous in the history books as being an invincible warrior, was knighted by Montrose. But he isn't the character his father was.

"That's where I heard the name before," said Kate.

"After his son's army had left Dunaverty, Old Colkitto returned to Islay, where he was commissioned by his son to guard Dunyvaig Castle. The Covenanter army followed him there, determined to finally catch him. They surrounded Dunyvaig and Colla asked for quarter for his men. I'm guessing at the time, he didn't know what they had done at Dunaverty, or he may not have trusted them.

"David Leslie allowed the quarter to stand this time, but they still wanted Colkitto. The story goes that he was tricked on coming out of the castle to greet an old friend and was finally captured and taken to Dunstaffnage Castle just outside Oban. Now Colkitto was an old friend of Lord Dunstaffnage, even though he was a Campbell. Colkitto had been imprisoned there before and was instantly granted parole as long as he promised not to escape. So, he went to work in the fields to help bring in the harvest.

"Meanwhile, his fate was being decided. He was sentenced to death at Inveraray Court by George Campbell, who was renowned for handing out only one verdict. The court was told that he was living free on parole again at Dunstaffnage. The Preacher had caught him living free there a couple of years before when he should have been in chains.

"Lord Dunstaffnage denied he was free to wander and quite a race then ensued to get back to the castle before it was discovered he was not locked up. Apparently, Dunstaffnage's men arrived only minutes before the court's men and shouted over the fields to Colkitto, 'Colla in chains! Colla in chains!' Colkitto understood and left the field immediately taking himself off to the dungeon and chaining himself up before he was discovered.

"They took him out of his cell and he was hung at Dunstaffnage Castle from the mast of his own galley," said Eden. "Mind you, he was nearly 80 years old by then, which was pretty good going for being a warrior in that century."

"That's quite a story, I'm intrigued but I can't help wondering what has it got to do with Seal Lodge and your family?" Kate asked.

"Well, it brings us back to the massacre at Dunaverty and the babies who survived. Now this story is all based on a legend, I discovered it in an old book of myths at the Scottish Library, it seems that the other child was old Colkitto's youngest son. He had also been left in the care of the nurse and Colkitto was planning to send for him once he had control of Dunyvaig Castle on Islay. No one knows who the mother of the child was, as Colkitto's wife had died years earlier, and he had just been released from his five-year imprisonment at Dunstaffnage Castle. I assume he was on parole and living free there during that time, as that can be the only explanation of how he managed to father a child.

"The child's name was Conall, and he was taken to the Isle of Sanda just off the coast of Kintyre. The MacDonalds had a strong foothold on Sanda, though that was lost just after the Dunaverty Massacre; however, the island was restored back to the MacDonalds in 1666.

"Conall grew up on the island and, led a fairly peaceful life. He kept his identity hidden, there were few who knew he was Colkitto's son, which was probably why he lived so long. Colkitto's other sons lived short and violent lives. Conall went on to father three children, two sons, who both left the island; and a daughter named Mary, who remained on Sanda. She went on to have two boys, one disappeared from record, but the oldest son continued the line.

"Anyway, we followed the family tree as much as we could. There were strange gaps but all in all, it seemed to lead us to the birth of Ewan MacDonald, our father, a descendent of Conall. That would make us direct descendants also. We are related to Colkitto."

"I couldn't see that one coming," said Kate, amazed. "I don't think I could have written that."

"You seriously underestimate yourself," said Jamie. "That's the reason I called you. I have seen the research you do to write your novels and I was hoping, as you're in the area, that you will maybe help us a little in finding out more about Colkitto and what happened to Conall."

"I would love to help," Kate blurted out, then kicked herself for seeming too eager. Why did this man make her feel like a complete muppet?

"I knew you would," piped in Eden. "I'm like a dog with a bone right now and can't wait to get down there to see the place."

"I'm going to be meeting local builders and drawing up plans, so I may have to rent a property down there. I don't want to stay in a hotel the whole time. Do you know of any?" Jamie asked Kate.

"You can stay with me. I have plenty of room and would love the company," said Kate.

"We can't just put you out like that," said Jamie.

"Nonsense, it's a fascinating project and I really would like to be part of it," said Kate. "It makes sense that you stay with me."

"Well that's settled then," said Eden. "When do we leave?"

Jamie grimaced and shook his head at her.

"Well, I can finish up here in a few days, I need to spend some time with my parents, or I will never hear the end of it. Then I can pack up and we can hit the road. We can make my house a base of investigation," Kate offered.

"Are you sure?" said Jamie, again feeling a little uncomfortable. "I wasn't expecting you to put us up. We had already found a hotel for the time being."

"I wouldn't hear of you staying anywhere else. I'll call you in a couple of days and we can organise the journey," said Kate.

Chapter Five

As neither Jamie nor Eden had ever been on the Kintyre peninsula, Kate had offered to drive, but Jamie decided to follow her in his car so he would have a vehicle at his disposal. Eden rode with Kate and chatted away happily about her plans for the Lodge. They stopped at the Loch Fyne Bistro near Inveraray for a freshly caught scallop and oyster lunch and to let Gizmo out for a run. The little dog insisted on sitting propped up on Eden's lap the whole way.

Eden chose to continue riding with Kate and Gizmo from the restaurant and turned the conversation to her father. "I've no idea why Dad kept Jamie secret from us all. He told me he came from Glasgow and that his mother had died when he was in his late teens. His father had apparently been killed during the war. I never questioned it or attempted to find out anymore. I wish I had now."

"It's something that doesn't dawn on you at the time. I guess you always think in the back of your head, you will have plenty of time, then suddenly, the person is gone," said Kate.

"I'm sorry about your husband, Kate. Jamie told me a little bit about him dying in a plane crash," said Eden.

"He loved to fly, it was a hobby he took up when my books started making us money. I don't like flying, so I could never understand his passion for it. Mike was a good man, I do miss him and what we could have had, but I guess, life goes on," Kate replied.

"Dad was 66 when he died and in very good health for his age. He had never been to a doctor's in his life. He was an open water swimmer and entered many events and races throughout his life. He loved the sea swims the best and every Saturday morning, for as long as I can remember, he would drive over to Gullane and swim from the beach. It didn't matter what the season or the weather, though he did stay away when there were storms. My sister and I went with him a few times during our lives. We are both strong swimmers because of it; anyway, I'm digressing. Dad had been very quiet over the last few months, which was unusual, as he was always the life and soul of the room. He was quite the social animal and was always out and about, even after Mum died. Then it just seemed to stop and Carly and I started to notice that he was spending a lot of his time withdrawn and alone.

"He just said he was tired and although we tried to persuade him, he refused to go and see the doctor. We always visited him on Sundays, Carly would bring her family and we would cook and talk about our week. Dad just sat and listened quietly, which was unusual, as we were used to seeing him rolling around the floor with his grandchildren. We were both getting very worried about him. He seemed to just close up, and the light went out of his eyes.

"Then one Saturday afternoon, I got a call from Gullane police. Dad had been spotted going into the sea down at the beach and had swum out, I suppose on his usual swimming route. He never came back and was presumed drowned. He must have got tired in the water, which was hard for us to imagine, as he was an excellent swimmer. They never did recover his body," Eden explained.

"I'm so sorry," said Kate. "That must have been very difficult for you."

"It was for a while, but Dad was a stubborn man and I guess if there was any way he would have liked to have gone, it would have been in his beloved ocean," said Eden. "It took a few months for the coroner to pronounce him dead, and in all that time, we never knew Jamie existed."

They had just passed the ferry terminals to Jura and Gigha when Kate had to take a left turn off the main A83 towards the other side of the peninsula. "Hold on, this road down to Carradale can be hazardous at times," she warned Eden. The one-track road was a mass of sharp bends and random sheep. Kate had got used to driving it now, but she was wondering how Jamie was faring behind her. Eventually, they swung around another steep bend and there was her house with its stunning views of Arran. As she opened the door of her car, Gizmo pushed his way out and ran straight down onto the beach to let the seabirds know he had returned.

They unpacked the cars and Kate showed them around her home, which they both loved. Later that evening, after they had eaten the monkfish they had bought in Tarbert, Kate took them for a stroll along the moonlit beach. She was very proud of her place, especially on a clear night like this. The sea was like glass with the lights of Arran reflecting on it. They had torches to find their way over the rocks, but the moon was full and gave off enough light as it was.

"I can understand why you chose this place," said Jamie. "It's so beautiful and peaceful."

"I love it here," replied Kate just as Gizmo darted past, chasing something up the beach.

"I wonder why Dad never brought us here," Eden said. "He never spoke of the Mull, ever. And yet he bought that hotel. It's so strange."

"Well, tomorrow we can go down to the Lodge and you can see what you're letting yourself in for and maybe find some clues about your dad," said Kate.

The next day, they all piled into Kate's car and headed down the narrow road towards Campbeltown. According to the distance on the map, it should have taken them no time at all, but the roads were so unpredictable and winding that it took a good 40 minutes to reach Campbeltown. They had a quick stroll around the harbour town, picturesque as it was surrounded with rocky cliffs and hills.

They didn't stay too long as Jamie was eager to see Seal Lodge, so they drove another 12 miles to Southend, on a much straighter road this time, and eventually saw Seal Lodge looming down on them. Kate parked up next to the locked gates leading up to the Lodge. There was no one about. Eden and Jamie got out of the car, both staring up towards the old building.

"It's quite something, isn't it?" said Kate.

"I never knew this is where Dad grew up," said Eden, her eyes filled with emotion. "How could he just leave and forget this place?"

"I don't think he did," said Jamie. "He wouldn't have bought Seal Lodge if he had forgotten it."

"Shall we walk up to the Lodge? We can squeeze through these gates, they are not exactly secure, and we won't be trespassing," Kate suggested.

They all squeezed through and hiked up the long driveway to the ruin of what was Seal Lodge. It was a huge, white five-storey building, completely deserted, apart from the seagulls that sat atop it. The windows were gone, and the stonework on the front patio was smashed. They walked up behind the building to the entrance. The door was locked, which was ironic considering you could have got in through any one of the giant windows. Jamie pulled out the keys he had and unlocked the door and they all stepped inside what once was the lobby.

"Be careful, I'm not sure how sturdy this floor is," he said, stepping carefully into the Lodge. There was nothing much left in the place, half the floor had been ripped up to get the piping underneath. It had been ransacked and there was so much rubbish around, it was difficult to tell what it was like before.

"Hey, guys, look at the view," said Eden, who had been fairly quiet during the walk. They turned and looked out the giant window frames at the stunning view in front of them. You could see everything from the Ailsa Craig over to Ireland. "This must have been quite a place."

"If I were to do this, I'm not sure whether tearing it down and starting from scratch might not be a better idea," said Jamie thoughtfully.

"What do you mean 'IF'!" said Eden. "You must do it, this is what Dad wanted, and you cannot tear it down. You just have to fix it."

Jamie didn't bother to point out that he had never met their father, so had no real allegiance to him, so he just laughed, "Well, it will take a lot of work and probably a good deal of time. I guess it will all depend on the foundations and how strong they are. I need to get surveyors out first and then figure out how to rebuild it. What do you think, Kate?"

Eden glared at Kate. "I think you should absolutely do it," said Kate. And Eden smiled victoriously while Jamie shook his head, obviously beaten.

Kate walked over to the staircase which still seemed intact. "Do you think it's safe to go up?" she asked.

"It looks firm, let me try it first. I'll know if it's going to collapse or not," replied Jamie. He started to climb slowly up each step of the staircase. The bannister had long gone, but the stairs themselves were quite solid. He made it up to the first floor. "It's okay, just be careful when you come up."

He started to explore some of the bedrooms on the first floor and could still see the garish wallpaper under the mould. "I would love to see pictures of this place before it shut," he called over to the girls. He walked to the bedroom at the other end of the hallway, it was slightly larger than the others, maybe because it was a corner room. Jamie felt a shiver and suddenly noticed he could see the steam from his breath, it was much colder in here than the rest of the rooms, even though they all had missing windows. Jamie walked over to what was left of the window frame and peered out. It looked out over the graveyard below. *Not a pleasant view,* he thought. Then suddenly, in the corner of his eye, he thought he saw a figure staring back up at him. A tall thin figure, all in black, with a large rimmed black hat.

He refocused and stared down, but the figure was gone. He shook his head. *What the hell was that?* he thought. He couldn't see anything around that could account for it and he felt very uncomfortable and cold. Suddenly, something grabbed him from behind, making him jump out his skin.

"What ya doing, bro?" laughed Eden. "Did I scare you?"

"I think jumping on people in old ruined hotels should be grounds for a good beating," said Jamie, laughing as Eden squealed and ran out the room.

"Have you seen enough?" said Kate. "Are we going to do this, I mean, are you going to do this?"

"You had it right the first time, Kate, you have to be part of this," said Eden.

"Absolutely, anyway, we need you to write a book about this place that will bring in the punters," said Jamie, his eyes twinkling.

"I'm glad you said that, my imagination has been sparked ever since I spoke with Ronan," replied Kate. "I wanted to ask if you would mind if I created a story around the place."

"I think that would be excellent!" exclaimed Eden, not bothering to contain her excitement.

They left the Lodge, Jamie locked the doors again, as pointless as it was, and they walked back down to the road. Kate got Gizmo out of the car and they walked along past St Columba's churchyard, Keil Caves and onto a lovely, long sandy beach. Kate pointed out Dunaverty Rock to them, the sight of the massacre, although the castle was long gone now.

As they walked along Carskiev Beach, they saw they were being watched by nosey seals who kept popping their heads out the water to take a look at them. The curious seals followed them along the beach, floating in the sea from just beyond the breaking waves. Gizzy was barking like crazy, trying to get them to throw rocks in the sea for him. When they got back to the car, they were all excited and energised.

"Now, we can either go for lunch or I can take you to the Mull of Kintyre Lighthouse at the end of the peninsula. I warn you now, it's quite a trek," said Kate.

"I'm up for it," said Eden immediately.

"Let's go then," said Jamie.

Kate drove them along the six-mile mountain track to the end of the road. They got out of her car and were hit by the Atlantic wind.

"I love this place, it's so wild," said Eden laughing as she, struggled to stand against the wind.

After their walk to the lighthouse, they left Southend and headed back up towards Carradale, where they stopped for lunch. The pretty town with its white cottages and palm trees looks as if it was straight off some Greek Island. There is a very steep hill down to a small quaint-looking harbour still used by the Langoustine fishermen. They were starving and had a very late lunch in the ornate conservatory of the beautiful old Carradale hotel, bowls of the locally caught langoustine in garlic butter with warm crusty bread.

Kate hadn't had this much fun since her husband had been alive. She had plenty of friends, but Jamie and Eden were really sharing her passion about this area. It was going to be fun working with them.

Chapter Six

During the next few days, Jamie was gone a fair bit. He had driven to Glasgow to see his family and organise some surveyors to view the Lodge.

Eden and Kate had been doing some more research on Colkitto, discovering that his wife, Mary, had come from the Island of Sanda, the same place that Conall, his son, had grown up on. They decided they wanted to go to Sanda and try to get a feel for the life the MacDonalds would have had back then. They also wanted to check the churchyard on Sanda to see if there were any gravestones with Jamie and Eden's ancestors on them.

Trying to find the owner of the Isle of Sanda to ask permission to visit was proving difficult. The island used to be open to the public, you could get boats on day tours from Campbeltown. There had been a hotel and bar on the island. The island was then bought by a Swiss billionaire and his wife and in March 2014, they tried to close the island off to the public. They erected threatening trespassing and private property notices; however, the law says everyone has a legal right to roam in Scotland, as long as you don't get too near the owner's residence. This meant, on Sanda, you cannot use the pier, which is situated directly in front of the owner's property. Therefore, all excursions to Sanda were stopped, and the island has been left to rot. So, for Kate and Eden, it would mean finding a boat that would be willing to take them across the Sanda Sounds, let them get a dingy to shore and come back for them later. This was proving a little difficult to arrange.

They left a message for the fishermen on the notice board at the harbour, asking if someone could take them to Sanda and pick them up again for a good fee. Kate left her phone number. They decided to drive back to Southend and made another discovery when they explored St Columba's graveyard next to the Lodge. A lot of the gravestones had fallen and many were lying flat on the ground. They found the grave of Ranald MacDonald, the other baby who had survived the massacre. He had made it to adulthood and gone on to have family himself, who were buried near him.

In the centre of the graveyard was a small building shrouded in ivy. This was called St Columba's chapel but was most likely built in the 13th century, a few hundred years after his time.

Kate and Eden walked around the building, looking for an opening, but the ivy was so thick, it was hard to find. Eventually, Kate noticed a grass bank sloping downwards and looking very worn. Pulling away the ivy, they found a small entrance that they both had to stoop down low to get inside. Eden squealed as she got tangled in the ivy; however, the sombre atmosphere inside the chapel made them both fall silent.

There was something haunting and mysterious about the place. There were old grave slabs embedded on the ground, with the carvings of knights on them dating back to the 14th century. Kate found a strange stone nestled in the ivy and scrubbed away the moss, to discover it was a tombstone with the skull and crossbones engraved on it.

Eden was trying to open a large iron gate that fenced off a separate crypt. It wouldn't budge, even with Kate's help. They could only just make out the carvings on the large stone tomb inside, it seemed to be of another knight holding a huge sword.

They brushed away the moss from some more of the old tomb stones and found more with the skull and crossbones etched into them.

"This place is quite creepy," Eden whispered, afraid to raise her voice any. "Do you think these are the graves of pirates? I mean, there was a lot of smuggling back in the day, to and from Ireland. This is probably the reason why the owners thought they could have a pirate's treasure hunt at the Lodge all these years ago."

"I'm not sure, but I don't think they have anything much to do with pirates. I've seen these markings on other gravestones, and there are the same skull and crossbones at Rosslyn Chapel and Greyfriars Kirkyard in Edinburgh. I know many historians suggest the stones were carved for the Knights Templar," whispered Kate.

"Surely, not here on Kintyre? We'll be having our own Da Vinci Code soon," whispered Eden.

"There is speculation that the Knights Templar were given a safe haven in Scotland when they were accused and persecuted for heresy in the 14th century by the pope. The stories and legends around them are so conflicting, and whether the Knights Templar ever arrived in Scotland is still debated. Some historians suggest that they fought with Robert the Bruce at the Battle of Bannockburn," Kate told her. "I used that storyline in one of my novels."

"We need to discover what these are about," whispered Eden. "We will need to know everything about this area, for when our guests come to stay. This whole place seems to be steeped in mysteries."

"I did some research on some gravestones I discovered for one of my books. They had the skull and crossbones on them, but not quite like these stones. I found out that they were put on the stones in the 17th century as a meaning of mortality and the ascension into heaven. However, they were not surrounded by tombs with knights carved into them, so I am leaning more towards the mark of the Knights Templar here," whispered Kate.

"Well, we can try to find out more, someone must know," Eden shivered slightly. "Shall we get out of here, I'm feeling quite closed in."

"Sure, lead the way," said Kate.

They both turned to where they thought the opening had been, but saw only ivy. "It's hard to see the opening with all this greenery," said Kate, trying to feel her way through the thick vines.

"I need to get out of here," said Eden, her voice now raised slightly.

Kate turned to look at her and saw her friend was in full panic. She was gasping for breath and hanging onto one of the tombs.

"Okay, take it easy and breathe slowly, I'll find the way out," said Kate, desperately trying to work out where they had come in. It seemed to be getting darker and Kate noticed a mist forming around her feet. She could hear Eden wheezing for air and she felt herself begin to panic. She told herself to get a grip and grabbed Eden's hand. She thought back to what she had first seen when they came in and retraced her steps.

The ivy had somehow completely covered the small doorway, but Kate managed to find it, pulled it away from the entrance and pushed Eden through first. Kate squeezed through after her and found Eden hanging onto a gravestone for balance. There was low mist covering the ground all around them, making it difficult to walk as Kate led them out of the graveyard. By the time they got to the road, Eden was breathing normally again, though she still looked shaken.

"Are you okay?" Kate asked.

"Yes, I don't know what happened. I'm not usually spooked by anything, but I honestly felt like something was in there with us. Something that wanted to harm me, it was horrible," said Eden. "For God's sake, don't tell Jamie, he'll think I'm a right muppet!"

"Are you up for looking at the Keil House ruin?" Kate asked.

"Yes of course, I'm fine now. I was just being an idiot," said Eden.

They walked over to the ruin which had once been the spectacular Keil House and Kate felt goosebumps appear on her skin as they approached. Kate had barely noticed the old ruin the first time she had come to Southend. But when she had researched the area, she found that it had once been a spectacular building.

"This place was initially a church back in the 12th and 13th centuries and was used as such until 1670. It was then bought and built into a palatial home by a Glasgow merchant named James Fleming. He made his money from cheap Indian cotton that he sold to Britain for inflated prices. He spent a fortune on the place and the completed house was said to have more windows than Buckingham Palace. They had to rectify that so as not to offend royalty, so two of the windows were filled in," Kate explained to Eden.

"So how is it in this state?" asked Eden.

"Well, Fleming went bankrupt and was a bit of a crook by all accounts. There was a warrant issued for his arrest and the house lay empty for many years before it was bought by Ninian Stewart from Glasgow, another merchant.

"When he died, the family sold it on to the Mackinnen MacNeil trust in 1915, who turned the building into Kintyre Technical College and it became a boarding school for boys. It was a very good school, but the boys were not permitted to leave the premises. They farmed, they swam in the sea and they cooked and kept the house clean as part of their schooling. Then one night in 1924, a mysterious fire started in their wood store in the house basement.

"There was a new boy named Rory MacDonald who had just started at the school. He called the alarm, but many suspect he had more to do with it than he let on. He never spoke a word of what had happened that night.

"The whole building burnt down, the 55 boys and 4 masters just managing to escape with their lives before the roof collapsed. It was utterly destroyed and the school was moved to Dumbarton," Kate told her.

"Another MacDonald story. Don't you think that's strange?" said Eden. "It's so sad, it must have been a magnificent building," said Eden.

They left the old ruins and Kate took Eden down to the Muneroy tearoom, which, this time, was full of customers. Lizzie was delighted to see Kate again and managed to squeeze them in. In no time, Eden was devouring a chocolate and coconut gateau, whilst Kate nibbled on some Millionaires Shortbread. Lizzie was busy, but Kate noticed a large hard book on the paper stand titled *Southend, Mull of Kintyre Reunited*.

The girls started to leaf their way through the book, which was the story of the Mull of Kintyre from the 1900s to the present day. It had incredible photographs of both Seal Lodge and the Keil House school before it was burnt down. Suddenly, they were looking at pictures of the Riley sisters outside the Lodge, in between them stood a small boy with a big grin on his face, it was Eden and Jamie's father, Ewan.

"Look how happy he is," said Eden, staring closely at the photo. "I still don't understand why he never mentioned this part of his life."

"We will find out, I'm sure there is a good explanation," replied Kate.

"Aw, he had a cheeky wee face," said Lizzie, suddenly appearing behind them. "Can I get you ladies anything else?"

"Can you tell us where we could find a copy of this book?" asked Kate. "Lizzie, I'd like to introduce you to Eden, she is Ewan's daughter. She and her brother are here to rebuild the Lodge."

Frances squealed with excitement, almost dropping her tray. The tearoom went quiet as everyone turned around to look at them.

"Yer really gonnae rebuild that old place?" said an elderly woman seated next to them, breaking the silence.

"Well, that was the plan," replied Eden nervously, not sure what sort of reaction she could expect.

"That's fantastic," said Lizzie, who then called her husband, Tim, in to tell him, as an excited buzz replaced the silence in the tearoom.

The girls were bombarded with questions and it was very clear that the local community were on board with their plans. Lizzie gave them a copy of the book, as they sold them in their store. Kate insisted on paying for it, so instead Lizzie gave them some cake to take home.

There was a strict policy in the tearoom that cakes could not be purchased for take away, so they were touched at the gesture.

By the time they got back in the car, Eden was grinning from ear to ear. "I think the locals like us," she said. "I'm so relieved, they are all so friendly, we are going to love it here."

A few days later, Jamie returned with the survey report and was delighted to find that the foundations were rock solid. He spent the next three days taking measurements and photographs from every angle. He worked continuously and the girls didn't see a lot of him. Kate and Eden had become fast friends, both as passionate as each other about unravelling the history at Southend.

Kate got a phone call from a local boatman named Donny who owned the boat marina at Southend, news had spread fast around Kintyre about the rebuild of the Lodge and Donny had seen Kate's number in Campbeltown. He offered to take them to Sanda, so the next day, they met him at the marina, Gizmo had been left behind, much to his disgust, but past experience told Kate he was not a sailor in any way, shape or form.

They boarded the small fishing boat and sat back as they set off into the Kilbrannan Sounds. It was a nice smooth ride, but the boat itself stunk of old fish guts, making Kate giggle as she watched Eden heave every now and then. To make matters worse, as soon as they left the shelter of the harbour and turned onto the open sea, the boat lurched and bounced in the rough waters. The weather was fine but as always, there was a strong Atlantic wind. Kate had the stomach for small boats as she had been out on many with her father, but for Eden, it was a different story. The poor girl soon turned green and threw up three times over the side of the boat in the hour and a quarter it took to reach Sanda. Kate felt a little guilty at enjoying the trip whilst Eden was so ill, but she loved the open water. She saw a basking shark making its way slowly through the waves, and bottle necked dolphins began to follow the boat, only to be disappointed as there was no fishing today.

Donny took the boat to the north of the island on the opposite side from its lighthouse. The new owner's house at the jetty looked completely deserted and so he took a chance and pulled in there, despite the private property signs.

Kate looked at her watch, it was already 11 a.m. and she didn't want to be out in the water when it got dark. It was late October now and the nights were drawing in. "Could you get us at three o'clock?" she asked.

"Make that 2:30, I dinnae wannae be stuck here by the tides," he said.

"Fine, we'll be here, thank you," said Kate. She looked at Eden, who was already getting some colour back in her cheeks.

Chapter Seven

The girls watched Donny's boat chug off, then they turned their attention towards the island. It was utterly deserted, except for the abundance of seabirds. Kate wished she was more of a twitcher, but as it was, she didn't know a seagull from a guillemot. This place had been a bird watcher's paradise for years, with Scotland's first bird observatory, but all that was gone now.

Eden pulled out the small map of the island she had photocopied from an old book in Campbeltown library. The sun had broken through the clouds now, and although there was a stiff wind, you could still feel the warmth in its rays. They passed by the farmhouse that was supposed to be used by the owners, but it looked like no one had been there for a very long time. They then passed the old pub, named 'The Byron Darnton Tavern' after a ship that had crashed on the rocks here in 1946, taking American servicemen and their families back to the US after the Second World War. The pub was also deserted, left to the mercy of the elements.

Passing the boat house which had been the base for the Sanda Island Bird Observatory, last used in 2013 and was now reduced to wreckage thanks presumably to the uncaring island owners.

"Why the hell does the Scottish government allow these foreigners to buy our beautiful Scottish islands and let them rot? There is so much history here, I'm absolutely disgusted," said Kate.

"Agreed," said Eden. "What on earth gives them the right to stop tourists coming here? These islands are part of our heritage, our ancestors lived here. I feel as angry as you do about what has happened here. It's utter sacrilege!"

They felt the heat from the sun as they walked up to the crumbling ruins of St Ninian's chapel. It was roofless now, but the side walls still stood to roof level, and there was an intact wooden lintel over the entrance. There was a stone alter slab inside and also a grave slab set in the floor that refers to 'Archibald – Son to MacDonald of Sanda and Cirstin Stewart'. Cirstin Stewart was the wife to Archibald Mor MacDonald who was killed in the Dunaverty Massacre.

"The man Colkitto left in charge at Dunaverty must have come from Sanda originally," said Kate.

They carried on exploring the churchyard and found in the burial ground one very early cruciform-shaped stone that was extremely eroded. There were also a few scattered grave stones dated much later with heraldic memorials to the MacDonald lairds, but they couldn't find one for Conall MacDonald.

Eden suddenly shouted over to Kate, "Look, I've found a stone for Mary, daughter of Conall MacDonald."

"Well, at least that's proof that he did live here," said Kate. "I wonder what happened to him."

Kate had been reading about St Ninian, who was supposed to have visited Sanda, but as with many other claims, nothing was particularly clear. There were many who claimed St Ninian was buried here, but then there were many other islands that also held the same claim. Naturally, there was a local legend to go with the story. It said that if you stood on the unmarked grave of St Ninian on Sanda, you would die within the year. The grave apparently used to be marked by an alder tree, but that has long gone, so now you just took your chances.

Kate and Eden walked over the island and found themselves sheltered from the winds by the hills on either side as they headed towards Wallace Rocks and the lighthouse. It only took them 45 minutes to reach the other side of the island. Kate clambered up towards the old abandoned lighthouse. It had been constructed in 1850. When seen from the sea, the natural arch of the rock with the lighthouse on it made it look like a ship, and so it was named 'The Ship' on marine charts.

In other stories about Sanda Island, Robert the Bruce, stayed here after fleeing Dunaverty Castle, where he was hiding in 1306. He was pursued by the English navy and had hidden on Sanda en route to Ireland. 'Prince Edwards Rock' just south of the lighthouse is named after his brother Edward Bruce, who was made, for a very brief spell, King of Ireland.

With all this wonderful history surrounding them, Kate felt nothing but disappointment, sickened by the state the island had been allowed to get into. She hoped to find perhaps more ruins of homes that the MacDonalds may have lived in. There seemed to be nothing here that would help Eden or Jamie find out any more about Colkitto or his son Conall. She turned to Eden, whom she had thought was standing just behind her, but Eden was gone. Kate looked around but couldn't see her anywhere. Bewildered, she started to climb back down from the lighthouse, calling to Eden as she went, and then Kate saw her standing down on Wallace Rocks, perilously close to the sea. The waves were crashing in over her and Eden just seemed to be standing there, staring out at the ocean, unaffected by the waves or the danger she was in. Kate doubted Eden could hear her shout above the sound of crashing waves and she couldn't understand what the hell Eden was doing.

Kate started to clamber over the slippery seaweed-covered rocks to where Eden was standing. The girl was just standing there as if in some sort of trance. Kate slipped and banged her knee hard on a rock. "Eden!" she called. "What are you doing?" But Eden just stood, as if in some sort of trance, gazing out towards the ocean, her face showing no sign that she was aware of where she was.

Kate pulled herself over the rocks, each one getting more slippery the closer she got to the sea. The sea spray had completely soaked her and water was running down her face. "Eden, what's happening?" she yelled again. Kate was close enough now that Eden should hear her, but still she stood as still as a statue, staring out to sea. She noticed that the spray from the waves seemed to avoid Eden as if she had a protective bubble over her. Kate was completely sodden, but Eden seemed bone dry.

Finally, Kate managed to reach out and grab Eden's arm. "Eden, wake up, it's me. You're going to get us killed!"

Eden turned her head slowly to face Kate and Kate stumbled backwards with shock. Eden's eyes were completely black, the whites of her eyes were gone, and they seemed empty and void of life. Kate grabbed her again and shook her hard. "Eden, wake up, what's the matter with you?"

Suddenly, Eden blinked and her eyes changed immediately. "Kate?" she said with a confused look on her face. Then a wave washed over them, and she woke up, "What the hell are we doing here? Oh, my God, how did we get here?" she half screamed.

A large wave crashed in again, covering them both with spray. Kate grabbed hold of Eden's hand and pulled her back the way she had come. It seemed even more treacherous on the way back, but eventually, they were crawling up onto the grassy slope.

They both collapsed, breathing heavily. "What the hell happened to you back there?" said Kate. "I thought you were behind me at the lighthouse, but when I turned, you had vanished."

"I don't know, I don't remember going there," said Eden, who was completely horrified. "All I can remember is climbing up to the lighthouse with you, then hearing that strange music."

"What music?" asked Kate, rubbing her leg. There was a hole in her jeans and she could see her knee was bleeding underneath.

"You must have heard it. It was… it was… honestly, I can't describe it now, I can't remember," said Eden, rubbing her head in frustration.

"I never heard anything at all, but whatever it was, it had you in some sort of trance. Has anything like this ever happened to you before?" asked Kate.

"No, never. I really can't explain it. It's really freaked me out," said Eden.

"Look, we better get back to the jetty," said Kate, looking at her watch. Donny will be coming for us, and we'll catch our death in these clothes. I'm soaked through, let's hope he has some blankets."

"I'm sorry, Kate," said Eden, looking really upset.

"Oh, for goodness' sake, I wasn't complaining," Kate started to laugh. "It's the most exciting thing that's happened to me for a while. I can't wait to hear what Jamie is going to say about the ghostly singing. Maybe it was some sort of harpy trying to lure you to your death from the rocks."

"I'm not sure I can laugh about it yet," said Eden. "But whatever it was, I don't think it was trying to harm me."

"Well, I'm just glad we are safe and have lived to tell the tale," said Kate.

The walk back across the island wasn't fun for either of them. They were both freezing cold and Kate's knee was really throbbing from falling on the rocks. She decided not to complain about it to Eden, who felt bad enough as it was. Eden seemed less shaken when they reached the jetty; thankfully, Donny was already there waiting for them.

"What happened tae ye?" he asked.

"We got caught in a freak wave on the shore," said Kate immediately and Eden looked relieved.

"I've some spare clothes in the cabin. Yer welcome tae them, yer gonnae get really cold otherwise," Donny offered and they gratefully accepted.

Eden was quiet on the trip back and, thankfully, not sick. Kate was standing in one of Donny's old sweaters and galoshes, dabbing her knee with antiseptic ointment from his medical supplies. She chatted to him about the island and why the new owners had left it to rot like that. He was as angry as she was about it, as were many of the people in Campbeltown. Not only was it letting the island fall into disrepair, but many jobs had been lost because of it.

When they arrived back at Southend marina, Kate promised they would drop his clothes back with him the next day. He wasn't too worried and gave them his number in case they needed him again.

By the time they had driven back to the cottage, they were both too tired to talk about what had happened. Jamie was still out, so Kate poured them a glass of wine and opened a can of beans to go on some toast. They were both in bed and asleep when Jamie finally got back to the house.

Chapter Eight

Jamie was also tired when he arrived back at Kate's. The whole rebuild of the Lodge was going to be a huge project. When he had first heard about his father, followed on by meeting his half-sisters, he had been swept up in the excitement of it all. Now the immense size of the project was hitting home. He had never taken on anything quite as big as this, and he hoped he wouldn't let the girls down.

Jamie was born in Glasgow, he had never met his real father, though he always knew that his mum's husband, Bill, was not his birth father. She had never hidden that from him and Bill had been a good father to Jamie. His parents went on to have twin sons, Cameron and Tom, and the boys grew up happily in the High Burnside area of Glasgow.

All the boys were tall and athletic, but as much as Cam and Tom were blonde and blue eyed, Jamie was dark haired with brown eyes. He was an excellent swimmer and won a lot of competitions for his high school. He was offered a chance to train with professional swimming coaches, but it all fell to the way side when his mum was diagnosed with breast cancer. The cancer had been discovered too late, but it still took an agonising six months for his mother to pass, leaving the boys and their father devastated.

A couple of years later, Jamie got accepted in Edinburgh University to study architecture. He moved into a flat in the Cowgate area of Edinburgh and lived the ultimate student lifestyle. This involved a series of pubs and parties, but somehow, he got his degree and got offered a job for a firm in London.

He moved down to London and managed to get himself a room in a shared house near to Manor House tube station in the predominately Turkish area of the city. He lived there for the next five years, making good friends with his housemates and truly developing a love of Turkish food. He also met Charlotte there, a young paralegal who happened to be in the same bar as him one

Friday evening. Jamie had never really been in love before. There had been plenty of girlfriends and a few one-night stands during his student days, but nothing very serious. So, it was a total surprise for Jamie when he fell hook, line and sinker for her dark grey intelligent eyes and short spikey blonde hair.

He and Charlotte moved in together a few months after meeting and a few months after that, they were married on a beach in the Bahamas. Jamie's dad and brothers attended the wedding, as well as Charlotte's family and a couple of friends. It had been Charlotte's idea, the whole wedding on the beach thing, and Jamie had taken some ribbing from his brothers because of it. The wedding went well though and he loved being by the ocean; in fact, they could hardly get him out of the water.

He managed to scrape up enough for a deposit for a flat in Crouch End in London, and never felt happier. Charlotte, however, must have felt differently. She was five years his junior, and it wasn't long until she resumed her after-work drinks on a Friday night.

As the months went by, she came in later and later, then it wasn't just Fridays, and often she wouldn't appear until after midnight, usually the worse for wear. Jamie tried to put his foot down, but it just caused rows. Charlotte was independent and strong willed, and to be honest, it was what had attracted him to her in the first place.

They started to live separate lives and soon, they were just ships that passed in the night. Jamie had tried to talk to her, but Charlotte told him in no uncertain terms to lighten up. She wanted to live her life while she was young. It wasn't long before Jamie suspected she was doing more than just living her life, and sure enough, in the third year of their marriage, she announced it was over. She had fallen for one of the lawyers in her firm, and she was sorry, but she had to follow her heart. Jamie was not surprised or as upset as he thought he would be. In fact, after suspecting something was going on, it was a relief to finally get it over with.

Having just turned 31, Jamie decided to get out of London and set himself up in Brighton. He wanted to move by the sea and as most of his work associates were located in the southeast, Brighton seemed a sensible choice. Through his contacts, he managed to get himself a couple of contracts for houses in the area, and over the last eight years, his reputation and his business had grown.

He loved Brighton, he would go for a swim in the sea every morning, then return to his huge sea view apartment to work on his drawing boards. He dated a few times but nothing serious, and he got to know the quirky locals exploring the lanes and local pubs. He had a nice life, he was a really friendly and approachable guy, but all the time, he felt something was missing. He had thought he should look at meeting someone and settling down, but he just wasn't convinced that was what he wanted to do. Both his brothers were married now and he was an uncle to two lively boys. Cam and Tom were still in Glasgow and Jamie tried to get home as often as he could to see them and his dad. It still wasn't enough he knew that. His dad was getting older, and Jamie felt guilty that he was leaving all the care to his brothers, though none of them complained and they were always pleased to see him.

Then, three months ago, he had received the letter from his birth father's solicitor and, suddenly, he felt that rush of excitement that he now knew he had been missing in his life. To top it all, it had led him to Kate. He remembered her from the Granary Bar in Edinburgh during his student days. She told him she was in her first year at Napier University, that made her about three years younger than him. He had tried to chat her up, but she had been working at the bar and it was heaving in there. He didn't stand a chance.

One day, about four years ago, he was walking through the lanes in Brighton when he saw a poster stuck up on a notice board saying she was coming to Brighton for a book signing. He thought he would go but had no doubt she wouldn't remember him, and that was confirmed after he had stood in a queue to get his book signed.

She had smiled politely and asked who to sign the book to. He felt like a fool when he gave her his name and more of a fool when he actually read the book. It was a historical romance, not his cup of tea at all. No wonder there were hardly any men in that shop. He would keep that one quiet for now, it still made him cringe, and he still had the book, *The Heiress of Dunrobin*, signed on the front cover, 'To Jamie, enjoy, Kate MacPhee'.

He had read about her husband's accident online, then saw she had moved to the Mull of Kintyre in one of the Sunday supplement's he always had delivered. He wondered what had taken her to the Mull of Kintyre but had not thought much more about it until he received that letter. Jamie was registered at Hamish's medical practice, though he had never been to a doctor's surgery, apart from an occasional check-up as a child. But he wondered if Hamish was still in touch with Kate, so he had made an appointment.

He had vaguely known Hamish as they had attended the same uni, albeit different courses, but they had socialised a few times together. Hamish, thankfully, did remember him and had been quite friendly with Kate, although they had not been in touch for years. He said he would write to her, give her Jamie's email address and they would take it from there. She emailed him a month later and said she would love to help, and now, here they were.

It was love at first sight when Jamie saw her again. Kate was a fresh-faced beauty, with lively blonde hair and bright, inquisitive blue eyes. He loved the way she blushed so easily, her eyes hidden under her dark lashes. He just wanted to scoop her up, but resisted. He would play the waiting game until he was sure she was ready.

The first meeting with his sisters had gone better than he could have ever imagined. Immediately, he could see the family resemblance, they all had the same eyes, though the girl's faces were more elfin shaped compared to his own chiselled jawline.

Carly was happily married to a local police inspector. They had two children, aged two and four, and Carly worked at home, inputting data for the overworked Scottish police force. She was a very attractive woman, with long dark hair and a warm and friendly disposition. She seemed delighted to meet Jamie and did not seem as shocked at having a half-brother as Eden was.

Eden was in complete contrast to her calm, mature sister. She was a 27-year-old bundle of energy, dark spikey hair tipped with purple, dark eye makeup and he could see at least one tattoo winding its way up her arm. He suspected there were more. She told him she was between jobs and he saw Carly smile and roll her eyes. Eden punched her in a joking way and went on to explain that she wanted to be an actress. She had performed in many small theatre productions around the city and had a few small bit parts on TV productions and even one major Hollywood film, but her dreams of being snapped up had not quite happened yet. She had been working for her boyfriend, who had a tattoo parlour down in Leith, but had recently split from him and was currently unemployed.

It was clear the sisters were very close, but Eden was more than curious about him. She bombarded him with questions and he found he was answering her happily, having nothing to hide. Carly told her off a couple of times, but in all honesty, Eden's infectious personality did not seem, in the least, intrusive. Before long, she virtually had his life story and a bond was formed.

Eden had been very close to her father, so had been upset when she had learnt he held back so many secrets from her. But as happened often with Eden, she got over it quickly and turned her confusion into a mission. She was going to find out all there was about her father and where he came from, and there would be no stopping her. She was fascinated with the photo Kate had returned to him. Ewan had never spoken of his mother, but her likeness to both the girls was uncanny.

Jamie got close to Eden in a very short time and hoped she and Kate would get on, as he doubted he could stop Eden bulldozing her way into his life. Luckily, they hit it off immediately, both of them with a limitless source of imagination and keen, inquiring minds. In all honesty, he had been more than impressed by what the two of them had found out through their joint investigations. They had been having a lot of fun together exploring the Mull and surrounding areas.

Jamie poured himself a large scotch and settled in the comfy settee in the conservatory. He had had a strange day up at the Lodge. Local builders from Campbeltown had arrived in the morning and they had been eager to get the contract for the rebuild, and Jamie found they had some good ideas on how to proceed.

Jamie was torn as he knew of a good team in Glasgow but was aware he knew nothing about the building expertise here on the Mull, and using local people for the work would build a good reputation for the Lodge. They wouldn't want outsiders in taking their jobs, so it was a relief when he had finally met Stuart Aiken and his local crew and realised how skilled they actually were. They had just finished a major job at another hotel and were ready to start the build.

Jamie thought of waiting until spring for the weather to be better, but they assured him that the weather on the Mull was unpredictable at any time of year, and as the foundations were strong, they could get the roof on quickly. They could get skips in and start clearing away the debris the following week. Jamie would have to get to his drawing board out and come up with some initial plans, it was happening way quicker than he anticipated, but he was caught up in the excitement of it now. Eden would be delighted to hear they could start so soon. Everything being well, they could have the Lodge open by next autumn at least, giving them time to choose the furnishing and get the décor done ready for opening.

After the builders had gone, Jamie walked through the Lodge, roughly drawing sketches of the floor layout. Although the roof was gone, the walls and staircases were still intact and he climbed up to the first floor to continue his sketches. He entered one of the many small box rooms that had been single bedrooms.

The old floral wall paper was peeling from the walls and the carpet was ripped and stained. It would be a massive job just clearing the old place out, but he was beginning to see the potential, the views across the bay from this level were incredible.

The room suddenly started to feel icy cold and Jamie began to see the steam from his breath. He felt something brush past him and he jumped around, but there was nothing there. He couldn't decide whether he was just tired or still slightly spooked by all the ghost stories he had been told about the Lodge. Jamie thought of the strange figure he had seen in the graveyard the other day. He laughed nervously at himself, what an idiot he was being, he went back to the stairs, carrying his notebook and large measuring tape as he walked carefully down the staircase.

A cold breeze swept past him again and he became very aware of some sort of presence close to him. Bewildered, he stopped and looked around but saw nothing but his breath, then he felt something shove him hard, he lost his footing and tumbled the rest of the way down the stairs. He landed hard at the bottom, bruised but no serious damage. He got to his feet and looked around but could see no one, the place was deserted. He picked up his tape and notebook and headed out the door, bruised and battered he just wanted to get outside.

The fresh air cleared his head, and he decided to walk along the beach just past the caves. He was a little shaken up but couldn't make sense of it, not unless he was going to fall into the trap of believing in ghosts.

He walked past the caves on his right and the rock pools on his left, where he could see seals watching him from beyond the rocks. There were five of them, he counted, and as he walked down the sandy slope to the beach, they followed him along the coastline, from just beyond where the huge waves formed into white foaming crescents. This side of the beach was deserted, as usual, and the wind was relentless. He zipped up his fleece and continued walking just short of where the waves rolled in. He got towards the end of the beach, feeling better and warmer from his walk. He looked out at the seals who were watching him still from their safe distance, but there were only four now.

As Jamie turned to head back, he thought he could hear something, some sort of music floating over the water. No, it was more the sound of a voice, a female voice singing; no, surely not, it must be the seabirds. But as he listened, he could hear the haunting melody become clearer as if it were travelling with the wind. It was the unmistakable voice of a young woman and it seemed so familiar to him. The hypnotic song offered him sanctuary and filled him with such a deep sense of belonging, that he yearned to go to it. His mind filled with images of the sea, of riding the waves and diving deep through its depths. He was swimming along the ocean floor, knocking over hermit crabs and chasing octopus out of their hiding holes. He was not alone, he was racing with the other seals, diving as deep as he could, then speeding towards the surface to break free of the waves and take a breath of fresh, sweet sea air.

"Hey! Come on, laddie, wake up, ye eejit!" a deep voice broke through the spell.

"I can see ye oot there, let the laddie gae before ye kill him!" shouted the voice. "Laddie, wake up, yer gonnae droon if ye dinnae get oot the water!"

The singing stopped abruptly and Jamie's mind jumped back into focus. He was standing knee-deep in the sea, the waves were crashing over him and he was soaked through. He felt the rip tide pull at him and he could hardly stand. Holding him steady was a giant of a man, seemingly not bothered about the rip tides that were pulling at Jamie with such a ferocity. The man steered him back to the shore, then stood and looked at him.

"What the hell was I doing?" Jamie shouted over the roar of the waves and wind. "I'm so sorry I've made you get soaked. I don't know how to thank you."

"Aye, well, there's some folks who shudnae be strolling so close tae the shore, especially roond these parts," said the man.

Jamie caught his breath and got his first good look at his rescuer. He was a giant of a man, with wild white hair and a full beard. Jamie thought he was tall at 6'2", but this man had to be 6'6" at least. His age was undeterminable, and he was wearing a well-worn kilt and matching plaid thrown over a thick woollen shirt. But it was the huge claymore hanging from his shoulder and the dirk that was tucked into his stocking that drew Jamie's eye. The man was also bone dry, whilst Jamie stood there dripping and shivering. He couldn't think what to say next as the stranger eyed him intensely with piercing blue eyes. "Are you from around here?" Jamie eventually asked.

"Aye, I suppose I am, and who might ye be, laddie? Yer nae related tae these Selkies, or are ye?"

"Selkies?"

"Aye, those fish-eating, soul-stealing spirits o' the sea, they're still watching ye, laddie, ye need tae be careful aroond here," said the man.

Jamie turned and looked towards the sea and saw the four seals floating there, looking curiously in their direction. This stranger was clearly a little insane, maybe Jamie should just introduce himself and find out who the man was.

"Thanks very much for helping me out, I don't know what was wrong there. My name is Jamie MacDonald," he said. "I'm going to be renovating Seal Lodge."

"Are ye noo? A MacDonald back at Seal Lodge, eh? Wonder will never cease," said the man.

"Well, I'm hoping to do it justice," said Jamie.

"Justice, ye say. Well, ye'll nae find a lot of that aroond these shores. Ye need tae be careful carrying the name MacDonald here. Watch yer back, laddie, and stay oot the water, if ye ken what's good fir ye," said the stranger.

"Do you have a name, sir?" Jamie asked, not understanding what this man was talking about at all. "I'd like to know who to thank."

"Colla, that's what people roond here call me," he replied.

"Well, Colla, I hope you'll come to the Lodge when we eventually open," said Jamie, who was now really cold and desperate to get back to his car. He turned to look towards the Lodge for just a second as he spoke, but as he turned back to Colla, the man was gone. He had completely vanished, there was no one on the beach, apart from himself.

Freezing cold now, Jamie didn't hang about and slowly jogged back up the beach and along the road to the Lodge. He always kept a change of clothes in the car in case he got muddy or soaked through during his site visits, so soon enough, he was changed and sitting in his car with the heater blasting.

He tried to get his head around what had just happened on the beach, but no matter what excuse he came up with, he had no idea why he walked into the sea. Perhaps he was more tired and stressed than he realised.

And then there was Colla. Where had he vanished to? And why was he dressed so strangely? He would have to ask around to find out who he was. It was getting dark now, and he felt exhausted, so he decided to drive straight back to Kate's.

When he got back, the chapel was dark and quiet. He'd seen Kate's car, so he knew they were in. Gizmo bounced over to him when he walked through the door and he let the little dog out to play. The girls must have had a busy day also, as they were both asleep.

Jamie finished his whiskey and let Gizmo back in the house and gave the dog a couple of biscuits. He wasn't hungry himself, so he took himself off to his room, undressed and got into bed. His mind was still reeling after the day's events, so he decided to read the book Eden had got on 'Colkitto'. After reading for an hour of murders, treachery and battles, his lids grew heavy and he fell into a fitful sleep.

Chapter Nine

Moire breathed a sigh of relief when the two women managed to scramble away from the edge of the sea on Sanda Island. She hadn't meant to put them in any danger, but she had been so sure about the young dark-haired woman. Moire had first spotted Eden on the beach at Southend when she and her friends had been swimming there. The young woman's aura, along with her dark hair and soft brown eyes, was instantly recognisable, and Moire knew this young woman, and the man she was with, had Selkie blood. Not only that, but their resemblance to Moire herself was uncanny.

It was as if fate had intervened when, a few days later, Moire spotted the same young woman on a boat headed for Sanda Island. The Selkie followed the boat and watched as the women got off and started to explore. Moire guessed they would head to the lighthouse, so she swam around to the other side of the island. She pulled herself up on to a rock that stood a little way off the coast, hidden from the lighthouse but close enough for her to see them coming. She then transformed into her human body, revealing a beautiful young Selkie woman, with elfin features and glorious dark hair blowing in the wind.

Selkies were ancient ocean-dwelling people who had lived for thousands of years in the seas and oceans of the Northern Hemisphere. Many legends were told of the seal people throughout the centuries, but none were completely accurate. The Selkie Folk lived in the water as seals, but they lived in air-filled caverns at the bottom of the ocean. Once they were out of the water, most Selkies could take on human form. They were a gentle race of magical beings, whose only downfall was their never-ending curiosity. It would get them in trouble with fishermen, and that is where a lot of the stories around the seal people came from.

Legends about the Selkies are well known in Canada, Russia, Iceland, Norway and Finland, as well as the British Isles. The land-dwellers believe that Selkies shed their skin to bask in the sun when they come out of the water. Some stories tell of how fishermen would come across beautiful Selkie women sunbathing on a beach. The fishermen would steal their skins so they could not return to the ocean, forcing the women to become their wives.

These stories are untrue, as Selkies do not actually shed skins, and it would be unlikely for any land-dweller to have the power to imprison a Selkie. However, Selkies do occasionally fall in love with a land-dweller and then they choose for themselves whether to live a mortal life. It is a difficult choice for them, as Selkies can live for hundreds of years; however, if they choose to live as a land-dweller, they will age as a land-dweller does. In many cases, the call of the ocean is too strong and the Selkie will return to the water. Their youth is restored; however, they no longer will have the ability to transform and must live out the remainder of their life as a seal.

Moire's curiosity about the land-dwellers had got her in many scrapes, and she was frequently in trouble with her mother for getting too close to them. Her mother, Isla, was the Selkie Queen to the pod they all belonged to.

The great white Selkie King Fionnlagh was Moire's father and their reign covered most of the west coast of Scotland. The main Selkie pod lived under Eileen Nom Ran, the Island of Seals, just south of Oronsay. It is uninhabited by the land-dwellers but a mating ground for the Atlantic grey seals, which give the Selkies perfect cover to travel to and from the island unspotted. Under Eileen Nom Ran was a huge underwater cavern, which the Selkie pod use as their home.

Isla had tried to make Moire remain with them at Seal Island, but as Moire got older, she and her friends became more curious about the land-dwellers. They were, after all, their ancient relatives, and it was a land-dweller body that they changed into when they transformed.

Moire and her friends would often explore the more inhabited islands and, sometimes, even the mainland of Scotland. Her mother would have been furious if she had known Moire had swum up the Firth of Clyde to the Isles of Arran and Bute. They could easily have been trapped with no quick escape to the open sea. The fisherman on the Firth did not like seals near their nets and would shoot them if they were spotted, so it was a hazardous place for Selkies.

There were other dangers for them in open water, not least of all sharks, and recently, a pod of orcas had been seen swimming close to the West Coast Islands. That never bode well for the Selkie Folk or the grey seals. Thankfully, it was rare for them to come this far south, but it happened occasionally.

From what Moire had seen of the land-dwellers, they did not seem as bad as her mother had described. She was wise enough to stay away from the fishermen and their nets, but the other land-dwellers often seemed excited when they saw her and her friends. The land dwellers would look at them through goggle-like things and peer down at them from the sides of their boats, shouting with excitement when Moire or her friends lifted their heads out of the water. It became quite a game for them.

Moire had often come across folk who looked like they could belong to the Selkies. Dark hair and brown eyes were not uncommon in the land-dweller world, but there was something different about a Selkie, they carried an aura that only another Selkie would recognise. Selkie woman were always beautiful in human form, their narrow faces and huge eyes were alluring to land-dwellers. The male Selkies were strong, handsome and very muscular as they swam great distances on hunts.

Moire watched as the two women arrived at the lighthouse. She could see them struggle in the wind as they climbed up the steps. Moire was certain that this dark-haired young woman was related to them in some way. There was a particular spell that Aegir, the great God of the Ocean, had given to the Selkie Mother thousands of years before to help the Selkies recognise their own. The spell would only be heard by those of Selkie blood, and Moire was desperate to find out who this young woman was, so she started to sing the haunting melody of the Selkies.

As she sang, her music drifted with the wind towards the island and Moire saw the dark-haired woman lift her head and turn in the Selkie's direction. Moire sang on, sure now this girl was one of them, and as she watched, the young woman climbed back down from the lighthouse and started to walk down the rocks towards the ocean.

Aware that the spell may pull the girl into the water, Moire changed the pitch of her song, preventing Eden from taking that final step into the sea. She held the young woman in a trance, sharing the wonders of the ocean with her and trying to form a bond on a deeper level. It was too soon to pull the young woman into the ocean to join her. Selkies did not kidnap half-bloods, they needed to be allowed to make the choice to come to the ocean themselves. This woman was half land-dweller after all, and she may wish to remain there.

Moire voice conjured images of the ocean, and she could just start to feel their connection forming when the other woman suddenly appeared scrambling over the rocks towards her friend. This woman was definitely not of Selkie blood. Moire could see she was very unsteady on her feet and dangerously close to falling into the rocky depths as the waves pounded her. Moire, realising the danger she was causing, stopped her song immediately, releasing the dark-haired young woman from her spell. She watched as the pair of them struggled back up the rocks, getting battered by the waves that Moire had previously been protecting the young woman from. She was relieved when she saw they were safe but felt a little guilty of the danger she had put them in. Next time she would have to be more careful, she couldn't risk putting lives at danger, that was against Selkie law.

Moire was now sure that the woman on Sanda was of Selkie origin, she wondered what she should do next. It was strange that the woman was on Sanda. That island had been deserted for years by the land-dwellers, and it had become a good meeting place for the young courting Selkies. She would have to report this to the Selkie Council, for they kept a log of missing Selkie children and, surely, there would be some parent wishing to be reunited with their daughter.

Moire slid back into the water, instantly transforming to her seal form. She swam around the island to the jetty at the other side. Their boat had come back for them, so she waited until they boarded, then followed at a safe distance as they headed back to the town on the mainland. She knew she could not follow them into the harbour of the town, so she broke off her pursuit and headed inshore towards her Selkie friends, who were swimming around Southend bay by the cliffs.

Her four friends were there, lying on the rocks opposite the caves they often snuck into when they transformed to their human bodies after dark. Uarraig called Moire over to them. He was a large, black male seal and considered himself the leader of their group. Maili was with him, a much smaller speckled grey seal, with large black eyes. She was due to be bonded to Uarraig at the next full moon ceremony.

Dand was also there, a chocolate brown seal, with mischievous hazel eyes, he was the joker of the group and the most daring. And then there was Sorcha, glistening smooth black skin, her land-dweller form was something to behold, with her intoxicating eyes and dark skin.

They were all watching a loan, handsome man walk along the seafront. It was the same man that Moire had seen with the two women the other day.

"Uarraig, you won't believe what just happened," Moire used telepathy, the language of choice for the Selkies when in their seal form.

Uarraig slipped off the rock to join Moire, and the others followed suit. "You see this man?" said Uarraig. "He was the one we saw the other day, with a female, and they both have Selkie traits."

"I have just seen the female on Sanda," said Moire.

She turned her attention to the man who was now walking on the beach. Uarraig submerged under the waves and swam around to the beach, the others following him. They raised their heads above the water just beyond the waves that would have dragged them in. They watched Jamie as he walked along the water's edge.

"He has the same look as the woman I saw on the island," Moire told them. "I think he is a half-blood."

"We should see if he can hear our call," said Maili. "I can swim to the cliffs and sing the Selkie call."

"I just did that at Sanda Island. The woman heard me, she had such a strong connection, I could have brought her right into the sea," said Moire.

"I don't know of anyone in the pod being found this way for years. Perhaps they are related, we need to see if he can hear us," said Uarraig. "Then we will have to head off to tell the others at the meet."

"Very well, it's safe here just now, there is no one else around, go try it, Maili," said Moire. "But be careful not to harm him."

Maili swam off to the shore facing her, towards the rocks that formed the coastline leading to the Mull of Kintyre lighthouse. She clambered on to a flat rock hidden from the shore and checked the coastline for boats. Once she was sure she could not be spotted, she transformed to reveal a petite young woman, with a startling mane of white- and blue-tinged hair cascading down her back. She was a stark contrast to the dark-eyed Moire, but beautiful nevertheless. Maili started her song, singing the same magical spell that Moire had used not a couple of hours earlier. The music danced in the wind, skipping over the waves towards the shore, while the other Selkies watched from the ocean.

The man stopped walking and turned his head towards them, Moire recognised the Selkie traits in his eyes, "He looks like the woman I saw earlier," she said.

The man started to walk slowly into the sea, the spell surrounding him, protecting him from the crashing waves and the rip tide current. He stopped when the water was just above his knees as Maili had changed the song slightly to stop him coming in further. She sent him images of playing with his brothers and sisters of the ocean, of riding the waves and chasing the fish. She could feel his connection was strong and so continued to sing, bringing him deeper into the Selkie world.

Moire watched him stand still in the waves, unaffected by the push and pull of the rip tide. "He has been under for a long time now," she warned the others.

"Perhaps he wishes to join us," suggested Dand.

"He needs to be given the choice, not brought under a spell," said Uarraig and then called to his mate, "Maili, let him go."

"I have tried," Maili called back to them. "But he won't let go of the magic."

"I told you he wished to come with us," said Dand.

They watched as the man, whose eyes were now completely black, was still staring out to the sea, completely lost in the Selkie spell. "We have to help him," said Moire, starting to panic, not least of all because of the wrath she feared from her mother. "We can't just leave him like this."

Then as if their joint wishes were answered, they saw a man appear on the beach. Moire gasped with recognition, as did the others when they clapped eyes on him. They watched as Colla Ciotach walked towards the man and called out to him. He then looked out at the sea and saw them watching. "I can see ye oot there, let him gae!" he yelled at them, then marched into the sea. He grabbed hold of the man and shook him hard, "Let him gae!" Colla roared at them, pulling the man away from the spell. At once, the waves crashed over them, and the Selkies could see the man was disoriented and in shock. Colla dragged him back to shore, cursing at them as he did so.

Uarraig was worried, "We need to leave this place now. Maili, come back to us, I think it's time we headed back to the pod. We are going to have some explaining to do, not least of all why we are so late for the meet."

"Do you think that Colla knew who we are?" Moire asked them, she was still worried about his reaction.

"I don't know," replied Uarraig "I hope not. If he tells your mother what we did, we will be in trouble."

Maili swam back to the group, once more in the form of a light grey seal. They set off around the tip of Kintyre and out into the open sea, heading north towards Eileen Nan Ron, the Island of Seals, at the south of Oronsay Island.

The Island of Seals, or Eileen Nan Ron as the local people called it, was not only their home, but also the ancient meeting place of the Northern Selkies. Every October, the Atlantic grey seal would arrive in their thousands to the breeding ground on Eileen Non Ran. The cries of the bull seals could be heard for miles around and conservationists left the island alone. It was a perfect time for the Selkies to have their annual meet. The Selkies could swim in with the seals and then dive down to the huge cavern hidden under the sea.

The visiting Selkie pods arrived safely in large numbers under the cover of the mating seals on Eileen Nan Ron's shore. The Scottish and Irish Selkies were usually first to arrive, then the Welsh and English pods would swim in. Selkies would come from as far as Norway, Finland, Russia and even Iceland to attend this annual meet.

The Selkies swam down to the deep cavern entrance and then re-emerged in an underground sea lake that filled most of the cave. They could transform and would spend nearly a month together as a group, feasting, socialising and attending the council meetings. Everything they had seen and done over the past year would be shared, bondings would take place and the Selkies who had been lost to the pods were remembered. That included the Selkies who had chosen to live as land-dwellers.

King Fionnlagh and Queen Isla were the heads of the Western Isle Selkies. They had been welcoming new arrivals at Seal Island for nearly two weeks now but were still waiting for the arrival of their daughter, Moire. Isla had a lot of news to share with her, not least of all that her son Ewan had returned to the pod. It had been a difficult decision for him as he had left a family behind, but in the end, the calling of the ocean had been too strong. Most Selkies came back to the ocean after living a full land-dweller's life. Usually, it was due to the death of their land-dweller partners. They had no need to remain on shore and they knew their youth would be restored once they came back to the sea, even though they would never be able to take human form again.

Ewan had considered this for many years before he finally made that choice, even though it meant he would never see his children again. Eden and Carly were young women now and had their own lives. He knew Carly would be fine with her husband and family, but he had agonised over leaving Eden. She could never really settle, and he often wondered if it was the Selkie blood in her. But Eden had never given any indication that she could hear the calling of the ocean, so he never approached it with her.

Before Ewan left, he had finally searched out Jamie and was saddened to hear his mother had died. She had been his first love when he went to university in Glasgow. They knew before Jamie was born that the relationship was not going to work and separated soon after. Although he paid for Jamie's child support throughout the years, he stood aside to let Bill raise him, which Jamie's mother was grateful for.

Ewan was pleased to find out Jamie had followed him in the career of architecture, and when he managed to buy Seal Lodge, it was with Jamie in mind. He had hoped that his son would fall in love with the place and remain on Kintyre.

He knew his daughters would welcome Jamie to the family and hoped they would all come to visit the Lodge. Ewan would be able to watch them from the sea, and maybe one day, one of them would hear the calling and decide to come and join him.

When Ewan had finally swum out at Gullane Beach, he felt he had all his loose ends covered and hoped he would be able to watch the rebuild of the Lodge from the Kintyre coast. His mother was waiting for him when he entered the water, she had known this day was coming and was here to lead him back to the ocean.

As he swam out to the deep water, Ewan felt a familiar shiver and then his body changed and, suddenly, he was racing through the currents, strong, free and more alive than he had felt for years.

Ewan was now at Eileen Non Ran with the other Selkies but remained with the others who had chosen to come back to the sea and were unable to transform. They stayed by the sea lake, and the council meetings were always held in the water, so they did not miss out. Ewan was also awaiting the arrival of his sister, Moire, whom he left all these years before when he and his mother had gone to the Lodge.

Isla had brought him to Seal Lodge so he could grow into a man and make his own decision about whether to return to the Selkies or live a land-dweller's life. She hated living on land and had gone to the ocean every night to see Moire and her husband, Fionnlach. She could not leave the ocean for long, for if she did, she would lose her ability to transform. Her son was swept away with the teenage lifestyle and had chosen a land-dweller life, so Isla returned to the sea on the eve of his 18th birthday.

Moire's father was the Selkie King named Fionnlagh, the name meaning White Warrior, and indeed he was a huge white Selkie. He had welcomed a very nervous Ewan back to the pod helping him readjust to Selkie life. They shared stories about their daughters, and Fionnlagh told Ewan that Moire was pushing the boundaries, as all young Selkies did. She was incredibly curious and he and Isla were constantly worried that she would be killed or captured by fishermen.

Moire and her friends were already a week late for the meet, and all their parents were getting worried. If they did not appear soon, a search party would be sent out.

Chapter Ten

The next morning, Kate was up before the rest of them, she made a pot of coffee. She hadn't seen Jamie the night before but had heard him come in. Filling her mug, and letting Gizmo outside, she walked into the conservatory just as a dishevelled Jamie appeared from his room. He wore only jogging bottoms, and her eyes were involuntary drawn to his chest, which was smooth and muscular. He was quite a sight with his dishevelled hair and dark morning stubble. Kate could feel herself start to blush and averted her eyes. She prayed he wouldn't notice.

"What are you blushing at?" grinned Jamie as he helped himself to a mug of coffee.

Damn it!

"Shall I go put some more clothes on?" he said with raised eyebrows that only made Kate blush more.

"I have to admit I'm not used to half-naked men walking around my house," she replied.

"What about fully naked," he laughed.

"Very funny!" squealed Kate, her face now as red as it could be.

Jamie disappeared, laughing loudly, only to reappear a second or two later, pulling a jumper over his head. "Better?" he said.

"Much," said Kate and then desperate to change the subject, "How did you get on yesterday with the builders?"

"Well, it's all good as far as I can see. They seem to understand the layout of the place and they showed me some of the other projects they have worked on. The boss, Stuart Aiken, has overseen some big hotel builds, so he is eager to get started. They are going to start clearing the debris away as soon as I give them the nod."

"Wow, that's quick, how are your plans coming along?" asked Kate.

"Pretty good actually, the Lodge was not a bad design to begin with. And with the foundations and walls in good condition, they have given me a good grounding on how the original plans were laid out. I will extend the dining area and build bigger kitchens for a more modern era. The bar is a good size, and the bar top fixture is still there, so I will see what we can do with it. The whole Lodge will eventually have fewer bedrooms than the original design, as they were quite small, so I think we will double them up and make them into luxury suites. I still have a lot of work to do as you can see," said Jamie.

"So, you'll be here for quite a while then," asked Kate, trying not to sound too hopeful.

"Aye, I suppose I will be, but to be honest, I've been thinking about returning to Scotland for a while and even if this project hadn't come about, I would have probably moved back to the west coast anyway."

"Are you planning to run the Lodge?" Kate asked, realising they had never discussed that before.

"I'm not sure if I'm hotel management material. I was going to suggest that Eden do most of the day-to-day running if she wants, she does seem really keen on the place. I would imagine she would be a really good host and I could carry on with my work and base my business here. I haven't really made any decisions I'm committed to right now; anyway, at least being here, I will get to see more of you," said Jamie, his steady gaze on her.

Why did this man have this effect on her? She could feel her colour rising again and was furious at the lack of control she had; however, he made no remark this time. "I will be glad to have some good friends here, I have to admit, sometimes it has been a bit lonely," she said.

"I always wondered why you cut yourself off so much from the outside world. This is a beautiful place, but let's face it, it's miles away from your family and friends in Edinburgh," said Jamie.

"Yes, I know, but I do love the solitude, especially after losing Tom so suddenly, it just seemed easier to shut myself away for a while. I have been going back to Edinburgh more and more frequently these days, though, to catch up with friends and enjoy a few nights out," Kate admitted. He was still staring at her intensely with his deep brown eyes and she found herself unable to tear her eyes away from his face.

"Well, hopefully, I can change that. I'd love to get to know you better, Kate. Perhaps when things are underway, we could spend some time alone?" he asked.

"Yes, I would like that," Kate replied.

"What are you two up to?" Eden's voice broke the moment between them. "Not getting all smoochy, are you?"

"We're just talking," replied Jamie. "And how are you this morning, lazy?"

"I had some weird dreams, did Kate tell you what happened at Sanda Island?" said Eden.

"No, we haven't talked about your day yet," said Jamie.

"It was so weird, you tell him, Kate, I'm going to get some coffee and toast, I'm starving."

Kate told Jamie about the island and what happened to Eden. She could see him look worried as she explained about the trance Eden had been in. When she finished her story, he sat thoughtfully for a short while, then looked up as Eden came in carrying a mug and a plate, with a piece of toast hanging out her mouth. Jamie shook his head and rolled his eyes at her. "Well, I suppose I'd better tell you what happened to me then, it was very similar." Jamie explained what had happened on the beach. He could remember more than Eden about the woman's voice and the music that enticed him into the water.

"I don't know what to make of it," said Kate. "The two of you bare remarkable resemblance to each other, you would never think you were only half-brother and sister, especially in your eyes. Perhaps there is something in your genes that attracts you to water. You said your dad loved the ocean."

"Our genes?" said Eden, laughing.

"God, that sound ridiculous, ignore me. I'm just grasping at straws here. It was quite frightening to see the look on your face on these rocks. You were completely out of it and I swear, your eyes had gone completely black," said Kate.

"I think I was too, thank God for this Colla character who pulled me out the water," said Jamie. "He was the strangest man I've ever met. He made me feel like a child when he spoke to me. He was dressed in old Scottish highland garb and he had a bloody great big sword hanging on his back."

"What on earth was he doing with that?" said Eden.

"To be honest, I never asked him. I was still kind of shaken from being in the water," said Jamie.

"Maybe he's another MacDonald, and he's scared the Campbells will come back, so he carries the sword for protection," said Kate, laughing at Eden's horrified expression. "I am joking."

Eden threw a cushion at her and Jamie laughed. "I don't know, at the time, it just felt like the sword belonged there, I didn't pay much heed until after he had gone. I don't know how he disappeared like that, but, no doubt, time will tell and we are bound to meet him again. There are not that many people living around there, so someone will know him."

"Maybe he was a ghost, an ancient MacDonald come to rescue you," said Eden.

"Well, he certainly gave me a good telling-off, but he seemed surprised when I said I was a MacDonald. Especially when I told him I was taking over Seal Lodge," said Jamie.

"I can't wait to meet this character, my story is just getting better and better," said Kate. "Now what are the plans for today?"

"Well, I'm getting the ferry across to Arran to pick up Ronan MacDougall. If you're up for it, he has offered to take me 'round the Lodge and then, hopefully, tell me all his ghost stories," said Jamie. "Would you like to join us, ladies?"

Eden threw another cushion at Jamie this time. "Would we? You know I've been dying to meet Ronan. Why didn't you tell us what you were planning? Of course we're coming."

"Well, I would have if you were not fast asleep when I got in last night," Jamie defended himself.

"I was going to suggest going to Machrihanish to look at the hotel there. It's been recently refurbished and I thought it might give Eden some ideas about the interior décor. Why don't you bring Ronan there when you pick him up and we can have some lunch, then head over to the Lodge?" said Kate. "We were going to explore the caves anyway."

Jamie had a quick shower and set off 30 minutes later. Kate took Gizmo for a walk along the beach, then she and Eden set off late morning, driving back down the coast to Campbeltown. They then headed five miles to the west of the peninsula, where they found the Ugadale Hotel next to Machrihanish Golf Course. They hotel was a grand building that was just off the beach and it also had a number of cottages and its own pub on the grounds. It was there that they decided to have lunch.

Jamie and Ronan arrived 20 minutes after the girls did. After the introductions and food ordering, Ronan, who was clearly enjoying his day out, and being badgered with questions from Eden, started to repeat his story about the Lodge. Kate sat back and watched as Jamie and Eden got sucked into the old man's tales just as she had previously. It was just as good listening the second time around and Kate was sure he had embellished slightly from the first time she heard it, probably due to the larger audience.

The food arrived, delicious and all local produce. "So, do you think we will see the ghosts?" Eden asked.

"Aye, I'm sure ye will, yer grandmammie certainly saw them, although she never said a word aboot them," said Ronan.

"What was she like?" Eden asked.

"I would say she wis the double of ye, a real bonnie lass. Her hair wis different tae yours, it wis long but she always wore it tied up," said Ronan, then frowned as he looked at Eden. "I dinnie ken why the young lassies chop all their bonnie hair off these days."

Eden laughed. "It's fashionable," she said, unoffended.

"Aye, well nae in my day," said Ronan.

"You said she never went out, except for her beach walks at night. Wasn't she lonely?" Jamie asked.

"Nae that she let on," said Ronan. "There were a few young chancers that tried it on wi' her, she wis a bonnie lass, but she didnae gie them a second look. She kept tae herself and spoke only wi her wee laddie and the sisters. She did start tae warm up tae me, but I still couldnae have a proper blether with her. Not like with the three of yoose. She wis very reserved, but had a lovely smile, though ye didnae see it that often."

They finished their meals with Ronan telling them stories of their dad's teenage antics at the Lodge. By the time they left the Ugadale, they were all in great moods and excited to get to the Lodge.

Chapter Eleven

By the time they got to Seal Lodge, the wind had dropped and it was a nice, crisp autumn sunny day. Ronan walked around the Lodge with them, describing the layout of the building. He then walked them down to the tennis courts and pointed out the ruin of Keil School House.

"The sisters never went near the ruin and never allowed any of the guests tae go there either. I dinnae really ken much aboot the place, but it still gives me the 'heeby jeebies'," said Ronan.

"It's not included in the sale anyway, so I think we will just leave it alone," said Jamie.

He took them in the Lodge and explained how the place had been laid out. They all could see he was a bit emotional when he saw the state of the Lodge, but Jamie assured him that things would look better once the rubbish was all cleared away. Ronan did not seem to want to spend long inside the building.

"Now, who is gonnae gie me a hand up tae the caves? I take it ye havnae explored them yet?" asked Ronan.

"No, we haven't, I was going to have a peek at them today anyway," said Eden.

They walked back down the lane and along the sea front past St Columba's chapel. "Have ye seen the footsteps?" Ronan asked.

"No not yet," said Eden. "I have read about them though."

"Well, they're up that wee mound there, just before the caves. You can see the steps. I'm nae going up there, not wi my old bones," said Ronan. "I'll wait here and have a wee smoke."

The steps were well laid up the side of a grassy bank and when they reached the top, they could clearly see the footsteps with the date 564 carved into the rocks. Eden had her book out and, as usual, filled them in with the history.

"The footsteps were said to be left by St Columba and his 12 followers when they were exiled from Ireland in 563 AD. They spread Christianity throughout Western Scotland. But historians reckon it's more likely that one of the footsteps was made in the Dalroiadan Era, as the Scotti fought the Irish Picts. They were known to leave prints in stone to swear allegiance to the Scotti kings. The legend just grew up around St Columba over the centuries. Then supposedly, a local stone mason in 1856 took it upon himself to add to the legend and carved another footprint in the stone and added the date of Columba's landing. Unfortunately, he carved the wrong date, as Columba's exile was actually in 563. Typical! It does say here that 'The Royal Commission of Ancient and Historical Monuments of Scotland' think that the footprint is as old as the first millennium BC, long before the Scotti and the Kingdom of Dalroiada."

"You are just a fountain of knowledge, aren't you?" said Jamie. Eden stuck her tongue out at him.

They stared down at the footprints. "I think it looks like he was wearing shoes, did they have shoes back then?" asked Jamie.

"Well, it would have been bloody cold if they didn't and a bit rocky on your feet!" quipped Eden. "If we go slightly inland, we should come across the Holy Well, set in the cliff," she said, looking at the map drawn in her book.

They found the well easily, it looked like a basin that had been carved into the rocky cliff to catch the water. Above it, they could make out a cross carved into the stone.

"The water is said to have healing properties," said Eden, scooping up a handful. "Go on, take a drink."

Kate complied to keep her happy, then looked out across the bright blue sea and over to Dunaverty Rock. There was a clear view today and she felt herself shiver as she thought of the massacre there. She looked down the slope at Ronan, who was puffing on a pipe and leaning heavily on his walking stick, also looking over to Dunaverty. "We'd better get back to him, he's going to get tired standing there."

They all walked down to meet the old man. "We'd better get going if ye want tae see the caves, there's a mist coming in," said Ronan.

The others looked out at the sea, it was a glorious day, with no sign of fog or mist. They all looked at each other, but no one corrected him. They helped Ronan up the grassy slopes to the biggest of Keil Caves, known as the Great Cave.

"Noo, lassie, what does yer wee book tell ye aboot this place?" Ronan asked her as they walked into the cavern.

"Well, St Columba reportedly stayed here when he arrived from Antrim, and the caves have been inhabited since prehistoric times. In fact, Kate, you will laugh at this. In the 1881 census, there was a family of MacPhees living here. John MacPhee and his wife, Margaret, he was a tin smith. There were six of them that lived here," said Eden.

"My God, what a life, I suppose it's a good shelter though. It's not particularly deep but it bends 'round and keeps you protected from the elements. It's quite a large cavern," said Kate, trying to imagine what it would be like. "I wonder if I'm related somewhere along the line. There are so many different spelling of MacPhee in Scotland, F E E, or F I E, or P H I E, when I looked into it, I found that the spellings didn't really matter. It just depended on who wrote it, the MacPhee Clan are one."

"Aye, well, now ye've seen yer books, let me tell ye a wee story aboot this place," said Ronan, making himself comfortable on a rock in the cave.

"I presume ye have already been tae St Columba's cemetery and seen St Columba's old wee chapel. If ye look at the gravestones ootside the chapel, ye will find one fir Ranald MacDonald, he wis a survivor of the Dunaverty Rock Massacre in 1647," said Ronan.

"Yes, we saw a grave stone for him and one for his wife," said Eden. "We have been trying to find out more about him."

"Well, I can help ye some wi that," said Ronan. "When Colkitto got tae Dunaverty, he wis 77 years old but still an opposing figure of a man. He had only just been released frae captivity and wis aiding his son Alisdair against that brutal Covenanter army. The MacDonalds had already suffered a great defeat at Rhunahaorine Moss, near Tarbert, and the remnants of their army were chased down the peninsula by General David Leslie's army and the Marquis of Argyll. The MacDonalds made it tae what they thought wis safety at the castle on Dunaverty Rock it had stood undefeated fir a thousand years.

"Now here is the bit of the story that few ken these days. When Colkitto wis pirating aroond the Mull of Kintyre and the Hebrides years earlier, he had met and had an affair with a mysterious lass named Lorna. He met her right here, in this caves, when he came ashore frae his galley one day. Colkitto was bewitched by this dark-haired beauty, but many of the locals were feart of her as they thought she wis a witch. They werenae tae happy with Colkitto, who wis married tae a local lassie, Mary, who wis still back on Colonsay with his bairns. He visited Lorna more and more often. Putting himself and his men in danger as rumours spread aboot his visits there.

"His men began tae think the lass had cast a spell on him and threatened tae have her killed if he continued tae see her. Colkitto went intae a furious rage wi his crew when they issued the threat, so bewitched by the lassie he wis, and, in a moment of madness, he cut the hand off his chief oarsman. He wis immediately ashamed of his attack on his friend, and it snapped him back tae his senses. He began tae think that he had bin put under a spell, but he kent he wudnae be able tae resist Lorna and so he stayed away frae the caves fir months.

"Lorna was devastated at being cast aside by Colla, and every day, she returned tae this cave, waiting fir him tae return. One night, she heard the tunes of the pipes coming frae the distance. Her heart leapt as she believed her lover had returned, she rushed oot of the cave tae find Angus McDougall, the castle piper, drunk and full of mischief. He had bin boasting earlier tae his friends that noo Colkitto wis done wi the fleusy, he wis gonnae have his way wi her. That wis the last anyone saw of Angus. Noo nae one kent what happened that night, but Angus wis never seen again, and Lorna disappeared frae the cave. It wis lucky for Angus that he never returned, because when Colla heard what had happened, he had murder in mind.

"Now that's why the cave next tae this one is called 'Piper's Cave'. Many folks still hear the ghost of Angus playing his pipes on a clear night."

"I wondered why it was called Piper's Cave," said Eden.

"Aye, well, the story didnae end there," said Ronan.

Kate laughed to herself, Ronan's stories never did end.

"So noo many years later, here is old Colkitto back at Dunaverty Rock and aboot tae leave on his galley, tae take charge of the garrison on Islay before the Covenanter army arrived. Before he left, Colla took a wee walk along Carskiev beach and up tae the caves, probably reminiscing aboot old times, when he saw a lass come towards him, carrying a wee bairn in her arms. It wis Lorna, looking not a day older than the day they had first met. Colkitto was overwhelmed with emotion and went tae embrace her, but she stepped back, her eyes cold and hostile.

"Lorna told him she wis frae the sea, a Selkie, who had been fool enough tae fall in love wi him all these years ago, Colkitto had brought shame tae her, as her Selkie family had warned he would dae, and she returned tae the sea heart broken. Lorna wis pregnant and had a son, but as a half-blood Selkie, the child didnae age in the sea and remained a young pup. Lorna kent her son would have tae return tae the land-dweller world. It wis the only way he would grow intae a man, and after waiting many years fir Colkitto tae return, Lorna could noo gie him his bairn, whom she had named Conall.

"Now I'm guessing that if she had kent aboot the slaughter that wis aboot tae take place at Dunaverty, she wudnae have left that bairn wi him. But she made Colkitto swear that when Conall was grown, the laddie would be allowed tae make his own choice of whether he wished tae return tae the ocean and his Selkie pod.

"Lorna showed no emotion as she returned tae the ocean, leaving Colkitto holding his bairn. He returned tae the castle and gave the child tae a nurse tae look after. He planned tae send for the bairn as soon as he had secured Islay. The nurse wis already taking care of wee Ranald, son of Archibald MacDonald, who wis in charge of the garrison, but she promised she would look after Conall also.

"Later that day, the nurse was struck by an overwhelming feeling that things were going tae end badly at the castle and took it upon herself tae sneak the two bairns oot. She managed tae get ontae the beach, but the Campbells had arrived already and a Campbell horseman approached her tae ask her where she wis going. She managed to convince the horseman that she wis a Campbell and had got separated frae the main army taking care of her twin boys. The nurse told him she wis trying tae flee the battle before it started. The horseman cut some of his tartan plaid off and tossed it tae her. 'You'd better cover them up and keep them warm,' he said as he rode off. The nurse wrapped the boys in the Campbell tartan, managing tae escape through the main Campbell army, pretending tae be a soldier's wife. It wis common fir the wives and families tae follow their men intae battle.

"When news of the massacre came tae Colkitto, he believed his son was slain at Dunaverty and never kent that the nurse had escaped wi him. She took the wee laddie over tae Sanda Island and brought him up as her own, and there, he grew in tae a man.

'Conall lived as a farmer on Sanda, he had a number of children, I believe, but when Conall was in his '60s, Isla appeared, a young girl of about 13, I'm nae sure who her mother wis. He told his family she wis his niece and her parents had died. But the story goes that nae long after, Isla was pulled in tae the sea whilst playing by the rocks. Conall went in after her and the pair of them were never seen again.

"Noo, I'm convinced that they chose tae gae back tae their Selkie family that day. I also believe it wis the same Isla that came tae the Lodge wi her son Ewan, your grandmother."

"How do you know all this?" asked Kate as she saw that Jamie was struggling for something to say. "I always heard that Selkies were some sort of fishermen's legends, like Mermaids or Sirens. They shed their skins and make men fall in love with them. You talk like they are real, and are you really suggesting that this Isla is Ewan's mother?"

"Aye, well, when ye've lived on Kintyre as long as I have, ye see and hear things that most people wudnae believe. I've seen Selkies and I ken these stories that yer talking aboot. But Selkies have existed as long as we have in this world, and they live fir hundreds of years. The stories of Selkies have been whispered in these parts fir generations. I ken ye find it hard tae believe, but some things cannae be explained. As for Isla, well, I swear I thought I saw that lassie coming oot of the sea that day with her wee laddie in tow. And like I said, Selkies live fir a very long time when they are in the ocean."

Kate looked at Jamie and saw him smother a smile.

"Well, I'm with Ronan," said Eden. "I believe in the Selkies, and wouldn't it be great if our grandmother was a Selkie. What would that make us?"

"Bloody idiots," said Jamie, laughing. "Honestly, Ronan. I love your stories, you should get Kate to write them all down. Maybe we could have some sort of Selkie fountain at the front of the Lodge. This place is getting more magical by the moment."

"Aye, well, fir a non-believer, I like ye, laddie. But ye'd better be careful and nae get tae close tae that sea. If the Selkies believe ye are one of them, they will try tae entice ye intae the water tae join them," said Ronan.

Eden looked horrified. "Do you think that's what happened to us yesterday?"

"Eden, come on now, you're getting spooked. Of course not, that's ridiculous!" said Jamie.

"Well, I heard music and so did you, it nearly drew us to our deaths!" said Eden.

"Did ye hear a woman singing?" Ronan asked.

"Yes, we both did," said Eden, glaring at Jamie. "Something very strange happened to us both."

"Well, I'm saying, just ye be careful roond that coastline," said Ronan. "Now we had better get oot of here before that mist traps us."

They helped Ronan up off the rock he was sitting on, then made their way out to the cave entrance. It seemed incredibly dark now, which was strange as it was only three o'clock, but when they arrived at the opening, they were met by a thick, swirling mist. It was impossible to see through it and it was impossible to go anywhere. They were completely trapped in the cave.

"We are gonnae have tae stay here," said Ronan.

"You can't be serious?" said Jamie, then looked at the old man. "You are serious, aren't you?"

"We cannae be going anywhere till it clears. Come on, let's build a wee fire. There's usually plenty of bits of wood left in here by the locals in case they get caught oot by the mist."

Ronan was not wrong, there was plenty of wood stashed in crannies around the cave. Ronan had matches, so they soon had a fire going, which cast a warm pleasant glow around the cavern.

Kate had sat down on the soft sand, with her back against a smooth wall surface. The warmth of the fire was pleasant and the whole effect made the cave seem cosy and safe. Jamie came over to her. "Budge up," he said. "You've got the best seat in the house here."

Kate shuffled along a bit as Jamie plonked himself right next to her. He was pressed up against her, causing her to shiver slightly at his touch. She was sure she was going red, thank goodness she was well covered up. Jamie turned and grinned at her. "This is cosy, isn't it," he said with a twinkle in his eyes. She was grateful of the firelight, which camouflaged her blushes.

Ronan had lit his pipe and was sitting comfortably on a rock, whilst Eden, who had eventually got bored, was pacing up and down, exploring all the nooks and crannies of the cave. "I can't see how far back this goes," she said, peering through a hole at the back of the cave. "It gets too narrow at the end to fit through."

"Dinnae be trying tae fit through anything, lassie," said Ronan. "You dinnae ken what magic there is in these caves."

Just as Ronan spoke, there was a stiff breeze that swept through the cave and the fire went out suddenly, leaving them engulfed in blackness.

Chapter Twelve

"What the hell!" yelled Jamie, jumping to his feet.

"Dinnae move, laddie," said Ronan. "Stay very still."

Kate grabbed towards Jamie's hand in the dark and, thankfully, found it. He pulled her up next to him and hugged her to him just as the sounds of a distant piper came drifting into the cave.

"Do you hear it?" whispered Kate.

"Aye, it's Angus McDougall, came tae play his pipes," said Ronan, his voice calm and matter of fact.

The pipe music became louder as it came closer. Kate hung onto Jamie, fear washing over her. Then she felt something brush past her, "Eden, is that you?" she called out. There was no answer.

They listened as the pipe music gave way to the sound of fighting and battle cries. They heard swords clashing and men shouting for mercy. Kate buried her face into Jamie's shoulder as she heard pleading screams of terrified women and children. The sound drifted away as if someone was turning the volume down, then a clearly spoken, grotesque voice froze them all to the spot with fear.

"God demands his enemies are punished, kill them all, give nae quarter. I dinnae want a MacDonald left alive on these shores! Put them all tae the sword, lest ye be judged by God himself. Send these pitiful creatures screaming tae hell!"

Kate clung onto Jamie as the noise of the screaming intensified, filling the cavern. She heard a poor woman plead for the life of her baby and then howl in bloody anguish. The sounds of murderous brutality were all around them, with the roars and cursing of men and the crying of children. The noise seemed to peak and then fade away once again. This time, there came an anguished woman's voice, full of venom as she cursed the soldiers. She turned her wrath onto the Preacher and her voice was full of pain, "John Neave, may ye never rest in God's eternal heaven. Fir yer wicked soul will never leave this place. Ye will die a monsterous death and yer tormented spirit will wander the pits of darkness, and the name of MacDonald will curse ye firever!"

Her voice was suddenly silent, but the malevolent Preacher spoke once more, "Burn this witch, then dispose of her body in the sea! Oor Lord God will nae abandon us this day. Her curses are useless!"

Jamie felt Kate bury her head into his shoulder and he was glad of her touch. The battle noise disappeared and the pipes ceased to play, they were left in a deathly silence. The fire suddenly sprung to life, lighting up the entirety of the cave in a split second.

They stood there blinking with shock for a second or two before they could gather themselves. Ronan was still sitting on the rock, holding his pipe, his face pale as he stared at the fire. For once, the old man had nothing to say.

"Where's Eden?" said Kate, still trembling and looking desperately around the cave. There was no sign of her anywhere.

"Eden, where are you!" Jamie yelled at the top of his lungs, making Kate jump.

Again, there was no answer. He ran to the cave entrance; unbelievably, the mist was gone as if it had never been there and it was just turning to dusk. Jamie called out again and again, checking the other caves, then eventually running down to the beach. There was no sign of his sister anywhere. He was in full panic now, what could have happened to her? Eden had been in the cave with them up until the fire went out. He couldn't think straight, he was still shaken and couldn't make sense of what had just happened.

Kate was helping Ronan out of the cave, her face anxious and full of worry, "Have you found her?" she yelled over to him.

"Eden!" Jamie yelled again.

"Maybe she was scared and ran back to the car?" cried Kate. "I'll go look. Ronan, you stay here."

Kate ran off in the direction of the Lodge, praying that she would find Eden terrified at the car.

Ronan walked slowly across the road to the rocky beach and saw a seal watching him from the water. "Jamie, look here!" he shouted, pointing his stick towards the seal.

Jamie turned expecting to see Eden but instead saw the seal in the water. What the hell was the old man pointing at? He'd seen seals before and this wasn't helping him find Eden. He looked along the coastline towards the Mull of Kintyre and saw a figure in the distance on the beach. He left Ronan and jogged towards the figure, hoping it was Eden, or at least someone who had seen her.

As he got closer, he recognised it as the man he had seen on the beach the day before, still wearing his kilt and heavy tartan plaid, standing waiting for Jamie to arrive.

"Hallo again. Colla, isn't it?" said Jamie as he arrived next to the giant of a man. "Have you seen a young woman around here? We lost her in the mist."

"Aye, she's gone, that devil's got her," said Colla. "Wis she yer sister, sonnie?"

"Yes, well, half-sister; what do you mean, she's gone? Gone where?" asked Jamie.

"That Bloody Preacher, John Neave, he took her. Yer gonnae have tae find her, sonnie, before that devil harms her. I'll dae what I can," said Colla.

"What Preacher?" Jamie was shouting now, he felt he was going mad. He still hadn't got to grips with what happened in the cave.

"You heard him in the cave, he came in the mist and he took her wi him. He's lost his mind and his thirst fir revenge against the MacDonalds holds nae bounds," said Colla.

"But where would he take her?" asked Jamie, now feeling desperate.

"She's in the caves, laddie, ye'll have tae hurry," said old Colla. "I'll dae what I can tae protect her, but he's tae strong fir me just noo."

"She's not in the caves, we've checked them. Look, if you can't help, just say. You're talking nonsense," said Jamie, getting aggravated.

Colla looked at Jamie calmly. "All is nae as it seems, search the caves."

Jamie suddenly realised he was talking to a mad man and this was not helping him find his sister. "Look, thanks for your help," he said, wanting to get away as quickly as possible. He turned to leave, then turned back, "If you see…" Colla was gone.

Where the hell he went, Jamie had no idea, but he was too worried about Eden to stop and think about it. He prayed that Kate had found her back at the car and he jogged back along the beach to where Ronan was standing, watching him from the road. As he approached, he saw Kate running back towards them. She didn't look happy.

"She's not at the car or anywhere around the Lodge," she shouted over to him. "Where can she be? Maybe she's still in the cave, maybe she squeezed into that cranny at the back or has gone to hide in another cave and is too frightened to come out. I'll go have another look and check the others' caves," she said as she ran up the slope towards the caves.

"Who were ye talking tae?" asked Ronan.

"Some guy called Colla. He helped me out of the water yesterday when I got myself in trouble. He is a strange character though. He's huge, all kilted up with a fierce-looking sword slung over his shoulder. I thought he might have been playing a part for the tourists. He said to look for Eden in the caves," replied Jamie.

Ronan stared back at him, searching his face, as if wanting to say something but holding back.

"What is it?" Jamie asked him, exasperated.

"Ye just saw the ghost of old Colkitto. They say he roams Kintyre and takes care of his own. Ye must be related tae him, laddie, that's quite an honour roond these parts," said Ronan.

"Look, Ronan, I don't know what's going on here and I'd be the first to say there has been some strange happenings today, but my first priority is to find Eden. I can't be thinking of ghosts and legends right now," said Jamie, trying to hide his frustration.

Kate reappeared from the caves, "She's not anywhere to be seen. I think we had better call the police." She looked at Jamie, recognising the concern and worry on his face. "Why don't you drive into Campbeltown and talk to the police and I'll stay here in case she appears," she suggested.

"I can't let you stay here on your own, not after what has happened to Eden," said Jamie.

"Look, I'm fine. I've been here many times and the mist has gone now. The caravan park is just over there and there are plenty of people about. Maybe the police can shed light on whether this has happened before, you have to get Ronan home anyway. I have my car at the Lodge, so I will drive it down to the coast and ask around to see if anyone has seen her.

"The Argyll Arms is just up the road, maybe she made her way there. We can stay in touch with our mobiles," said Kate, not taking no for an answer.

It was just about dark now, Jamie wasn't comfortable with her suggestion, but Ronan did look tired, it had been a long day for the old man, and Kate had her car, so she could drive back at any time. In the pit of his stomach, he knew they wouldn't find Eden at the pub, nor anywhere else around. She had her mobile, so she would have called if at all possible, Eden would know they would be worried.

"Okay, Kate, you go get your car, ask around a bit, but don't be sitting out in the dark, especially not in that carpark by the caves. You won't be able to see anything anyway and I think we have established she's not there. I will phone you before I take Ronan back across to Arran and if you haven't seen her by then, then head home," said Jamie.

It was pitch black and cold when they got back to the Lodge carpark. Jamie headed off in his car with a stricken-looking Ronan, and Kate followed but turned off at the pub as they drove on. The Argyll Arms was deadly quiet and the landlord was the only one at the bar. He hadn't seen Eden, but he suggested that if she didn't appear during the night, that they return in the morning and he would organise a search party with the locals. They wouldn't go out at night.

Kate got back in her car and drove back along the coastline with her full beam on. She got the shivers, it was definitely quite eerie around there in the dark. She was still reeling from their experience in the cave, and as she drove by the old graveyard, her headlights hit the gravestones, casting long shadows that added to the eerie atmosphere. She drove past, then pulled into the carpark just beyond the caves, she wasn't sure how brave she would be sitting there in the dark on her own. She turned her car around to face the beach, left her engine running and switched on the full beams. The headlights' rays stretched out for quite a way over the beach, lighting the white tips of the waves cascading onto the shore.

For the first time since Eden's disappearance, she seriously thought about what had happened in the cave. She had put it to the back of her mind as she couldn't make any sense of it.

The mist had come on so quickly, she had never experienced anything like it in the whole two years she had lived on the peninsula. The fire going out had been scary, but what was really terrifying were the battle cries and the screaming that was going on around them. Then there was that hideous voice of that preacher. It seemed that Ronan's tales of ghosts were true, because Kate couldn't think of any other explanation.

So where had Eden gone? Kate remembered holding onto Jamie and feeling someone brush against her. Was that Eden? Maybe she was in some sort of trance again, the same as on the Isle of Sanda the day before. Whatever was going on, there was something strange happening and it seemed to centre around Eden and Jamie. She was beginning to feel a little scared as she sat with her engine running to keep the heater and lights on, then she thought she could see the figure of a man standing by the shore.

It definitely wasn't Eden, this man was too big, so she sat and watched him just stand there when suddenly her mobile started to ring. Thankfully, it was Jamie. The police had suggested the same as the pub landlord. If they hadn't heard from her by the morning, then they would organise a search party for the area. Jamie hadn't told them about the ghosts in the cave, but when they heard the mist had come down so quickly, they had nodded, looking at each other with a sense of understanding that only the locals could have. He had also been told that the Skipness ferry had stopped running for the night, so Ronan would have to stay with them until the morning if Kate didn't mind. She told him she didn't and that she would head back to the house and see them there. She turned her car around and drove slowly back towards Campbeltown.

On the beach, old Colkitto stood, watching Kate drive off. He had seen her with his kin earlier and knew she was looking for the girl. That murderous Reverend John Neave had been awoken once again, and this time, Colkitto would not let him harm his kin. The preacher had haunted all of Colla Ciotach's kinsmen for generations, kidnapping and murdering them when possible. This time, Colkitto was going to stop him.

Chapter Thirteen

Kate hardly slept, she had given Ronan her bed, the old man was shattered and looked very grey. She tried to dose in Eden's bed but ended up counting the hours until daylight. She couldn't get the sound of the ghosts she had heard out of her mind. That preacher man's malicious voice as he ordered his men to murder those people made her feel sick to the stomach, let alone the nightmarish horror of hearing the terrified cries of anguish and screams of children. She checked her mobile, it was 5 in the morning and she couldn't lay there any longer. She got up, went to the kitchen and put the coffee on.

"Couldn't sleep either?" said Jamie, who was sitting alone in the dark in the conservatory.

"No, I'm sick with worry, I just don't know what to do," replied Kate, flicking on a small lamp to light up the room. Jamie looked awful, his eyes were red and his face was drawn. An empty bottle of scotch lay next to him. He saw her look at it. "It wasn't full, love, I just had a couple of drams."

"I'm not judging, I wish I'd have known, I'd have joined you," said Kate. She went back to the kitchen and poured them some coffee and returned handing Jamie a steaming cup. "I guess we should head out as soon as it's light. Hopefully, the police will be more helpful this morning."

"I will have to drive Ronan home, unless you could do that?" asked Jamie hopefully. He was desperate to get back to Southend.

"Nae need, sonnie, I'm gonnae stay until the wee lassie is found," said Ronan, appearing in the doorway. "I feel responsible taking ye in tae these caves, I could see there wis a mist coming."

"You couldn't have known, Ronan, but I appreciate all the help we can get today," said Jamie.

An hour later, they were heading in a convoy towards Campbeltown, having decided to take two cars. Jamie called back in at the police station while Kate and Ronan headed straight back to Seal Lodge. It was just getting light, it looked like a clear day, but there was a low mist covering the beach. Kate decided to park by the caves instead of driving up to the Lodge. She had brought Gizmo with her this time in some futile attempt to transform him into a search dog and perhaps be able to track down Eden. She opened up the rear of her car and he leapt out and ran straight onto the beach, disappearing in the mist; however, she could tell where he was from the screeches and cries of seagulls who were rudely interrupted during their morning low-tide feast.

Ronan stayed in the car, the old man was tired still from yesterday's excursion, he said he would keep an eye on Gizmo while Kate went back up to search the caves. She felt a shiver of fear as she climbed over the wall and started to walk up towards them, the memories of yesterday still haunting her. She headed straight for the 'Great Cave', the one they had been trapped in, and entered slowly, aware of every footstep she took.

The cave was deserted, the only indication that anything had happened there was the burnt-out remnants of their fire. It was much easier to see inside the cave with the low sunlight pouring directly in and Kate walked over to where she last saw Eden sitting before the fire went out. There in the sand were hand prints that looked like they had been dragged along towards the narrow crevice at the back of the cave.

She instinctively knew they were Eden's, she could see where the girl's fingers had dug deep in the sand, trying to get a hold against whatever was pulling her. Then, as if to confirm what she already knew, she saw a small silver ring flickering inside the crevice. She reached in to retrieve it and saw it was Eden's lip ring. Kate pulled out her mobile and flicked on the torch. She reached into the crevice as far as she could and saw it went on a lot further than she could have imagined, but there was just no way she could squeeze through or anyone else for that matter. Just then, Gizmo appeared in the cave, clearly looking for her. He came bounding over and was immediately interested in what she was doing. He climbed up into the crevice to see what she was looking at and somehow managed to squeeze himself through. He disappeared, but she could still hear him snuffling around on the other side.

"Gizmo, come back!" she called, but the dog paid no attention. He started to bark and whimper excitedly and as she strained to see what was going on, she thought she heard a groan.

"Eden, is that you!" she yelled. Gizmo was still barking but she could now hear another noise, like someone moaning softly.

"Eden, it's me, Kate! We're going to get you out!" she yelled.

"Kate, help me," Eden's voice was weak.

"Eden, don't try to move, I'm going to get help. Gizmo will stay with you!" shouted Kate and she ran out the cave, trying to find Jamie's number on her phone. They would need men and tools to dig her out of the cavern, how the hell did she get in there? Just as she was going to dial, she saw his car, followed by two police cars, driving along the coast. She ran down to meet them.

"I've found her, she's stuck in the cave, Jamie," she yelled. "I think she's hurt, we'll need some tools to get her out."

They all made their way back to the cave, Jamie tried to squeeze through as much as he could. "Eden, can you hear me?" he shouted.

"Yes," said Eden in a weak whisper. "Please shine the torch again, it's so dark."

Kate handed him her phone and he shone the torch as far as he could into the dark crevice. The police were already on their radio, sending for help, and within half an hour, Stuart Aiken and his team of builders arrived, carrying all sorts of drills and digging equipment. They went to work, widening the entrance to the narrow crevice. The noise from the drills was deafening inside the cave and they had to keep stopping to check that the roof was secure. They couldn't risk it collapsing in on Eden.

It took them three hours to widen the gap so that Kate could just squeeze through. She borrowed one of the police officers' torches as her phone battery had long since died and crawled through into what was a huge cavern, bigger than the Great Cave itself. Gizmo was pleased to see her, jumping up at her, then running over to Eden and licking the semi-conscious girl's face.

Eden was lying in the centre of the cavern, and Kate rushed over to her. She couldn't move and there was a huge gash on the side of her head. But apart from that, there didn't seem to be any broken bones.

"Eden, I'm here, we're going to get you out," said Kate, throwing her coat over the girl and putting Eden's head gently on her lap. The sound of the drills started again and Kate waited.

"Has he gone?" whispered Eden.

"Has who gone?" said Kate, stroking her friend's face.

"The Preacher," said Eden, her eyes barely open.

"Yes, he's gone," said Kate.

"He'll be back," replied Eden just as the men managed to break through into the inner cave. Jamie and the paramedics came rushing in and before long, Eden was on a stretcher, wrapped in blankets as she was carried down to the ambulance.

"You go with her," said Kate to Jamie. "I'll see Ronan back to Arran."

"Thanks, love, I'm so grateful you found her. I'll see you later," said Jamie and before she knew what was happening, he had reached out and pulled her in for a deep, long kiss. She felt feelings come alive that had been long buried when he let her go suddenly and she found herself gasping for breath. He touched her cheek, looking straight into her eyes, then kissed her forehead and strode out of the cave after Eden, leaving her shaken and slightly confused.

Gizmo stood looking at her and she pulled herself together. Suddenly, the cave seemed very dark again as everyone left, but she wanted to have a look around. She shone her torch towards what seemed to be the far end of the cavern and started to explore other nooks and crannies that there was an abundance of. Scratches on cave walls were carved into the rock by the entrance as if someone was trying to get out. Had someone been trapped in here before? Her eyes drifted around to another area in the cavern, it seemed to be hiding something with large boulders blocking her view. Moving slowly forward, she shone her torch in that direction, trying to see what was behind the boulders.

Gizmo began to growl, then there was a sudden breeze that blew through the cavern. She felt her hair stand on end as a feeling of something evil and malevolent had just washed over her. She took a deep breath and tried to calm herself, but Gizmo was now barking and growling like crazy. It was getting colder and Kate decided she just wanted to get out of there. She left the cave, walking back into the outer cavern and then finally into the bright sunlight. She sighed heavily with relief as she realised that Ronan was standing, watching her.

"Are ye all right, lassie?" he asked as she climbed over the wall to join him.

"Yes, I'm fine, thanks, it's been quite a morning. Are you ready to head home, Ronan?" she asked.

"Aye, I'd better be off before my wife sends the cavalry oot looking fir me," he replied.

Kate put Gizmo in the back of the car, then she and Ronan drove back up to Skipness. The ferry port came into view and Kate glanced over at the old man. Ronan hadn't talked much on the way back and Kate suspected he was more tired than he let on. She hoped he didn't blame himself for what happened.

"Are you okay, Ronan? You seem very quiet, has it all been a bit much for you?" Kate asked kindly.

"Aye, I'm fine, lass, it's brought back a lot of old memories. Hearing the Preacher again turned my blood tae ice. He's an evil soul that one," said Ronan.

By the time Kate dropped Ronan off home, it was nearly two o'clock. She phoned Jamie, he said Eden was doing fine in the hospital. She was badly concussed from the head injury, she also was suffering from hyperthermia and was quite dehydrated, but apart from that, she would be as right as rain. There was no point on Kate driving back to the hospital, he would stay with Eden until early evening, then he would pick them up some Chinese food and see Kate back at the house. He said they had a lot to talk about, which immediately caused a knot to form in Kate's stomach.

She decided to go for a walk along Blackwaterfoot Beach again before she headed back home as the ferry wasn't for another couple of hours, it didn't run as often now, it was heading towards the winter months. It was a beautiful autumn day; the sun was warm but the breeze was cool and Gizmo was in his element, chasing all the seabirds along the beach. Before long, Kate felt the cobwebs blow away as her mind turned towards that kiss. Jamie had kissed her, and she had wanted to kiss him again. For the first time since Tom's death, Kate felt like she could move on again and she hoped Jamie felt the same way. Although it had been such a relief to get Eden back, that it could have been just emotional overload that caused him to kiss her like that. But what did he mean by saying they had a lot to talk about? Did he mean the future of the Lodge or did he mean his feelings towards her? By the time Kate got back to her car, she had told herself to play it cool, she was not going to give away her feelings. Jamie would have to take the first step.

Chapter Fourteen

It was just after 6 when Kate got back. Jamie wasn't in and she figured she probably had a couple of hours, so she fed Gizmo, then took a long shower. Kate stepped out of her bathroom, towelled herself dry and slipped into her bath robe, deciding to get herself a glass of wine to sip while she was drying her hair. Kate wanted to make an effort this evening. She left her room to head towards the kitchen just as Jamie let himself in the door with a Chinese carry-out bag in one hand and a bottle of wine in the other. She looked at him with surprise, "I didn't expect you back so soon."

"Eden was asleep and there was no point in me staying," said Jamie, looking at her strangely. He went to put the food in the kitchen and she followed him in, aware of her wet hair and lack of makeup.

"Can I get you some wine?" she asked as she reached up to grab a glass from the cupboard. Her robe fell slightly open and she felt Jamie watching her. She turned to face him and he was steadily gazing at her with those deep brown eyes of his. She felt a longing sweep through her, she swallowed hard, hoping that she wasn't reading him wrong. He dropped the bag of food and took three purposeful steps towards her and pulled her to him, kissing her with an urgency that she shared as she kissed him back. Kate didn't know how they got to her bedroom, but she was pulling off his clothes as he loosened the cord of her robe.

They were primal and frenzied at first, as if they had waited forever for this moment, but as the night went on, they touched and explored each other with a warm gentleness that they had both missed out on for so long. Eventually exhausted, they slept comfortably in each other's arms, the horrors of the last 24 hours forgotten.

It was after 9 when they were awoken by Gizmo scratching at the door to be let out. Kate slipped out of bed and shyly pulled her robe back on. She left the room to let Gizmo out, then returned to hear the shower running.

Feeling a tinge of disappointment, she headed back towards the bed, but Jamie suddenly grabbed her as she passed the bathroom door, pulling her into the shower with him. "Where do you think you're going?" he laughed.

It was another hour before they finally got dressed. Jamie decided to cook breakfast, they were both ravenous as neither had eaten the day before. Kate sipped her coffee from the breakfast bar and watched him cook. "You really are a man of many talents," she said.

"And you know this how?" asked Jamie wickedly.

"What's the plan for today?" said Kate, ignoring him and changing the subject. She knew she was blushing again. "Do you think Eden will be allowed to come home?"

"Yep, they said she would be fine after a night's rest and lots of fluids. If she's awake, she'll be desperate to get out of there, and I still want to know what happened. There are too many unanswered questions," replied Jamie.

Kate was thinking the same. She still wanted to go back to the caves and finish exploring the cavern they had found Eden in. "I think we may find some answers in the cave we found Eden in. I had a look around after you'd gone and found some strange markings on the wall, as if someone else had been trapped there. There was something else, but Gizmo got spooked and I just wanted to get out of there. Maybe we should take another look."

"We can take a look at it later, I still want to find out what happened with Eden. We haven't spoken about the voices and sounds we heard yet either," said Jamie.

"Yea, I know, it's a bit of an elephant, but I can't rationalise it, and I didn't want to say the 'ghost' word in case you thought I was nuts," said Kate.

"Me either," agreed Jamie. "But I can't think of any other explanation, and did you see Ronan's face? He just went grey. He hardly said a word, and that is unusual."

"We can go see Eden after breakfast. Maybe we should take two cars again in case one of us has to take her home. She may not want to go back to the Lodge with us after her experience," Kate suggested.

"No, not today. I think today we will stick together whatever. If we have to bring Eden back, we'll do it together. I don't want you out of my sight today and I definitely don't want you going off investigating spooky caves on your own," Jamie said.

Kate smiled, it was nice to have someone care about her like that again. They had a huge breakfast, then feeling stuffed, they headed off in Kate's car, with Gizmo in his bed in the back. Campbeltown Hospital was a small modern building but not really a fully equipped hospital. They dealt with a lot of tourist accidents and easily treatable illnesses, but the serious stuff was helicoptered to Glasgow. Eden was sitting up, grinning from ear to ear, and fully dressed, waiting for them.

"I thought you would never get here," she said, clearly dying to get out of the place. "They wouldn't let me leave until you came for me, I've lost my phone, so I couldn't call you."

Kate and Jamie looked at each other with a slight guilty grimace. It wasn't missed by Eden, "What have you two been up to?" she asked, then noticing Kate's slightly pink colouring, "Ah, I see, I'm lying here, possibly at death's door and you two are playing Mr and Mrs."

"You're not at death's door, ye eejit," said Jamie, laughing. "And, yes, Kate has decided that we should be a couple now, so I agreed," he said grinning, looking directly at Kate, who was now squirming in her shoes.

"Aw, leave her alone, you bully," laughed Eden. "It took you long enough. Now let's get out of here, I need some air."

They left the hospital and went down to the harbour, collecting hot take-away coffee on route. They sat in the car, watching the boats, as the weather had turned colder and it was too chilly to be sitting outside. Eden had a dressing on the wound on her head but apart from that, seemed completely as right as rain.

"So, are you going to tell us what happened?" asked Jamie.

Eden's normal cheery face dropped slightly, "Honestly, it's all pretty vague. I've been trying to remember how I got in that cave. I remember the fire going out and then hearing the pipes. I couldn't move, I think I was frozen to the spot, all those battle noises and screams were terrifying. When I heard the Preacher's voice, I was sick with fear. I backed up against the cave wall, but then I was pushed forward and I fell to the ground. I felt something grab my ankles, pulling me back towards the wall. I tried to grab hold of anything to stop him, but I could hear his laughter in my head. He said he was going to crush me as all filthy MacDonalds deserve, and then I was pulled with such a force, I hit my head on something hard and everything went black.

106

"When I awoke, I was in complete darkness, but I knew I wasn't alone, I couldn't see him but I could feel him all around me, and I tried to sit up, but something seemed to be over me, preventing me from moving. It felt like something or someone was protecting me, but all the time, I could hear the Preacher mumbling and cursing all around me. Then I saw him, he was horrific," said Eden, shivering. "His face came screaming towards me in the darkness. It was horrible, like an insane beast ready to rip me apart. I must have passed out, because the next thing I remember is Gizmo licking my face and barking at me. Then you know the rest."

"That's awful, you must have been so scared. I'm so sorry, we had no idea where you were," said Kate.

"So, we seem to be dealing with some sort of dark, malevolent spirit who has a real problem with the MacDonald Clan. Do you think it is actually the ghost of John Neave, the Bloody Preacher from Dunaverty?" asked Jamie.

"I know it was him," said Eden. "I can't explain it but it was like I had met him before. Something was definitely protecting me from him."

"Perhaps it was Colkitto looking out for you. According to Ronan, I have apparently seen the ghost of Colkitto twice now," said Jamie with a grimace. "That giant of a man I told you I had met on the beach that day when I went in the water. I saw him again yesterday when I was looking for you. He warned me that this Preacher character had taken you and told me to look in the caves. I didn't believe him, I thought he was out of his mind. I wish I'd listened now."

"Why would you believe him, we had searched the caves and we wouldn't have found anything in the dark. Thank goodness for Gizmo," said Kate and the little dog raised his head at the sound of his name.

"Does this mean that the Preacher is going to be coming after us again? Is he really haunting those from the MacDonald Clan? It just sounds too bizarre," said Jamie.

"We heard that woman cursing the Preacher when we were in the cave," said Kate. "It could be quite dangerous for you and Eden if he is after MacDonalds. I can't believe I'm actually saying that, but we all heard the voices in the cave and Eden was taken by him. Is this going to affect the rebuild of the Lodge?"

"No, absolutely not! We can't be held up by the threat of ghosts, but I think perhaps we need to find out more about this 'Bloody Preacher' and find a way to get rid of him," said Eden. "Perhaps Colkitto could help with that, if we knew how to contact him."

"Well, I have come across him twice now, so it might not be as hard as we think. I have a feeling he will find us if we are in trouble again," said Jamie. "Eden, are you up for going to the Lodge? We could take you home first, if you'd rather?"

"I'm fine, and anyway, I need to try and find my phone. I must have dropped it in the cave," said Eden.

"You're not going back in that cave," said Jamie. "Not yet anyway."

"Just you try and stop me," said Eden. "If some monster is after my clan, he is going to have a battle on his hands."

Jamie went to argue but Kate grabbed his arm and shook her head. She could see Eden was determined. "If we all stick together and carry torches, we should be okay," she offered the compromise.

Jamie sighed. "Okay, I see I'm not going to win this one, buckle up, let's go see if we can find a ghost!"

Chapter Fifteen

As Moire and her friends approached Eileen Nan Ron, the ocean was churning with thousands of Atlantic grey seals performing acrobatics through the frothing water, trying to get to fish who had unfortunately come in too close to the shore. Moire was nervous about confronting her mother, knowing she would be furious at her daughter's late arrival to the meet. Her father, Fionnlagh, would be angry too, but she always got around him and he would forgive her much more quickly than her mother would.

The Selkies dived deep through scores of other seals, soon breaking away from them, heading deep under the island. They then swam up into the huge lake inside the Selkie cavern. They were greeted by some of the other Selkies as they pulled themselves out of the water, transforming into their land-dweller bodies. Before long, the whole cavern was buzzing with news of their return and Moire's parents arrived to find her.

"Where have you been?" demanded her father.

"I'm sorry, we lost track of time," she said. "I didn't mean to worry you."

"Well, you did, as usual, but I'm glad you are eventually here. We have news," said her mother, hugging her.

Moire was stunned, she had been expecting much worse and, clearly, so did her father, as he gave Isla a strange look, then pulled Moire in for a huge bear hug. "I'm glad you're here, Mo, I miss you when you're not."

"Me too, Father," said Moire, hugging him back. "We also have news."

"Well, it will have to wait, your brother has come back to us and I'm sure he has waited too long already to see you," said Isla.

"Ewan's come back to us? Where is he?" said Moire.

"He's at the far end of the lake, he can no longer take land-dweller form, but he is waiting for you," said her mother.

Moire dived back into the water, once again changing into a speckled grey seal as she swam through the lake. Moire saw Ewan before he saw her, he had grown, he was a small pup when she had last seen him.

"I didn't think I would see you again, Ewan," said Moire. "I am so happy you've come back to us. We have so much to catch up on."

"Moire, you haven't changed. I hear you have been getting in trouble again, looks like I will have to keep you under control," said Ewan.

"Mmmm, well, you can try," said Moire. "What made you want to come back?"

"I think I lived long enough as a land-dweller. I always thought I would die a human, then be buried next to my wife, but the calling of the ocean got too strong. The older I became, the more I had to resist returning to the water. It wasn't an easy choice, Moire, I've left behind my children and grandchildren. I only hope one day they will hear the calling also and perhaps visit our world," said Ewan.

They swam together alone in the lake, talking about the years that had gone by. Moire still a young Selkie and Ewan growing into old age as a land-dweller. He told her about his children and the sadness and loneliness he felt when his wife died. Moire listened with interest at Ewan's description of his daughters and the love they had shared. She was glad Ewan had returned but could feel the sadness in him when he spoke of his family.

Dand swam over to them, "Moire we have to go to the council meeting. Uarraig told them about the man on the beach at Kintyre."

"What man?" Ewan asked, his ears pricking at the mention of Kintyre.

"There was a man on the beach we believed to be a half-blood Selkie. He seemed to hear our call, there was also a young woman," said Moire.

"A man heard your call from what beach, was he near the old Lodge?" asked Ewan.

"You mean the big white building on the cliff? Yes, he was there, near the caves," said Moire.

"Moire, that may be my son, Jamie, I bought him Seal Lodge. He's probably there looking it over," said Ewan.

"Well, that would explain things," said Dand. "We had better go and tell the others."

The meeting was reconvened by the lake so that Ewan could be present. Uarraig explained to the Selkie council what happened on the beach. He then asked Moire to tell them about the woman on Sanda Island. From her description of the young woman, Ewan was sure it was Eden and wanted to leave immediately for the Kintyre coastline.

"Maybe after hearing your call, Moire, Eden will be thinking about coming into the ocean. If there is a chance, I want to be there," said Ewan.

"If they are indeed your children, Ewan, then we have a lot more to worry about than whether or not they wish to come back to the ocean," said Isla. "Do you remember me telling you when you left Kintyre that if you go to the city, you must promise me that you would never return to the Lodge?"

"Yes, you made me promise and I always felt guilty about that, I should have helped Janette more when Betty died," said Ewan.

"You have no need to feel guilty about Janette, I visited her many times after you left, I always looked out for her. We owed her a lot, and she understood why you couldn't come back," said Isla. "Seal Lodge was protected by the Riley sisters from the ghosts on Kintyre. They had come over from Ireland during the land-dwellers' war and went to work at the Lodge as nurses when it was used as a hospital. Janette and Betty were descended from a long line of Celtic Good Wives, or Witches as some called them.

"They had limited power, but they did have incredible knowledge of the magical world and the realms between life and death. They developed a connection to Kintyre and the ghosts of the past. I suspected that they were perhaps related to those who escaped the massacre, fleeing to Ireland all those centuries ago.

"It was during the land-dwellers' war that I first met the Riley sisters. A young naval officer named Ross MacDonald had been badly injured during the fighting, he was being cared for at the Lodge. As he started to recover, he took to walking along the beach with his walking canes, I would watch him struggle to walk along the sand, admiring his determination. I became a little infatuated with him, so one day, I decided I would meet him."

"You! I can't believe you would risk our secret to meet a land-dweller," said Moire incredulously. "You will not let me swim near a boat, yet you were prepared to risk everything."

"I was young once also," said Isla. "And I made a mistake, one I try to make sure you don't repeat."

Isla ignored Moire's protests and carried on with her story. "I transformed in the early light of dawn and waited by the caves for him to come on his morning walk. I will never forget our first meeting, I told him I lived in a nearby farmhouse, it was not long after we fell in love. We met regularly and one day, he introduced me to the sisters at the Lodge. They knew what I was immediately, and although they never told him, they warned me that no good could come from our relationship.

"Of course, they were right, the calling of the ocean was too much for me and I started to spend more and more time back in the water. What I did not realise was that Ross being a MacDonald had awoken the ghost of an evil preacher. Reverend John Neave had been responsible for many of the murders on Kintyre but had met a brutal end himself in the caves at the hands of a MacDonald, but not before he cursed all those who carried the name MacDonald for years to come.

"While Ross was with me, he was hidden from the Preacher by my Selkie magic, but the spirit was growing in power as time went on. The sisters could sense his presence and knew they were dealing with something evil, but back then, they did not know exactly how dangerous the Preacher's spirit was.

"One day, I had arranged to meet Ross but had changed my mind, remaining in the sea. Ross went looking for me on the beach. When he couldn't find me, he went to the cave where we had spent a lot of our time together. The spirit mists came in quickly, and Ross was trapped in the cave. He was never seen again, although many of the staff from the Lodge hospital searched for him. They hunted everywhere and then Betty discovered Ross' walking canes in the cave.

"The sisters could feel the ghost of the Bloody Preacher around them, but it wasn't until they bought the place after the war that they found out about the curse on the MacDonalds. I was devastated and filled with guilt, if I had only been there. I had to explain to the Selkie council what had happened. The older Selkies knew of the curse at Southend and about this Preacher. They told me his story, which I later shared with the sisters in some effort to stop this from happening again," said Isla.

"So, Eden and Jamie are in danger because they carry the name MacDonald?" said Ewan. "My father was Ross, wasn't he?"

"Yes, now let me continue. You will need to know this," said Isla, silencing her son.

"Well over 300 years ago, there was another brutal land-dweller battle in which this Preacher, full of blood lust, had demanded the slaughter of all who lived at Dunaverty Castle. As he stood and watched the slaughter, one of the castle Good Wives cursed him with an agonising death. He ordered her burnt as a witch, but not before her curses had done their damage. He managed to escape punishment for his part on that gruesome day and went back to his home in Ayrshire. But when the MacDonald boy who had been saved that day by a nurse grew into a man, he hunted down the evil preacher and dragged him back to Southend as his prisoner. Ranald MacDonald took the Preacher to Keil Caves and hung him high from the roof of the Great Cave. They set a fire under his feet, slowly sending him screaming to hell, the curse of the Good Wife coming true. But as the preacher died, he offered the devil his soul if he may return to take his revenge on every MacDonald who came to Southend. I had been too late to save Ross, but I made sure I told the sisters what I had discovered. They were then very careful over the years about who they allowed to stay at the Lodge and turned away many with the name MacDonald.

"And as for me, well, I was already carrying Ross' child," said Isla, looking over to Ewan. "I carried an enormous amount of guilt for many years. I finally fell in love again and bonded with Fionnlagh, who wished to remain in the sea.

"I gave birth to Moire and watched as she grew but you, Ewan, did not. A half-blood Selkie must grow to adulthood on land, for in the ocean, they will remain pups. I had to let you live your land-dweller life so you could grow into a man, but I was frightened the Preacher would know who you were. The sisters helped me, and between us, we kept the Preacher at bay with wards and Selkie magic. But once you left, and I could return to the ocean, the sisters knew you could not come back."

"And now I have sent my children into danger," Ewan groaned. "I wish you had told me this before. I would never have bought the Lodge. We need to warn them."

"I saw Colla Ciotach there on the beach, perhaps he will protect them?" asked Moire.

"Colkitto has awoken, has he? That may be a good thing. He will stop the Preacher if he can," said Isla.

"In the meantime, I am going back to Kintyre, I need to warn my children," said Ewan.

"You can no longer take land-dweller form, how would you get them to hear you? It's up to me to tell them. I have caused all of this," said Isla.

The Selkie council unanimously agreed that Isla would have to return to the land-dweller world once more to warn her grandchildren of the curse. Fionnlagh insisted he would go with her, along with Ewan, who refused to be left behind.

Moire and her friends watched them leave, then when they were sure they would no longer be noticed, they too headed out for Kintyre.

Chapter Sixteen

Colla Ciotach stood atop Beinn Na Lice, the mists swirling at his feet while the Golden Eagles screeched around him, his presence disturbing them on their mountain. His gaze was on Ireland, the land of his birth, before he came to his beloved Colonsay. Now here, he was on the wild hilltops of Kintyre, this peninsula and these islands were his home, this was where his heart belonged, it was the place he would defend for all eternity if he must.

The Preacher's return had awoken Colkitto from his resting place once again, as it had done nearly 70 years before, but he had been unable to save his kin then. The Preacher had been too strong, driven by his bitter hatred of the MacDonalds. Perhaps that was Colkitto's problem, he had never really had any hatred in his heart. He had followed his God and king throughout his life, sworn to defend them to the end, he had done this remaining true to his convictions. His death, although brutal, had been honourable, even at the hands of those murderous Campbells. They had never made him bow to their beliefs, he had never changed sides to save his own skin, and he saw nothing but regret in the eyes of his captors as they put that rope around his neck. He had forgiven them as God intended, but the Preacher was another story.

Colkitto spent many years causing trouble for the Argyll Lairds and Clan Campbell. He had sailed his galley up and down the Hebrides, ransacking Campbell claimed land, stealing away their cattle and grain supplies. He was a huge thorn in the side to the Duke of Argyll, but more to the duke's bitter and twisted son, Lord Lorne. Colla Ciotach had many loyal men follow him into battle, he feasted and drank with the best of them. If truth be told though, the great Colkitto was a romantic, his life would have been preferable living peacefully on Colonsay, but life had not dealt him that card.

Colkitto first came across Reverend John Neave in Inveraray, where the Preacher was dealing out punishment to a young woman whom he accused of straying from her husband. The poor girl was stripped naked in front of the town square, bound by ropes around both her wrists and ankles, then she was doused with freezing water from the sea over and over again. Colkitto, with six of his men, was riding through the town, trying to keep a low profile as they were in prime Campbell territory. He saw the poor girl being tortured, but he also noted the look of smug pleasure etched on the Preacher's face. Against the advice of his men, he decided they should liberate her. So, he confronted the Preacher, asking him what the lass had done that God would demand such a cruel penance.

Reverend Neave was enraged at his intervention, ignoring Colkitto completely, the furious Preacher ordered the girl to be thrown into the sea. Colkitto pulled out his claymore and sliced through the ropes whilst the townspeople looked on. He lifted the poor girl onto his horse and fled the town, followed by his men, before the Campbell soldiers realised who they were. The Preacher cried bloody murder, startling the sleepy soldiers, who then gave chase. Colkitto's galley was only a little way up the coast, so before the soldiers could reach them, Colkitto and his crew, along with the saved girl, were sailing back down Loch Fyne.

That had been Colkitto's first meeting with the cruel reverend, but was certainly not his last. As the years went by, the evil reputation of the Bloody Preacher grew, soon he was more feared than the Duke of Argyll himself.

The Preacher became an intricate part of the Covenanter army, orchestrating many a massacre, even on one occasion ordering his soldiers to rip the unborn babes from their dead mother's wombs. If they were lucky, his enemies were killed outright, but often they were captured, then were stripped and flogged to an inch of their life, which usually led to a slow and painful death for them days afterwards.

The soldiers' families did not escape the punishments either. Their women were fitted with the Scold's Bridle, an iron device that was placed over their heads, with a two-inch metal plate that was forced into their mouths, holding their tongue down, making it impossible to speak or eat. It was a device used for nagging women, not meant to be used to starve the poor creatures to death.

Even his own men had their stomachs turned by his level of cruelty, but no one dared to stand against him, as he was the prophet of God. Colla Ciotach made it his mission to interfere with the Preacher at every opportunity. Soon, just the mention of Colkitto, or his son Alisdair, was enough to send the crazed Preacher into a rage.

Colla Ciotach was Laird MacDonald of Colonsay due to a deal he made with the old Duke of Argyll many years before. The duke received a yearly rent from him, and in return Colkitto kept the MacDonalds under his control fairly well behaved. As far as the duke was concerned, it was the lesser of two evils.

This enraged the duke's son and heir, Archibald Campbell, who held the title of Lord Lorne. He had nothing but contempt for this rogue MacDonald that plagued their shores. When the duke, his father, finally died towards the end of 1638, the new duke decided to send Reverend Neave to investigate the blasphemous ways of the Colonsay islanders. As far as the duke was concerned, Colkitto had humiliated the Campbells at every turn, so he could not begin to understand why his father had been so lenient. Colkitto was now coming up on his 70th year and had friends everywhere, so was warned well in advance of the Preacher's imminent arrival. He set a trap, capturing the angry Reverend Neave and his small force of men as they landed.

Colkitto knew well that the reverend was still furious with him over the incident at Inveraray, when he had rescued the young woman from punishment. He also knew of the reverend believed himself to be the voice of God. The Preacher had outlawed feasting, drinking, dancing and merriment of any kind. That was a sin in itself as far as Colkitto was concerned. So he had his daughters prepare a huge feast to welcome the reverend and his men, inviting the whole of the island, including the local Catholic priest, who blessed the meal they were about to enjoy.

Colkitto also made sure that the woman he had rescued years before from the reverend's punishment at Inveraray served him his meal. The Preacher refused to eat or drink, instructing his men to do the same.

Amused by the Preacher's reluctance to join in, Colkitto ordered his piper to play, then the dancing and feasting went late into the night, whilst his unimpressed guests were forced to sit amongst them. The Preacher sat in utter silence, not a morsel passing his lips, his fury apparent to all that were there.

The next day, the MacDonalds escorted the humiliated Preacher and his men to their boat, then bid them farewell. Once out on the water, the Preacher roared at them, spouting verses from his Bible, promising the destruction of this devil's island. Colkitto and his men roared with laughter at the reverend, some threw stones at the

Preacher's boat from the shore, one hitting Reverend Neave under his eye, leaving him with a nasty scar to remember that day by.

The Duke of Argyll was given all the proof he needed, so the following year, he laid waste to Colkitto's beloved Colonsay, capturing Colkitto and his two sons-in-law. The MacDonalds had to flee and Campbell farmers were put there in their place. Colkitto and his sons were taken as prisoners to Dunstaffnage Castle just outside Oban as prisoners, remaining there for six years.

Colkitto reflected on his life on Colonsay. They were some of the most peaceful years of his life, though his beloved Mary died in childbirth there, which had broken his heart. Mary MacDonald was from the Island of Sanda, the mother of his children, the strongest woman he had ever known. She never lost her youthful looks, with her blonde hair and bright blue eyes. He had always carried some guilt for lying to Mary over his affair with Lorna during his pirate escapades. If he had known Lorna was a Selkie, he would have left her alone. But her wild, dark beauty had bewitched him. The affair had been a disaster from the start, with him risking even the lives of his crew just to get a moment with her. It was a madness he had never forgiven himself for. He always thought Lorna had been murdered by Angus, but then he saw her again years later on the beach at Kintyre, with his son. She had not forgiven him but had entrusted him with their child. A child he believed had been murdered at Dunaverty, though he knew now that Conall had survived.

During his imprisonment in Dunstaffnage Castle, Colkitto enjoyed a rather a free reign. He was well respected, a good friend of the Campbell Laird of Dunstaffnage, who was embarrassed at having to imprison him. He was there a few years, though was never in chains, roaming free during the day, after swearing that he would not flee his captors; an oath he kept. Although he slept in a cell, it was made comfortable for him, Colla Ciotach wanted for nothing.

Colkitto always thought that Dunstaffnage's kindness to him was due to the fact that the Campbell Laird was married to Beatrix MacDonald, some kin of Colkitto's. But he later discovered that Beatrix hated him, holding him responsible for embarrassing her amongst her Campbell friends and nobles.

Beatrix had a daughter named Janet who shared her mother's views on the MacDonald Clan. In fact, after her own father's death, she ordered her men to sneak out at night to kidnap any man, woman or child that bore the name MacDonald. They were tied up, carried off in boats, then left to drown on small rocks just above the sea level, too far for them to swim back to shore. Many perished, but many were rescued as the news spread of her evil deeds.

Boats would go out regularly looking for these unfortunate souls, then sail them to the safety of Ireland. The locals called this hateful woman 'The Black Bitch of Dunstaffnage'.

Janet was furious that her father had allowed Colkitto so much freedom, so in the summer of 1644, she sent a message to the now Marquis of Argyll (In 1641, the Duke of Argyll was made the 1st Marquis of Argyll. He was also the only marquis), complaining that Colla Ciotach was walking free. The marquis had more to worry about as he had joined forces with David Leslie's Covenanter army who was at war with Montrose. So, it was not until the following years that he could send Reverend John Neave to assess the situation.

When the Preacher arrived unannounced, he found Colkitto was not under lock and key. He ordered him to be locked up straight away, instructing them to use the jougs. A metal collar clamped around his neck and hammered into the wall. Once old Colkitto was secured, the Preacher came to visit him. It was then that Colkitto finally witnessed for himself the depths of this man's black soul. The Preacher had him branded with a large upside-down cross on his chest, promising him that he would crucify him like the apostle Peter, upside down, as he was unworthy to face God. This was an insult to his faith, but Colkitto did not utter a word, nor cry out when the burning iron touched him.

He then spent an uncomfortable few days attached to the wall by the jougs, given only water until Reverend Neave left. That Bloody Preacher visited him daily to read from the Old Testament in some futile effort to redeem his soul. Colkitto knew better the preacher was only there to revel in his discomfort. He smiled as he remembered the smugness that was etched into the face of the Preacher each day as he arrived, only to be turned to scorn and anger as Colkitto tormented and questioned his Bible. Finally, the reverend had to leave to return to the army. The Laird of Dunstaffnage had Colkitto released from the jougs immediately, against the wishes of the Preacher and Janet, his own bitter-faced daughter. Lord Dunstaffnage was a good man, he sent a goodwife to attend to Colkitto's burns, but he could no longer allow Colkitto the freedom of his castle. Colkitto shuddered as he remembered those days, it was a fate worse than death for the old Highlander to be trapped in a cell, unable to see his beloved country, but he understood that his old friend did not dare let him loose.

A year later, he was finally freed, but his great strength had dwindled and he was beginning to feel his age, he was now 76 years old.

Colkitto had always known his death would not be a smooth passing. He accepted his death would be brutal, that of the warrior. He rode with his son Sir Alisdair under the orders of Charles 1st, fighting General Leslie and the Covenanter army. He was commissioned as the king's senior representative in Scotland, then was sent to Dunyvaig Castle on the Island of Islay. He knew his time was coming to an end and he was ready for death, the news of the murder of his kin at Dunaverty Castle had broken his spirit. That was not the way of the Highlanders, to commit bloody murder at a call for parley.

After the murder at Dunaverty, David Leslie's army followed Colkitto to Islay, surrounding his garrison in the castle. Colla Ciotach then arranged a parley for all his men in the garrison. Allowing his officers to go free, though the foot soldiers were to be sent to France to fight.

Leslie had him surrounded, so Colkitto knew he would not be allowed to leave with his men. The Covenanters thought they had tricked him into leaving the castle, offering him parley to go visit an old acquaintance, by all accounts, the son of his old friend, Laird Dunstaffnage. Colkitto was under no illusion when he left the safety of the castle, he already knew how dishonourable David Leslie's army could be. He was captured as soon as he left the castle, Leslie again dishonoured the parley. Colkitto was taken to Edinburgh, but the Marquis of Argyll arranged for him to be brought back to the west coast, there he found himself once again imprisoned at Dunstaffnage.

His old friend allowed Colkitto his freedom once more whilst he awaited his fate. Colkitto worked in the fields, helping with the late summer harvest. They sentenced him to death at the Campbell court in Inveraray, attended by Laird Dunstaffnage, but as the sentence was given, the marquis looked at the laird accusingly and asked, "Is Colla under restraint?"

Dunstaffnage said he was, but Argyll did not believe him, threatening him with prison if it was found to be untrue. A race then ensued across the country, with Dunstaffnage's men arriving at the castle minutes before the Campbell soldiers. They called across the field, "Colla in chains, Colla in chains!" Colkitto understood the cries, going directly to the castle cells and locking himself in.

He walked proudly to his death, they hung him from the mast of his galley and buried him as he wished, under the second step that led to Dunstaffnage tomb. It was kept secret from the marquis and from the Preacher, who had demanded Colkitto's head be displayed at the gates of Inveraray. The marquis was informed that Colla Ciotach's body had been given to the sea before the Preacher's order had arrived.

Colkitto thought of his great warrior son with pride. Sir Alisdair MacDonald was fighting for the Confederate forces in Ireland after he had escaped Dunaverty. He was captured, then murdered not long after Colkitto had been hung. The great warrior had been stabbed in the back as he allowed his horse to drink from the river. A cowardly act that was later discovered to be a murderous plot.

Sir Alisdair was buried in Ireland where Colkitto's grandsons grew up to be good, peaceful men. Colkitto still had a bond with Ireland, but it was the Colonsay MacDonalds who had raised him to be the man he was.

And now the Preacher had awoken, once again Colkitto's kin were in danger. Colkitto was sworn to protect them, and this he would do, but as the Preacher was getting stronger, it would be hard to contain him, but he would find a way.

The Preacher's curse only extended around the cliffs, rocks and the caves around Southend. That included the Lodge and the churchyard, but not Dunaverty Rock. The Preacher was banished from the rock, the ghosts of his victims were too strong there.

His thoughts then turned to the Selkies. It had definitely been them casting that spell of theirs on the beach. Colkitto suspected that Jamie had Selkie blood, how else would he have heard their call?

The Highland warrior tuned his head and listened to the wind. He could sense that Jamie and his sister were heading this way again, they would soon be at the Lodge. So, he let go of his physical form, becoming a mist wraith, allowing the wind to carry him back towards the beaches. He would watch over them, protecting them if he could. They would draw out the Preacher, then he would fight one last battle before he could rest forever.

Chapter Seventeen

Jamie pulled the car up the long driveway and parked up by the Lodge again. The builders were obviously keen to get started, as there were at least five industrial-sized skips set up around the place; however, there was no sign that the work had started yet.

"Well, they did say next week," said Jamie. "It's Friday, so they are probably just getting the skips in place."

Eden was more than eager to get going. "Well, I want to go back to the cave to try and find my phone."

"Are you sure you're up to it today? You've had a hell of a time, I can always go look," said Kate.

"I know, but I really want to see it properly. I feel like there is something there we may have missed," said Eden.

They set off on foot down the drive again, soon they were climbing up to the Great Cave. Jamie glanced nervously behind him.

"Are you looking for mist?" Kate asked.

"You read my mind, but I think there is a strong enough wind blowing that will make sure it stays away," he replied.

Eden headed straight for the back of the cave, then through the hole that had been widened into the cavern deep into the hillside. It was very dark, but they all had torches and had also brought a lamp that lit up the cavern nicely. They searched over the cavern floor with their torches for Eden's phone, then found it completely dead with a smashed screen. "Oh well, maybe it will come on if I charge it," said Eden disappointedly. "I'm not sure if they will replace it this time, it's the third phone I've managed to smash."

Kate had gone back to the entrance and was looking at the scratch marks again on the wall. "Do you think someone was trapped in here?"

"If there was, wouldn't there be a body?" said Jamie.

Kate shivered, she hadn't thought of that. Her eyes were drawn back to the boulders that she had seen before. They were set right back against the wall and looked like they were surrounding something. Eden had spotted them also, she was already making her way towards them. Gizmo starting barking at something as Kate realised he wasn't in the cavern.

"Look over here!" Eden shouted. "Behind these rocks, there's another cave. I think Gizmo has found it."

Eden shone her torch through a small tunnel that was about three feet high, its entrance hidden behind the boulders. Gizmo was still barking at something on the other side, so Eden started to crawl through the tunnel, followed closely by Kate. Jamie grabbed the lamp, then he followed them through. This cavern was about the same size as the one before, but as the lamp lit up the interior, there was much more to see. Not least of all a decomposed body lying against the wall, dressed in some sort of old military uniform. There was not much left, except the skeleton with some hair attached, which they could see had been dark. The three of them stood and stared, none of them particularly squeamish, but none of them finding the right words. Kate went over to the body to examine it closely while Gizmo was still growling at it.

"How the hell did he get in here?" said Jamie.

"He must have got trapped. He was probably the one who made these scratches on the wall. What a horrible way to go," said Eden, swallowing hard. It was a fate that had nearly befallen her the night before. "Do you think the Preacher dragged him in here also?"

"I don't know what to think at present, but we are going to have to report this," said Jamie.

"Look on his jacket, there is some sort of badge with some writing and a number. I can just make it out, it says 'MacDonald 546, Seal Lodge Hospital'. He must be a soldier that was nursed here during the war, when the Lodge was a hospital," said Kate.

"And he was a MacDonald," pointed out Eden. "Poor soul, I wonder who he was, maybe we should look to see if there are any records of him being missing. That number must have been his identity number, I'm sure we could find out."

Jamie was looking around with his torch for any other clues when he spotted something else hanging from the roof of the cave. At first, he couldn't make it out, but as he got closer, he saw a pile of bones at his feet, it didn't take an expert to work out they were human. He shone his torch up to the roof, there was a skull hanging there, attached to some sort of chain. He jumped back, properly spooked this time.

"What is it?" said Kate.

"I don't know if you want to see this, but I think we may have found another body, but this one is much older," said Jamie. The girls came over and saw what he had been looking at and Eden gasped, "It's the Preacher."

"How do you know?" asked Kate.

"I don't know, I just do. This is where he was murdered, this must be where he cursed us all," said Eden, who looked dreadful, visibly shaking now.

"I think that's enough for today, let's get Eden home, we can contact the authorities," said Jamie.

"No, don't contact anybody yet," said Eden suddenly.

"What? Why?" said Jamie, confused.

"We need to talk first. I remember more of what happened now. Can we get out of here?" said Eden.

They crawled out of the cavern, heading back to the outer caves, then back out into the daylight. Kate was relieved there was no mist. Eden was white as a sheet, she looked like she would throw up. Kate linked arms with her while they walked slowly back to the car in silence.

They drove back along the coast a little way and decided to stop at the Argyll Arms. Kate ordered a pot of tea; after downing a cup, Eden began to look much better.

"I'm sorry about that, it just all came rushing back to me," she said, nestling her hot cup.

"What do you remember?" asked Jamie.

"There was another entity in the cavern. I told you I saw the Preacher's face come at me before I blacked out; well, I also felt his rage, but he couldn't get near me. I think the entity that surrounded me must have been the ghost of that dead soldier. I'm sure whoever he was, he saved me from the Preacher. I remember feeling safe just at that moment before I fell unconscious. The Preacher had grown weak, it was like he had drained all his energy pulling me into that cavern. But I also know that the Preacher's power is growing stronger, I could feel it in that cave. The longer he remains here, the stronger he gets, I think it's our fault he's here."

"There are just too many ghosts for me to get my head around," said Jamie, sounding as frustrated as he looked.

"I know it sounds crazy, I don't want to believe it all myself. But the Preacher is definitely out to hurt members of the MacDonald

Clan. What I don't understand is how our dad, or our grandmother, lived here all these years without being harmed. And why would he buy the place if he thought it was dangerous," said Eden.

"Perhaps they found a way to protect themselves, but that still doesn't explain why he bought the place if he knew about the Preacher," said Kate, trying to make sense of it all.

"We still need to contact the authorities, there might still be family looking for that body, trying to find answers to what happened to him," said Jamie.

"I know, but please can we just hold off for a couple of days? There is some reason that all these spirits are remaining on Kintyre, we have to find out why, then find a way to release them. I don't think moving these remains will help at present. I want to find out who this MacDonald is, perhaps finding his identity will answer a lot of our questions," said Eden, pleading with them.

"Well, I don't suppose it will make much difference if we leave them there for another few days. It's not like they are going anywhere," said Kate, looking at Jamie. "Unless some tourists stumble across them, but it's very quiet around here at this time of year."

"Okay, I'm out voted, but I'm not altogether comfortable," said Jamie.

"I think we need to go to the library to try to find out who the body is. He must have gone missing when he was at the hospital in Seal Lodge, so there will be records of it there," suggested Kate.

"Well, why don't you two go and do that, but drop me off at the builder's yard on route. I want to have a word with Stuart about the work," said Jamie.

They left Jamie at the builders' depot and carried on into Campbeltown centre. The library was situated on the ground floor of the Aqualibrium Leisure Centre; thankfully, it was open, so Kate asked the librarian at the desk if she could help them find information about the Lodge when it was used as a hospital.

"The Royal Navy requisitioned the hotel in 1939 to be used as a hospital during the Second World War. It says here that the five-storey white building became a useful navigational aid for the navy ships, although it was kept for the most part in the dark, they would light up the building to help guide Atlantic convoys," Kate read aloud.

"Some ships still use it as a navigational aid now," said Eden.

"Wow, I never knew this," said Kate, who was still reading. "In 1940, during the Second World War, the HMS Nimrod submarine training base was moved here to Campbeltown. The Luftwaffe bombed it several times, lots of people were injured or killed here. That would be the reason for the naval hospital."

"This place is just saturated in history," said Eden. "Perhaps there are records of who stayed at the hospital?"

They asked the librarian who was hovering near them, obviously curious about what they were looking for. So, they explained that they were looking for stories of anyone who might have gone missing from the naval hospital during the war.

"Records like that will be kept in the Navy archives, not for public perusal. But I do have a collection of all the local newspapers dating back to 1918. Perhaps there will be something in there," the librarian offered.

"That would be wonderful," said Eden. They were taken to a back room, the walls were shelved and full of old files. The librarian pointed out the files that covered the Second World War and the girls pulled them out. They sat at a table, painstakingly going through each paper, scanning for missing person reports.

"This town really pulled together through the war," said Kate. "It's horrible reading about all these bombings, but in a funny way, I feel a sense of pride at how these Highlanders dealt with the tragedies."

"Here!" said Eden suddenly. "I think I've found it. Listen."

'19th August 1941

Ross MacDonald, the only son of Drew and Fiona MacDonald from Skipness, a naval officer in His Majesty's Navy, has been reported missing from Seal Lodge Naval Hospital at Southend. He had a serious leg wound that impaired his mobility greatly. Janette Riley, a nurse at the hospital, said he would exercise his leg daily walking by the sea. It was on one of these outings that he vanished. A search party concluded that he may have been swept out to sea, but a body has never been found. Ross was from a long line of Kintyre MacDonalds and will be sorely missed by his friends and family.'

"That's it, it's him, it must be," said Kate. "Let's take a copy of this and show Jamie. I wonder if he has any family left here on Kintyre. Though it does say he was their only son."

"Maybe he had a sister?" Eden suggested.

"Maybe, I never thought of that. When we finally report that we've found the body, any family he has will probably resurface then," said Kate.

"Yes, but not yet, remember you promised me a couple of days at least," Eden reminded her. "I need to go and speak with Ronan again. I think he may know something about Ross MacDonald."

Chapter Eighteen

"Aye, I kent the story, but I wis only a wee laddie when the war struck. I remember having oor door blasted off in one of the bombing raids. We hid under the kitchen table, as we didnae have time tae get tae the bomb shelter," said Ronan.

It was the next morning and Eden and Kate were sitting in his floral living room at Pirnmill on Arran. His wife, Sheena, had made a fuss of them when they arrived full of apologies for coming unannounced. Seemingly unflustered, she had baked scones, serving them with a pot of tea and shortbread 15 minutes later. She then politely said she was going out, leaving them to it.

"I'm awfie glad ye arenae hurt, lassie. I did feel responsible taking ye in tae that cave," said Ronan.

"I'm fine, thank you, and it wasn't your fault. We would have gone there anyway," replied Eden.

"I didnae ken aboot this curse on the MacDonalds, but it all fits noo when I think aboot it," said Ronan. "The sisters didnae seem tae take notice of the ghosts I could see aroond the Lodge, but I remember them turning away more than one MacDonald that tried tae book in tae the Lodge, even though we werenae full."

Ronan went quiet, suddenly lost in thought, then spoke as if he were careful how he was wording the next sentence. "There wis one time, but I swore I would never talk aboot it. I met the Preacher's ghost, but I didnae ken who he wis. I wis somewhere I shudnae have bin, and I wis lucky, because the sisters found me."

Ronan then changed the subject and did not elaborate on what he had just told them. "The sisters kent more than they let on," he said. "I always suspected they had some sort of charm keeping the ghosts at bay. I ken ghosts appear, especially here in Scotland wi all the old stories, but I always wondered why there wis so many ghosts on Kintyre. It wis like the people there couldnae be put tae rest. If it is a curse, then I dinnae think ye'll be safe until it's broken, lassie."

"You told Jamie that he had spoken to Colkitto down on the beach. Have you seen his ghost before?" asked Kate.

"Aye, I've seen Colla many times over the years. He's usually on the beach, looking oot tae sea. I think he's watching for Lorna sometimes. I've spoken wi him. He respects us MacDougalls, as we came tae the MacDonalds' aid many times against those murderous Campbells. There wis more of us MacDougalls murdered at Dunaverty than there wis those that carried the name MacDonald. I never did speak wi him for long, I always got terrible chills in his presence, and he would just gae when he saw me shiver."

Ronan suddenly got up from his chair. "Ye ken, I have a briefcase somewhere wi some of the sister's paperwork and old hotel journals. I havnae gone through them fir years, but I took them when the new owners took over. They werenae interested in how the sisters ran the place, and I didnae want it all destroyed."

"Ronan, you're a legend," squealed Eden. "Could we please go through the briefcase?"

"Aye of course, I forgot all aboot it. Maybe ye'll find something that will help ye get rid of that spirit," said Ronan, leaving them for a couple of minutes, only to return with a battered old briefcase bursting at the seams with whatever was in it.

The girls hugged the old man goodbye before setting off back to Kintyre. Both of them feeling a step closer to the mystery around the Lodge now, and eager to start going through the briefcase.

***

Jamie was at the Lodge again with the builders. Stuart was inspecting the top floor, it seemed the staircases were still secure, but nowadays, a lift would have to be installed, no one climbed five storeys in a hotel anymore. Jamie was still a little nervous of climbing the stairs himself after his fall the other day, but now that he was in the Lodge, he was able to shake off his reservations. To be honest, all these ghost stories that Kate and Eden had been uncovering were giving him reservations about the idea of rebuilding the place. But now with the men here and the work in progress, he was feeling the familiar buzz he felt from a restoration project. This was going to be a fabulous building, as the original design was certainly unusual for its day, definitely very art deco.

The builders were keen just to get started with clearing out the place, they were uncovering all sorts of memorabilia from under the rubble. In one of the upper rooms, there were quite a few paintings hidden in an old closet that must have hung around the place one day. Most were just cheap copies, but some were really nice paintings of the Kintyre coastline, obviously done by a local artist, though Jamie couldn't make out the name signed on the canvas. He would definitely have these reframed and put back in the Lodge.

The furniture in most of the rooms was removed but, occasionally, one of the men would holler that they found an old chest of drawers or wardrobe. One of the wardrobes was still full of women's clothes, definitely '60s' style. Jamie decided to bag them up, he would let Eden and Kate go through them, you never knew what they would find.

Jamie began poking around the bar area. The mahogany bar top was ruined beyond repair, but the wooden shelving underneath was still in good nick. As he continued to check it along the length of the bar, he noticed something set into the wood right at the back of the shelf. He wouldn't have seen it if he hadn't been on his hands and knees. It looked like a small wooden safe that was screwed into the bar.

It was locked and he couldn't pull it out. He went out and got a crow bar from his car, then tried to loosen the box from the wooden frame. It took some doing, it was at an odd angle which made it difficult, but, finally, he managed to pry it loose without damaging the wood.

The box was square, about ten inches in height, Jamie was tempted to just smash it open, but something stopped him. He decided to try his set of skeleton keys that he kept for just this purpose. He sat in his car, trying the keys and, eventually, he heard the lock click as the door of the box swung open.

There were a couple of bags of change inside. Jamie saw it was old money, old shillings and sixpences, way before his time. It must have been here since the sisters had the place. There were a couple of envelopes in there also. Jamie opened the thickest one to find it had old black and white photos of the Lodge when the sisters must have owned it. There was a picture of Janette and Betty Riley standing by the bar, Jamie was surprised at how glamorous they were.

Both were probably in their 40s, slim, both with short dark curled hair, one dressed in a tight jacket and pencil skirt, whilst the other in a looser dress pulled in tight to show off a slim waist. Both ladies were posing with cigarettes in long cigarette holders, they looked like quite the party animals. He assumed, as they were called the spinster sisters, that they would perhaps be slightly on the frumpy side. How wrong he was.

There were more pictures of Janette and Betty posing obviously with some of their guests, then Jamie came across a picture of a young, strapping-looking Ronan out mowing the lawn. There were pictures of a boy and Jamie guessed it was his father. A few showed him playing on the beach when he looked around 11 or 12, then some of him as an older boy wearing a school uniform, standing next to the sisters. There was also one picture of Isla, his grandmother. It was a haunting black and white photograph of Isla standing on the beach, gazing out to sea.

The other envelope was still sealed shut and addressed to his father. He wondered for a brief moment whether he should wait until Eden was with him, but that moment passed quickly. His curiosity got the better of him and he carefully tore it open. It was a letter from Isla to her son.

My beloved Ewan

I have left this letter with Betty should you choose to not heed my warnings and visit the Lodge once again. I miss you more than you could ever know, but I understand you must follow your life's path. I will always hope that one day, you will decide to return to us to live out your life in the ocean, but until then, I pray that you will have a good life and many children.

Ewan, I need to explain some things to you that I have regretted not doing before we parted. The reason I made you promise not to return to the Lodge was for your own safety. The area around Southend and Dunaverty has been cursed for centuries. With so many brutal murders around these cliffs and mountains, malevolent forces trapped the poor souls of the murdered so they could not move on to the afterlife.

The ghosts of the dead haunt these shores and Seal Lodge was built just next to the unmarked graves from the massacre. The bodies had been thrown into pits, without a priest being given the chance to free their souls.

We Selkies knew where the bodies were, also why the ghosts had remained. There was one spirit who did not belong amongst them. He was a monster during his land-dweller life, responsible for the murders at Dunaverty Castle. He is known as 'the Preacher', a dark soul who was tortured to death in the caves here, but not before evoking black spirits that gave him the power to seek vengeance on all that carried the name MacDonald.

I met your father during the land-dweller war. I have told you about him but not what happened to him. Ross was a lovely man from Kintyre, he dreamt of living a quiet and peaceful here. He was badly injured during the great land-dweller war, which meant he would always walk with a limp. I watched him on the beach from the sea, struggling with his injury, and decided that I had to meet him. At the time, I was an impetuous Selkie and although I knew of the ghosts around the Lodge, I did not know of the Preacher.

Janette and Betty were nurses at the Lodge, but they recognised me for what I was. I realised they were Good Wives, or witches as the land-dwellers called them. Their magic was limited to spells and potions, so they were excellent nurses. They knew of the Selkie Folk, and they befriended me, although warning me at the same time that the call of the sea would be too strong for me to ignore. I, in turn, told them what I knew about the bodies buried around the Lodge, as they had seen the ghosts and were curious about why there were so many of them. The sisters cast some warding spells around the Lodge to protect it from the spirits, but what we didn't realise was that Ross' arrival had awoken the Preacher. He was a MacDonald and the longer he remained at the Lodge, the more powerful the dark magic of the Preacher grew.

While Ross was with me, he was protected from the dark magic as I was a full-blood Selkie, but then the call of the ocean became louder, I couldn't resist spending more and more time back in the water. Then one day, when I chose to remain in the ocean, Ross had gone to look for me alone. He was in the caves when he was taken by the Preacher. No one knew what had happened, I searched everywhere for him. Eventually, I came across the spirit of Colla Ciotach. Every Selkie around these parts knew of Colkitto. He and my mother Lorna had been lovers, he was the father of my brother Conall. He told me what had happened to Ross, explaining about the Preacher. The Preacher had dragged Ross through into undiscovered caverns behind the caves, trapping him for days, then had crushed his heart. Colkitto had tried to protect Ross, but he could not *overcome the dark power of the Preacher. He needed more time to draw on his own power.*

I had to tell the sister what happened, from then on, they then made it their mission to protect all that carried the name MacDonald. The Selkie council decided the sisters should remain at the Lodge after the war and gave them enough land-dweller money to buy the place. Janette and Betty warded as much as they could against the Preacher, avoiding having MacDonald clansmen stay at the Lodge.

The sisters also worked hard trying to find a way to help release the other lost spirits from Dunaverty but came to realise that as long as the Preacher was able to rise, the souls of his victims were trapped here.

When I arrived with you, I was unsure whether you would be safe at first. You were not a full-blood Selkie, but with my own magical protection and the sisters' warding, we managed to keep you undetected by the Preacher. But I knew once I left, you would be in danger, which is why I made you promise that you would not return.

I hope this letter explains my reasons. If you are at the Lodge, you must leave immediately, for I am sure you will have awoken him. Please be safe, my son.

Fionnlagh and Moire send their love and we all hope, one day, that you come back to us.

Your loving mother.

Jamie sat back in his car seat. He couldn't quite believe what he had just read. How on earth could he be expected to believe that there were Selkies and he was related to them? Yet somehow, all the pieces seemed to fit. She had described exactly what had happened to Eden, except Eden had someone or something protect her. Colkitto must be stronger now, but that didn't fix the danger they were all in. What was he going to do? He couldn't just give up on this project because of a ghost. But it was obviously a ghost that could do great harm. He would need to talk it through with Kate and Eden.

Jamie got out of his car and went to find Stuart Aiken. The builder was at the rear of the Lodge. "Stuart, I've got a few things to do, so I'll be gone for the rest of the day," said Jamie.

"Aye, okay, we'll just keep on clearing, ye dinnae have tae be here," said Stuart.

Jamie started walking back to his car, then a thought struck him. "Stuart, you don't have any men working here who's a MacDonald, do you?"

Stuart looked at him in surprise. "Nae MacDonalds here, except ye," he replied. "Why dae ye ask?"

"Oh, no reason, I'm just being daft," said Jamie.

"So, ye've heard aboot the curse, have ye?" said Stuart, chuckling.

"Aye, something like that," said Jamie, laughing.

"Och take nae heed," said Stuart. "Auld wife's fairy tales."

Jamie waved goodbye and went back to his car. So, some of the locals did know about the curse, but, obviously, not all of them believed it.

When he got back to Kate's house, he could see the girls were back from Arran. He let himself in and found them sitting in the conservatory with an old briefcase lying wide open, piles of yellowed papers were stacked around the room.

"What's this then?" he asked, going over to Kate and kissing the top of her head.

"You won't believe all the stuff we have found in here. Old menus and cocktail lists, recipes and staff rotas. There is just loads of paperwork crammed in here. But we also found what looks to be a spell book. We were just trying to make sense of it," said Eden, clearly overexcited.

Kate looked up and rolled her eyes at him, smiling. She made his heart skip a beat every time he looked at her.

"Well, I can see your briefcase, and I will raise you a wooden box," said Jamie, holding out his find. "I found something in here that you two are going to have to read."

Jamie opened the box and pulled out the two envelopes. "I'm going to take a shower and get all this dust off. You two please read this letter, then I think we really need to talk."

Chapter Nineteen

It was after 3 in the morning before they finished discussing Isla's letter. Eden was already convinced that they were half Selkies, which explained their love of water and why they were such good swimmers. Jamie laughed at her, but if he were to be honest, the thought had crossed his mind already. He just wasn't ready to believe he was a descendent of a sea creature from some ancient myth. Kate googled Selkies but didn't find out much more than what Ronan had already told them.

The tone of the conversation changed when they started to talk about the Preacher. Eden would not hear of putting the rebuild of the Lodge on hold. She was convinced that they could find a way of getting rid of him for good. Jamie sighed, he didn't want to hold up the work, but they couldn't put themselves in harm's way. "Maybe you should google exorcists," he said to Kate.

"I think we may be a bit hard pressed to find one of those on the Mull of Kintyre," said Kate dryly.

"Look, the two of you promised to give me a couple of days before we make any decisions. Let me go through this weird little spell book. It's hard to read but it may hold some clues," said Eden. "Now I'm going to bed. Don't make any decisions without me," she added firmly.

The next morning, Kate awoke first, Jamie's arm draped over her. She snuggled close into his body, then felt him stir. He kissed the back of her neck and she felt his erection. Smiling, she turned and Jamie pulled her on top of him. They made love late into the morning, forgetting the horrors of the last few days or dwelling on what was to come. Eventually, they got up, feeling a little guilty that Eden was on her own.

Kate was showered and dressed first, then went into the kitchen to put the coffee on. Eden didn't seem to be up, but then Kate noticed Gizmo was gone. She had a look in Eden's room, Eden wasn't there. Maybe they had gone for a walk.

Jamie appeared, rubbing his head with a towel, "Where's Eden?"

"I'm not sure, Gizmo's gone, so they probably have gone for a walk," said Kate.

Just then, Jamie's phone rang. "It's Stuart Aiken," said Jamie. "He's probably wondering where I am."

Jamie took the phone call in the conservatory just as Gizmo and Eden appeared back at the kitchen door. "You're up at last," said Eden, looking wind swept and much better than she had done the last couple of days. "I didn't want to disturb you."

"Well, the plot thickens," said Jamie, appearing looking slightly bewildered. "Stuart says there's a woman waiting for us at the Lodge. She was there when he arrived with his men this morning. She won't leave until she has spoken with us apparently, and get this. Her name is Isla MacDonald."

"What the hell!" said Kate. "It can't be, surely."

"Well, there's only one way to find out," declared Eden. "Let's go, what are we waiting for?"

Minutes later, they were on the road in Kate's car to the Lodge. None of them spoke much, as no one really knew what to say. To admit that it was Ewan's mother seemed ridiculous, but with everything else that had happened, could it be possible?

Kate pulled up the drive, they saw Isla seated on one of the old stone benches at the front of the Lodge. She looked exactly like her photograph all these years before, apart from her clothing which was much more modern as she had on jeans and a simple sweater. They all got out of the car as she turned towards them and smiled. She had always looked so solemn in the photographs, but the smile transformed her dramatically. Isla had an uncanny resemblance to Eden and it was her that she hugged first.

"You must be Eden, it's so wonderful to finally meet you," said Isla with a warmth they did not expect. "And, Jamie, you are so like your father."

Kate stood back a little, unsure what to say. Then the Selkie turned towards her and held out her hand. "I'm sorry I don't know your name. I understand you must have many questions about my arrival here."

"This is Kate, my girlfriend," said Jamie awkwardly. "I think we all have a lot questions, not least of all, how can this be?"

"Shall we go for a walk along the beach. I feel better next to the water, and Ewan will be able to see you there," said Isla.

"Our father!" said Eden. "You mean he is here?"

"There is a lot to tell you, please shall we go?" replied Isla, taking Eden's hand, leading her down towards the water.

They walked down towards the shore, then noticed the seals watching them from the water. Kate felt a shiver down her spine as she suspected they were more than just seals.

"I don't know how much you know of the Lodge, but I suspect you have done your investigations. My daughter and her friends have seen you with Ronan MacDougall, so I suspect he has told quite a lot about the history here," said Isla.

"Yes, he has. Are you really a Selkie?" Eden blurted out.

"Yes, child, I am a Selkie, but I am also your grandmother. You are also part Selkie, you share our ability to transform, you could come to the ocean to remain with us if you wish," Isla explained.

"Don't even think about it," whispered Kate in Jamie's ear.

"Our father went back to the sea?" said Eden. "Why didn't he tell us?"

"He couldn't, the Selkie secret is one we must keep sacred. You, nor your sister, had shown any desire to spend time in the ocean. He was not sure whether you heard the calling. All Selkie half-bloods usually do at some point in their lives, but few recognise it. He could not risk our safety by telling you," said Isla.

"If he is here, where is he then?" asked Jamie, looking over to where the seals were watching.

"He is there, but he can no longer take land-dweller form. His choice to live as a land-dweller meant that if he ever chose to return to live in the sea, he would never be able to transform again. But he has his Selkie family with him now, and we have missed him. You have to understand that giving up the Selkie life in the ocean is abhorrent to many of us. His love of your mother and of you kept him away from us for many years. As he grew older, his yearning for the ocean became too strong to ignore. He only left you when he felt you were strong enough to carry on without him," Isla told them.

"So, I can't talk to him," said Eden, her eyes full of tears.

"You can if you come into the water. You can still transform, I can show you how," said Isla.

Jamie grabbed hold of Eden protectively. "Well, she will need to think about that, long and hard!" he said, glaring at his sister before she did something rash.

"I understand," smiled Isla. "You also have the magic in your blood. We can discuss it another time. Right now, we have more pressing matters."

"The Preacher?" said Kate.

"Then you have come across him. That is a worry. I came to warn you about him. Ewan did not know the extent of the curse when he lived here. Otherwise, he would never have put you in such danger," said Isla.

"Yes, we know, we found your letter to him. The one you left with Betty all these years ago, she had it locked away, so we only discovered it yesterday," said Jamie.

"You know more than I thought you would. What have you decided to do? You cannot stay here, your lives are in danger," said Isla.

"We have already started the project, we're not planning on stopping now," said Jamie.

"We are looking for a way to get rid of him for good," said Eden. "I was reading the sisters' journal last night, they seemed to have quite a few spells to ward against ghosts."

"Yes, they did a good job with the ghosts that live around the Lodge. With all the tragedies that have happened here, along with the Preacher's curse, this area has been overwhelmed with trapped spirits. The sisters spent a lot of their time trying to find a way to help them. But they were always hindered by the Preacher. He would not let any escape. If he was to live trapped in torment, then so must they. This Preacher was born with a black heart, an ancient malevolent soul risen again to torment all those who came across him. The dark power he wields is not to be scorned at. I'm not sure there is a way to destroy him," said Isla, grimacing. "But I can see you will not leave so I will help you all I can. I can look through our ancient folklore, maybe I can try to find a way to send him back to where he came from. Your father won't be happy that you are remaining at the Lodge, I will try to make him understand."

Eden looked at the seals just as a grey speckled seal pulled himself out the water and onto a rock. It started barking at them, throwing its head from left to right.

"Please don't be sad, child. I know you miss him, but he is happy with us. He is finally home," said her grandmother. "Now I must leave you for now. I have been out of the water too long whilst waiting for you. We will not leave the coastline, one of us will be watching at all times. If the Preacher emerges, try to call out for us, we can help. That devil has no power over us," said Isla.

"Thank you for coming," said Eden, hugging her grandmother once more.

Jamie remained where he was, not sure what to make of it all. Isla simply smiled at him, then turned to walk into the sea. When the water was up to her knees, she let herself slip under the waves, there in her place was a sleek brown seal. Isla swam out to join the other Selkies while Jamie, Kate and Eden stood on the shore and watched.

"Well, that confirms the Selkie story," said Kate, flippantly breaking the silence.

Jamie just shook his head. "This world is becoming weirder by the second. Though I have to say, I'm kind of enjoying it. Apart from when you went missing," he added quickly when he saw Eden's horrified face looking at him.

"We need to get rid of the Preacher!" she said stubbornly.

"Yes, I understand that, I'm just not sure how," replied Jamie.

"There has to be a way, I'm sure we will find it," said Kate.

"Okay, let's get back to the Lodge. I need to speak with Stuart," said Jamie.

"Why don't you do that, Eden, and I could do some more exploring around here," Kate suggested. "You never know, we may have missed something."

"Yes, I'd like to do that," said Eden gratefully.

"Okay, just don't get in any more trouble. I've had all the ghosts and legends I can take for one day," said Jamie. He squeezed Eden's shoulders, then kissed Kate before he strolled back up the beach. The seals were still watching them.

Chapter Twenty

The girls walked along the beach a little further, the wind blowing steadily as they were watched by the seals. They weren't sure where they were headed, but it was cold in the wind there, so Eden suggested that they go to 'Bloody Rock', the sight of the massacre. They turned back towards the road, then followed Jamie up past the entrance to the Lodge. They walked half a mile, then found their way back down to the sandy horse shoe bay that hugged the coast all the way around to Dunaverty Rock. The rock was a huge mound, speckled red, and was nicknamed Bloody Rock after the massacre. It was surrounded on three sides by the ocean and jagged-looking rocks, which would have protected the castle that once sat upon it. The golf course was behind them, with quite a few golfers out playing. The girls found they were more sheltered from the Atlantic wind on this beach.

They came to the end of the sand, then climbed up the grassy slope past the lighthouse station. There they walked up the steep mound that led to the rock. The path across to it was narrow and uneven, the girls were careful, aware that a strong gust could blow them over. Sadly, there was nothing left of the castle that had been initially built in the 12th century.

"Apparently, there was a drawbridge here across to the castle," said Kate. "With all these cliffs surrounding it and only one drawbridge, you can see how the castle was impenetrable."

"Impenetrable as long as you have enough food and water, it's such a shame they dismantled it. They took the whole castle apart in 1685," said Eden. "It was just after the Earl of Argyll's failed rebellion against King James VII."

Kate pointed to what looked out over the landscape behind them. There was a stone cottage-shaped building over in a field south of the village. It was too low to the ground to be a cottage. "That must be the tomb where they say the victims of the massacre were buried in a mass grave, I saw a picture of it online. It's quite a way from where the castle was," said Kate, suddenly feeling an icy chill go through her body, she shivered.

"Yes, but we know they were not all interred there. Many of the bodies are over by the Lodge," said Eden. "Are you okay? You look like you're freezing."

"The bodies lying in that tomb didnae meet their end on these cliffs, they died of the pestilence that swept through these lands afterwards. A plague brought by the English army that killed more people aroond here than that Bloody Preacher managed at Dunaverty."

Kate and Eden turned around in surprise at the man's voice. They hadn't seen anyone while they had walked up. There stood a giant of a man, with striking pale blue eyes and long white hair. He was towering over them, dressed as a Highlander, with the hilt of a sword raised up over his shoulder. There was a strange mist hanging like a net curtain around him, making his features slightly blurred when Kate tried to focus on him.

"C–C–C–Colkitto?" Kate stuttered, still shivering.

"Aye, that's what they called me. But ye may call me Colla," he replied.

"How are you here?" she said, aware that Eden was standing behind her silent for once.

"The question isnae how, it's why, lassie," replied Colla.

"I'm s–s–s–sorry, this is a l–l–l–lot to t–t–t–take in," replied Kate, trying to catch her breath, she had no idea if she felt afraid or safe. This giant of a man ghost seemed to pose no threat, but was he a ghost?

"Aye, it cannae be easy for ye, take yer time, let it settle," said Colkitto, not moving from the spot in which he stood.

"I'm Eden," said Eden, suddenly finding her voice, saying the first thing that came into her head.

"Aye, I ken who ye are, Eden MacDonald. Yer my own kin, lassie, a descendent of my own, MacDonald bloodline, and the reason behind the awakening of John Neave. That would be why I'm here," he said.

"C–C–C–Can you s–s–s–stop him?" asked Kate. "He n–n–nearly killed Eden, we d–d–don't know how to g–g–g–get r–r–rid of him."

"I will catch him this time, he cannae evade me forever," said Colla.

"This time? Have you tried before?" asked Eden, she had her arms around Kate now, trying to warm her up.

"It's nae the first time my kin has come back tae Kintyre. I wisnae strong enough tae harm him last time, he murdered yer grandfather, in the same cave he tried tae murder ye in, lassie. I wis strong enough tae protect ye then, but nae strong enough tae dae him harm. My strength is building the longer I remain here. This time, I will put him back in hell where he belongs."

"That was you. The presence I felt over me in the cave. You stopped him, thank you," said Eden.

"Aye, that wis me, but I dinnae need yer thanks, lass, nae until we put him in the ground fir good," said Colla.

"How d–d–do we d–d–do t–t–t–that?" asked Kate, feeling sick with cold now.

"We'll draw him oot, he's hiding frae me, he has tae be careful tae pick his moment tae attack. He is a sneaky, cowardly soul, even in death. He will fail this time, then the rest of Kintyre can finally gae tae sleep fir eternity," Colkitto told them.

"We can't put anyone else in danger," said Eden. "We need to know how to protect ourselves from him."

"Yer nae safe anywhere by Columba's graveyard and the caves. He can appear as I can, but he hides. He plays games, he knows the Selkies are watching over ye. He won't mess aroond with Selkie magic, it scares him," said the old ghost. "Just wait until I call on ye, I will be watching him, I will ken when he appears. Ye cannae fight him on yer own, lassie, so dinnae try."

"But that doesn't tell us what we should do," said Eden, then looked at her friend's face. "Are you doing this to Kate, why is she so cold?"

"Ye have Selkie blood, my magic disnae affect you, I have tae gae before I dae her harm. Just watch yer backs, dinnae be alone and remember tae call on me," Colkitto said as he started to fade into the mist.

"But how do we do that?" Eden called as the mist started to dissipate, then vanished as if it had never been there. They stood alone on top of the rock now, the wind had dropped, but Kate was now shivering uncontrollably.

"Are you okay?" asked Eden.

"I'm j–j–j–just s–s–s–s–s–so c–c–c–c–c–c–c–cold," stammered Kate, unable to form words properly.

Eden ripped off her jacket and threw it around Kate's shoulders. It didn't make much difference as she led Kate back down the hill, then along to the golf clubhouse. Eden ordered some hot tea for them, but Kate couldn't hold the cup, she was shaking so much, so Eden called Jamie. He arrived minutes later and they helped Kate into the car.

"Shall we take her to the hospital?" said Jamie.

"N–n–n–n–no, p–p–p–p–p–please j–j–just h–h–h–home," begged Kate.

Eden sat in the back of the car with her arms around Kate's shoulders, trying to rub heat into her. Jamie drove as fast as he could on these hazardous roads, finally making it home. He carried Kate into her bedroom and put her in bed, stripping her cold clothes off her, then wrapping the duvet around her. He lay next to her, stoking her hair as she was still shaking violently, but after a while, the shivering subsided and Kate began to feel warmth flow through her body again. Her head was thumping now, so she closed her eyes. Before long, she was fast asleep. Jamie kissed her forehead, then went to join Eden in the conservatory.

"How is she?" his sister asked him.

"I don't know. She has stopped shaking and is asleep now, thank God. What the hell happened?" he asked.

"We met Colkitto's ghost on Dunaverty Rock. His energy must have had some sort of effect on Kate. I feel fine," said Eden. "But he said it was because I had Selkie blood."

"What did he want?" asked Jamie. "I thought he was supposed to be on our side."

"I'm not sure he wanted anything in particular. He was warning us about the Preacher and wanted us to know he is getting stronger and believes he will be able to defeat the Preacher. He told us we had to be vigilant and, if we were in danger, to call on him," said Eden.

"Nothing that we didn't know already," said Jamie. "There seems to be a lot of people warning us, but we still have no idea how to protect ourselves. What happened to Kate?"

"He said something about his spirit affecting her, she just started shivering really hard and could hardly speak. Poor Kate, she is going to have to be careful if these ghosts keep appearing," said Eden. "He didn't stay long because of the affect he was having on her."

"This is beginning to sound like a Stephen King horror story. Old hotel, ghosts and an evil Preacher. People will think we are nuts.

Stuart Aiken laughed at me the other day when I asked him if any of the men working at the Lodge were MacDonalds. He asked if I had heard about the curse, and if I believed it. People seem to know the story but they don't take it seriously," said Jamie.

"I think I can explain that," said Eden. "Colkitto mentioned the plague that had been brought to Scotland by the Covenanter army from England. I had read about it before but I didn't think it was significant. You see, the plague virtually wiped out the entire population on Kintyre. They say that there were only three houses left that had fires lit in Southend and the surrounding area. With the Highland clans either murdered at Dunaverty or wiped out by the plague, there was no one left to farm. Kintyre has always had very rich farmland, so the Scottish parliament sent Lowlanders from the borders to farm and repopulate Kintyre. They had names like Johnson or Smith. The MacDonalds and MacDougalls are now few and far between on the Mull. Our grandfather's family was up in Skipness, so they were safe from the curse. It was only when he came to Southend did he place himself in danger. That would be the reason why people don't take it seriously around here."

"Right, so what your saying is that because they're not many clansmen around here anymore, this has kept the Preacher at bay," said Jamie.

"Exactly. The other thing Colkitto said was that when he finally gets rid of the Preacher, the stranded ghosts on the Mull will be able to be put to rest. Which, let's be honest, would be a good thing for the Lodge," said Eden.

"Yes, agreed. I guess we are just going to be waiting for the Preacher to make his next move then," said Jamie.

"Well, we have to make sure we are not caught out anywhere on our own when we go to the Lodge. I think Kate will be safe, it's you and me that have the MacDonald blood. I also think that we are safe here, it only seems to be around Southend that the Preacher has any power," said Eden. "I've been thinking a lot about our father. I know you didn't know him, but he was a really great guy. He would never have put us in danger if he knew. I have been thinking about going into the water with Isla just to be able to talk to him."

"You can't be serious, Eden? You have no idea what that will do to you," said Jamie.

"I have to be honest with you, Jamie. Ever since that day on Sanda Island, I have been dreaming of the ocean almost every night.

It seems to be calling me, now I know that Dad is there, the feeling is stronger than ever," she said.

"I get it, Eden. But we have only just discovered this, we haven't had time to work out what impact this knowledge will have on our lives. Please just hold off with these thoughts until we get this Preacher business sorted. I couldn't cope with you disappearing again," said Jamie, his head in his hands.

"I promise I won't do anything without telling you first. Of course, I won't leave you to deal with the Preacher on your own, but I just want you to understand how I'm feeling. You have Kate, the two of you are going to have a fantastic life here, but I am still searching for something. I have been all my life. I've never been settled or happy anywhere, I've never held a job down long, nor held onto a relationship. I used to think there was something wrong with me as I just didn't seem to fit anywhere, but now I know what it is. It's like a lightbulb has gone on in my head, and the desire to go to the ocean is overwhelming. Please try to understand," Eden tried to explain.

"I kind of know what you're talking about. I felt something like it myself that day on the beach, but it's just all happening too fast. Eden, you need to know more about what you would be letting yourself in for. Look, let's talk about this again another time. I think we both have a lot to sleep on. I'm worried about Kate, so I'm going to go to bed now. I'm not being dismissive, I do get it. I just need some time to get my head around it all," said Jamie. He got up and ruffled Eden's hair affectionately before leaving to join Kate.

Chapter Twenty-One

Eden sat there for a while, looking out the huge glass windows at the stars reflecting across the firth to Arran. Gizmo was curled up next to her, "Do you want to go out?" she whispered to him; immediately, he jumped up, pawing at her eagerly. She slipped on her jacket and trainers, then opened the door quietly to head out to the beach, with Gizmo tearing ahead of her. It was a clear, frosty night, with no wind and silent, apart from the occasional hoot of an owl, there were no waves splashing on the shore, everything was still. Eden felt invigorated in the cold air, glad to be out of the house and next to the water. She longed to go in, but she had promised Jamie, so she just stood at the water's edge, breathing in the sea air. She heard a splash next to her, she looked down to see Gizmo watching her curiously.

"Hallo, Eden," said a voice behind her, making her jump with fright.

***

Moire and Dand were hidden behind rocks close to shore at Southend. They had been watching Isla all morning as she waited at the Lodge for Jamie and Eden. Moire's other Selkie friends had got bored waiting, they had decided to swim after a tourist boat that passed them earlier on its way to Ailsa Craig. Dand stayed on with Moire, then they spotted Fionnlagh and Ewan near to the beach, so they avoided them by swimming a little further north, taking shelter amongst the sea rocks. Moire wasn't sure how her mother would react if she knew they had followed them to Southend, Moire decided it was probably better not to find out.

When her niece and nephew arrived at the Lodge, she struggled to get a good look at them. She saw Isla start to walk them down to the sandy beach, so she and Dand pulled themselves up onto a rock, watching them from afar. Moire recognised Eden immediately as the girl she had encountered on Sanda Island, feeling the now familiar pull of the connection between them. Moire hadn't mentioned to any of the other Selkies, but somehow, she hadn't been able to completely let go of the connection that she established with her niece. Eden was in her dreams every time she slept, the pair of them swimming together across the ocean floor. Moire wondered if it was due to the fact that Eden was her niece and the potent Selkie magic had somehow recognised they were blood relatives. Whatever it was, the urge to meet Eden in the flesh was overwhelming, Moire was just biding her time until she got her chance.

When Isla returned to the ocean, Moire hoped they would leave and return to Seal Island, but the older Selkies followed the girls along the beach. Then the girls suddenly changed direction, heading back up towards the caves and the road. Moire watched as her mother, Fionnlagh and Ewan headed back out to open water.

"Look," said Dand. "They're going to Dunaverty Rock. Come on, we can beat them there."

The young Selkies dived from their rocks, back into the water, then headed around the bay towards Bloody Rock. They were there way ahead of the girls, so they just waited in the water below the cliff. Eventually, they caught a glimpse of them on top of the rock.

"Look, Dand! A spirit mist!" cried Moire. "You don't think it's the Preacher, do you?" as she watched a mist swirl to form an entity behind the girls.

"No, I think it's Colla. Look," said Dand as the mist took shape and Colkitto appeared on the rock.

"I wish we could hear what they're saying," said Moire.

"He's probably warning them about the Preacher. They are his kinfolk as much as they're yours," Dand pointed out. "That blonde lady doesn't look too well."

"The magic is too strong for her, he needs to leave them before he really hurts her. Does he not see what he's doing? She doesn't have Selkie blood, he's too powerful to be around her," said Moire.

Moire watched as Kate was clearly struggling to stand. Eden was holding her upright, trying to keep her warm. Thankfully, Colkitto dissipated into the air, Moire breathed a sigh of relief. She watched Eden help her friend down the rock, then lost sight of them.

Uarraig and the others swam over to join them. "Did you see them?" he asked.

"Yes, they've just left, Colkitto was here also," replied Dand.

"What now?" said Maili. "We can't hang around here all day. We need to return to the meet."

"You go ahead. I'm going to stay here a while longer," said Moire. She had no desire to return to the meet just now. She still had this connection with Eden and could feel it leading her.

"I don't like leaving you alone," said Uarraig. "It's safer when we are in a pod. You know that, Moire."

"I'll stay with her," offered Dand.

"Really? You don't have to. I know how to take care of myself now," Moire argued feebly. In truth, she was glad of his offer.

"No argument. Anyway, your niece is someone I wouldn't mind taking another look at," Dand laughed.

"You keep your hands off her!" Moire warned, Dand just laughed even more.

"All right, we are going to head back to the meet. We shall just pretend we don't know where you are if anyone asks, but don't be too long, because they won't believe us," said Uarraig.

Moire watched them go. She already knew where she was heading, her connection told her that Eden was heading back up the peninsula.

"Follow me," said Moire, then headed out to open water up the Firth of Clyde. The water was calm here, the Selkies remained deep under the water as they travelled. Dand didn't question where they were going, Moire was grateful for that. It would have been difficult trying to explain that she was following a feeling.

By the time they arrived at the small fishing town Carradale, it was dark. The sky was clear, there a frost was beginning to form over the land. They swam a little further north until they got to a small beach partially lit by the lights of a house set back from the shore.

"What are we doing here?" asked Dand.

"I think Eden is here. I can't really explain why, but I can sense her presence," replied Moire.

"Let's go then," said, Dand swimming towards the shore.

"Go where?" demanded, Moire wondering what he was doing. She watched as he hit the shallow water, then transformed into his land-dweller body. She felt a surge of excitement as she followed him onto shore, changing into a lovely young woman as she did so.

They both walked up onto the beach, remaining in the dark, avoiding the parts that were lit up by the house. They had no land-dweller clothes with them, so were only covered lightly by a sheer cloth left by their seal skins that allowed them to hide their modesty. Selkies rarely felt the cold.

It wasn't long before the door to the house opened as the figure of a young woman appeared. She had a dog with her, so the Selkies stood silently in the darkness, trying to remain undiscovered by the dog's powerful senses. Moire watched with fascination as Eden strolled down to the water's edge, the young woman was staring at the water and Moire felt her longing. Moire stepped forward, but Dand grabbed her arm with a worried expression on his face. She put her finger to her lips to silence him, then nodded towards Eden. He let her go reluctantly, remaining hidden in the darkness as Moire stepped into the light behind Eden.

"Hallo," she said and saw Eden jump with fright. "I'm sorry, I didn't mean to startle you."

Eden looked at Moire with astonishment at first, but then recognition suddenly appeared on her face. "I know you," she said. "You are in my dreams."

"As you are in mine," replied Moire. "I am your father's sister, Moire, so I suppose that makes me your aunt."

"Have I ever met you before? I mean, somewhere not in my dreams," asked Eden, having an enormous déjà vu moment. This dark-haired young woman in front of her was like looking at a mirror image of herself, except this woman's hair was long and her body had a strange sheen to it.

"I suppose we have, sort of. I sang to you when you were on Sanda Island, somehow that seems to have left some sort of connection between us. I believe it is because we are of the same blood. I have been longing to meet you since that day, I think it was our connection that drew me here," explained Moire.

"That was you on Sanda? You could have killed me, pulling me so close to the sea," said Eden.

"It would be unlikely that the sea would kill you, Eden. You have Selkie blood, which means, like your father, you may live in the water if you wish," said Moire.

"Is my father here?" Eden asked, looking out over the water.

"No, I'm sorry, he is not. He doesn't know I'm here. We followed Ewan and my mother to Southend so we could watch you from the water. My mother would be furious if she knew, but I just wanted to meet you," said Moire, feeling a little nervous. "I hope I've done the right thing."

"Of course, I'm sorry if I seem off. I was just taken by surprise. I have been feeling a strange pull to the ocean, I'm relieved to have someone explain it to me now. Honestly, I was getting really confused," said Eden, beginning to ramble on. "Wait a minute, you said 'We', is there someone with you?"

"That would be me," said Dand, stepping out of the darkness. Gizmo rushed at him, barking, and Dand took a step back.

"Gizzy, come here!" Eden shouted. The man walked towards them with a huge grin on his face. He was tall and muscular, with dark shoulder-length hair and had the same silvery sheen to his skin as Moire had.

"I like dogs," he said with his voice full of humour. "They don't seem to like me very much though. It must be the flippers."

Moire laughed. "This is Dand, one of my best friends."

"So, you risked getting in trouble too," said Eden, feeling herself tingle slightly as she looked at him.

"Well, from what I saw, you were worth the risk. Tell me, does it hurt when you put these metal rings through your skin," Dand asked, bending down to look at her closely and pointing at her lip ring.

"Erm, a bit," replied Eden, wishing for the first time in her life she didn't have it in.

"Sorry about Dand, he has no filter," said Moire, glaring at him.

"But I love it, I've never had a chance to see them up close before. You look exactly like Moire, except for the hair, and these drawings on your skin, do they come off?" Dand continued, seemingly unaware of how forward he was being. Moire reached over and punched him hard on the arm.

"Leave her alone, Dand, you're being rude," she said.

"No, it's okay," said Eden, laughing. "It must seem quite strange to you. In all honesty, it's strange to some of the other humans also. I guess I just like to be different."

"Then we have a lot in common," said Dand. "We like to be different also, don't we, Moire?"

The three of them spent the next couple of hours sitting on the beach, talking. They shared their life stories, Eden described her father's life as a land-dweller, Moire and Dand both listened with fascination. They asked question after question of things that had not even occurred to Eden. After a while, she was beginning to feel like she had been bombarded with enough questions, so she turned the tables and asked her new Selkie friends to describe their lives.

Life in the ocean seemed adventurous and much less complicated than a human life. Moire described their travels through the Northern Hemisphere, how many Selkie pods existed and how the Selkie magic worked when they transformed. Dand went on to describe swimming with ancient giant whales, escaping sharks and fishermen, not to mention the dreaded orcas.

They described their home at Eileen Nan Ron with its giant hidden lake. They told Eden of their schooling, how they learnt of all the creatures in and out of the ocean. They spoke of their gods and the power bestowed on them that gave the Selkies huge advantages beneath the waves. Eden listened, feeling envious of their magical lives. They only cemented her desire to go to the ocean, and she promised herself that when the Preacher was dealt with, she would go with them. Eden suddenly realised she was beginning to feel really cold, even Gizmo was shivering, despite being curled up on her lap.

"We Selkies don't feel the cold," said Dand. "You look frozen, I think we should perhaps call it a night."

They reluctantly said goodbye to one another. Moire stepped forward to embrace Eden, and as she did, Eden could not help but notice the strange, cold smoothness of her skin. Moire made her promise to meet them again, Eden said she would. As she watched, the two beautiful Selkies walked silently into the moonlit sea, sinking beneath the water. She heard a splash, then saw the flick of a tail.

She and Gizmo let themselves back in the house. They were freezing, much colder than she was prepared to admit. She would have to wrap up really warmly next time. Next time? Eden wondered if she should tell Jamie about her meeting. She decided not to. There was something pleasurable about having this as her own secret. After all, she hadn't broken her promise, she hadn't gone into the sea. It was all about spending time with her aunt and with Dand. Dand was funny but very forward and he had made her squirm at first, but she had begun to love the attention he gave her. Anyway, she wasn't doing any harm, Jamie had Kate to keep him occupied. Why shouldn't she explore this new side to her? She would not go into the water yet, not until she was sure the Preacher was gone. But the day was sure to come.

Chapter Twenty-Two

In the shadows of the Great Cave at Southend, the Preacher stood in his physical form. His sunken eyes peered out from straggly black hair that hung in dark curtains around his ancient face. His yellowed teeth snarled inside his withered lips as his essence filled the cavern with an all-consuming rage, burning as strong as it had the day he was dragged to his death here by that accursed MacDonald all these centuries ago. His desire for revenge had festered throughout the ages and now, once again, the kin of his enemy had returned.

He had almost destroyed the MacDonald female, but that damn Colla Ciotach had prevented him, a mistake that would not happen again. It would only be a matter of time before his full strength would return, the longer the MacDonalds remained, the more powerful his curse on them became. Soon, Colkitto would not be able to stop him.

The ghosts of the Preacher's victims were trapped on Kintyre, but they stayed clear of him, watching him from a distance, with the desire to avenge their deaths burned into their souls. The ghosts longed to move on to the afterlife but could not leave. They had longed for the Preacher's death to finally release them, but the Preacher had cursed them all, trapping them here for eternity. The only way for the ghosts to be released was to destroy him, sending his dark soul back to hell.

The Preacher sneered at their ghostly forms, God had abandoned them, the same God he had served throughout his life without question. In turn, God had turned his back on him, leaving him to burn in agony. No, the Preacher would not forgive God, any more than the filthy MacDonalds who had dragged him here. The Dark Lord had come for him, taken away his pain, then given him the power to avenge his death. Though even in death, he could still sense the presence of his old adversary, Colla Ciotach. The old goat was still haunting his every step.

John Neave was the third son of a strict Presbyterian reverend running a small parish named Ballantrae in Ayrshire. His two older brothers had been healthy strapping lads, the youngest of them was eight years his senior. John was a sickly, needy baby who became spoilt and protected by his mother, who, by all accounts, was a spiteful, vicious woman. Her wagging tongue had caused a lot of trouble in the parish over the years, she was only tolerated because being the reverend's wife brought her a certain status in the community. It was a status she ill deserved, but no one dared to speak out against her. John's father was a hard, unforgiving man. He had little compassion for his fellow man but his position in the community demanded respect, although the lines between respect and fear were somewhat blurred.

John's brothers were close in age and held a strong bond together, both of them suffering brutal punishments dealt out by their father. On one occasion, John watched on as his older brother was beaten to an inch of his life. His father had been told that the teenage boy was seen flirting with a young Catholic farm girl. The beating John's brother suffered rendered him with broken ribs, as well as a broken leg. His father refused his son any treatment from the local goodwife, leaving the bones to fester and not heal properly. A year later, the once strapping young man was a shell of himself, his strength dwindled daily. John brought him some food one morning to find him dead in his bunk.

John's parents did not shed a tear for his brother. After the funeral, his remaining brother upped and left without a word, never to return. There was a lot of whispering in the parish, but again, no one dared to speak out against the minister.

John grew into a tall, thin man who was not blessed with a muscular frame. He was extremely pale and his hair was almost black, hanging in curtains around his pinched face. He had intense grey eyes and a nose that appeared too big for his face. In short, he was not a handsome man.

His mother pressed him into following his father's footsteps in the church. He spent many long nights studying the Old Testament with his father in a dark, humourless fashion. As his father's health started to fail, John took over the weekly sermons on the Sabbath, revelling in the power being up on the parapet gave him. Soon, that taste of power in this tiny parish was not enough for John.

John wrote to Reverend Alexander Henderson, a well-respected Presbyterian reverend and scholar in Edinburgh. John managed to secure a position training under the reverend in Edinburgh, so against his mother's protests and his father indifference, he left for the city.

Edinburgh was crowded and dirty, but his work with Reverend Henderson was all he could have hoped for. Though his master's forgiving nature and compassion for the poor was a strange concept to him. His father had always taught him to believe that the poor were lazy Christians who deserved their lot in life. The good Reverend Henderson was well respected, with many friends. It was through him that John first met the son of the Duke of Argyll, Archibald Campbell, who had the title of Lord Lorne.

John listened to Lord Lorne's stories of the rogue Catholic Highlanders that constantly plagued the west coast of Argyll and the Hebrides. The clansmen seemed to have no respect for the law, starting fights whilst stealing one another's belongings. He admired the young Lord Lorne's no-tolerance approach to them, understanding Archibald's frustrations at how lenient his father, the duke, seemed to be with these lawless Highlanders.

Archibald Campbell was himself a tall, thin man with dark hair, and heavily hooded eyelids. His given title, 'Lord Lorne', was usually awarded to the first-born son of the duke, giving him lordship over the coastal and islands areas between Loch Leven in the north and Lochs Awe, Avich and Melfort in the south. He seemed to be constantly at odds with his father about the antics of the clansmen tenants. In due course, that would earn him the name of 'Gillespie Grumach' or 'Archibald the Grimm'.

A few years went by as John continued his studies in Edinburgh. He found himself in conflict between the forgiving nature of his master and the words of the Old Testament that had been drummed into him all his life. He had few friends, but as he never had any before, it was not something he missed. Then something happened that would change his position and thrust him into an important role.

It was the reign of Charles 1st, who was, by all accounts, a conceited king, convinced of his own divine right above God. He angered many people, not least of all when in 1637, he introduced his own 'Book of Common Prayer' without involving the general assembly.

This angered the Scottish Presbyterian church, who viewed this as a direct threat to the freedom of the church. In response, the church looked to their covenant, initially written in 1581, and they decided to rewrite it. Reverend Alexander Henderson was asked to become one of the authors of the new covenant with a hope that his wisdom and moderation would counterbalance the fanaticism of many of the Presbyterians at that time. John Neave got to play a huge role in the coordination of the signing of the new covenant. On the 28th of February, 1638, the covenant was made available to sign in Scotland, some 60,000 people from all over the country travelled to Edinburgh to sign it. John worked late into the evening that day, collecting the signatures.

Amongst the people who travelled to the city was the young Marquis of Montrose, James Graham, who had arrived from Aberdeen to sign the covenant, along with three other nobles of the day. John disliked the marquis as soon as he set eyes on him. He was a handsome, flamboyant character that was too loud and wore too much colour for the reverend's liking. However, John's master was clearly delighted to have him there, inviting the marquis to sup with them after the signing. John made himself scarce.

Soon after the initial signing of the covenant in Edinburgh, John was commissioned by the church to take the covenant around the west coast of Scotland, retrieving as many signatures as possible. John left Edinburgh, never to return, although, at the time, he did not know this would be the case. The Covenanter movement was well under way, with as many as 300,000 signatures collected that year.

John Neave was in his element. He travelled for three months and was welcomed almost everywhere he went, but none more so as when he arrived at Inveraray. He received a warm welcome from Lord Lorne, then after a few short weeks using Inveraray as his base, John was asked if he would remain as head of the local clergy. He accepted without hesitation, writing to his old master, sending the letter back along with all the signatures he had collected for the covenant.

It became clear that John had learnt nothing about compassion during his time in Edinburgh and was soon to be feared by many. The power he wielded went to his head, with him dishing out punishments as often as one would dish out porridge. Those who complained to Lord Lorne were sent directly to Reverend Neave himself, who would punish them as he saw fit. He had carried the covenant, there were none who would oppose him or his methods. No one, that was except for Colkitto and his heathen band of pirates and savages.

Colla Ciotach had always been a constant thorn in his side. He had first met that forsaken clansman on the day Colkitto had tried to humiliate him in the town square of Inveraray, when he was rightfully dishing out punishment to some harlot. The old duke seemed to hold some sort of respect for Colla Ciotach, something John, nor Lord Lorne, could understand, but the duke would allow no interference with Colkitto's tenancy on Colonsay. John would have to bide his time until the old duke died.

When that day finally came, Lord Lorne became the 8th Duke of Argyll, and John soon persuaded him, as one of his first duties, to send the reverend to Colonsay. He planned to gather evidence on the heathen behaviour of Colkitto and his kin. John should have guessed that someone would betray him and give Colkitto forewarning of his arrival. John despaired of the misguided loyalty the Highlanders had for Colla Ciotach and found himself captured as soon as he landed on the island.

He had not forgotten what he had to endure that night, nor would he forgive them. That filthy clan may have allowed him to leave unharmed the following morning, but not before they had almost taken his eye out with a rock thrown from the shore. The Preacher paced the Great Cave as the memories of that day festered, his rage was bordering on insanity as he howled into the darkness. This clansman would not stop him having his revenge, he would make Colkitto suffer.

It had delighted John Neave when Colkitto and his men were eventually banished from Colonsay and Colkitto himself imprisoned at Dunstaffnage. Unfortunately, John still was kept from him as he was required to join the Duke of Argyll and David Leslie's Covenanter army as they battled the might of Montrose. Another faithless royalist who had dishonoured himself by siding with the king, even though John had witnessed Montrose signing the covenant in Edinburgh two years before. John applauded himself for being a good judge of character, and although the Covenanter army suffered many defeats from Montrose and his wild Irish army led by Colkitto's son, when they were victorious, John made sure there would be no quarter for the soldiers or their families.

The Preacher watched on with a sneer of satisfaction as the Covenanter army slaughtered women and children, many women heavy with child. He told the soldiers to rip the bairns from their mothers' bellies to make sure none of the heathen offspring would live. Even the duke, who had a bloody name himself, recoiled from the barbarism in front of him and wondered at the character of his preacher who seemed to revel in the bloodshed.

Of course, with John Neave away with the army, Colkitto was spared his wrath for the time being. He lived a far too easy existence under the watchful eye of Lord Dunstaffnage. If the Preacher had only known the extent of the friendship between Colkitto and his captor, he would have sent men to make sure Colkitto's life was not so comfortable. Fortunately for Colkitto, John was too busy with the Covenanter army to take time out to seek revenge on his old adversary.

When Reverend John Neave returned to Argyll, he made it his priority to visit Colkitto at Dunstaffnage Castle to see how he was faring. John was appalled at how healthy and sunburnt the old goat was. He ordered him locked away, jouged to the wall, but had to tread lightly with his torture methods. There was still too much respect for Colkitto and John knew people were watching him closely. Still, he had sworn to have his vengeance, watched or not, it did not stop him branding him with the upside-down cross of a traitor. Lord Dunstaffnage was furious and complained bitterly of his prisoner's treatment, but John acted for the now Marquis of Argyll, and he had the last word.

Even after the branding, Colkitto still had the same fearless, mocking look in his pale blue eyes, and John wanted to tear them from their sockets. But even John knew he was treading on thin ice, there were a lot of angry rumblings around Dunstaffnage, and John decided to leave promptly for the safety of Argyll.

John left with the Campbell army, a mistake he decided as Colkitto escaped him again. Lord Dunstaffnage arranged for the old Highlander's release after they heard of the defeat suffered by Montrose. He was gone before John could return to Inveraray. Colkitto joined his son and the remaining royalist army and fled down Kintyre peninsula. The Covenanter army were charged up after their victory at Philiphaugh near Selkirk, and they set off in pursuit after the king's men, arriving finally at Dunaverty Castle. John was livid when he discovered that Colkitto and his son had escaped them only hours before. He spat poisoned text from the Old Testament at the marquis and Leslie, then preached to the army, making them feel cheated of a victory. The Preacher knew the marquis and David Leslie had little stomach left for massacres after the fields of Philiphaugh, but he pressed them on, driving the army into a frenzy of righteousness.

The Campbells had cut off water supplies to the castle; eventually, thirst had driven them out. The MacDonald army had asked for quarter, but John made sure none was given. He then watched on with satisfaction as the MacDonalds were slain, feeling aroused by the screams and cries of dying around him. The ones who had begged for water, John had his men tie them together, then throw them, screaming, onto the cliffs and sea below. The land was soaked in blood and it was then that David Leslie turned and asked him, "Now, Mr John, have you not, for once, got your fill of blood?"

John knew the marquis was sickened by all the slaughter, but still undeterred, he followed David Leslie to Dunyvaig Castle on Islay and finally witnessed the capture of Colla Ciotach. John tried to have him executed there on the island, but David Leslie was growing tired of his preaching and was having none of it. There had been enough blood spilt and fearing more blemishes on his record, he insisted that Colkitto be sent to Edinburgh to have a fair trial.

Disappointed, John returned to Inveraray, but he noticed that the marquis stayed away from him. Something had happened to tarnish their relationship and he was refused entry to the castle on more than one occasion. People began to notice, rumours started to spread and for the first time in his life, Reverend John Neave felt he was losing control.

Colkitto was returned to Dunstaffnage, but this time, John was not given permission to visit him. He felt cheated and angry, and even though the death sentence was pronounced, it had been none of his doing. John had been robbed of his own personal revenge, yet somehow, Colla Ciotach had managed to keep his dignity and his Highlander hero status.

A few weeks after Colkitto's death, John was in the church when the marquis came to see him. He was taken by surprise and attempted to make the marquis welcome but was soon to discover that his visit was not a friendly nature. The marquis had requested the general assembly send another clergyman to take over John's post in Inveraray. He accused John of relishing in the death and torment of his fellow man, that it had become apparent that his actions were not always fairly executed. There had been a number of complaints in the district of his unreasonable punishments and it was time for a new clergy to take over while the Marquis rebuilt relations with his people.

John's anger simmered under the surface as he listened to the marquis' betrayal. Suddenly, all the power he had held was being taken from him, he was being cast aside after all his work for the Campbells and the Covenanter army. He was, by all accounts, a wealthy man by now, but money had never really impacted on him, it was the power he relished.

John returned to Ballantrae and to the parish church he had grown up in. There was a new chaplain at the church, his parents had long since died. He had no intention of becoming the Reverend of Ballantrae, he was way beyond a small-town clergy.

He decided to retire and write his memoirs of the Covenanter war. He got himself a pleasant house by the sea with an elderly housekeeper, who cooked and cleaned for him. John Neave had returned home with no friends or family, yet still, he cared not.

John lived his life alone, no one came near, apart from his housekeeper. He was 66 years old when a boat pulled up on the beach not far from his home. He watched as three young men jumped ashore and headed directly to his home. He knew, deep down, they were up to no good, but in his wildest imagination, he could not have foreseen this as the end of his life. The men broke into his home and roughly bundled him up in a MacDonald plaid, then tied him tightly with rope. He called out to deaf ears, but none heard, he was taken across the water to Kintyre once more. They took him to the caves near Dunaverty, the place seemed deserted, so there was no one there for him to call for help. There were about 12 or so people waiting in the dark cavern for him. Torches were burning and as they threw him to the ground, he could see the Celtic MacDonald eyes staring coldly at him.

Ranald MacDonald, one of the two surviving children of Dunaverty, introduced himself as they hung John from chains in the roof of the cavern. They lit the fire below him.

The ghost of the Preacher stood in the cavern where he had died that day in agony. His charred bones still remained there untouched, his dark curse had closed in the cavern then as it took hold on Kintyre. Now the cavern had been opened again, his remains had been discovered, but it changed nothing. Soon, his victims would feel his wrath and Colkitto could watch again as his kin are slain.

The Preacher found he could now set foot in the Lodge, the sisters had prevented him from going there before using some sort of Selkie magic. Now all John had to do was wait until the MacDonalds were alone. He wanted their deaths to be slow and agonising, but it was their fear he cherished most. It wouldn't be long now, he could sense the arrival of the man and his sister at the Lodge. They had come alone.

Chapter Twenty-Three

Eden and Jamie drove up the long stony drive to the carpark of Seal Lodge. It was a grey, misty Sunday morning and there was no sign of any of the builders, which relieved Jamie. Stuart's team seemed to have working hours of their own, and although Jamie was pleased they were keen to get the work finished, it was good to have the place to themselves. Kate was still recovering from her meeting with Colkitto, and Jamie had insisted that she stayed at home. He knew she wasn't happy but had given up the argument easily, which confirmed to Jamie that she really didn't feel too good.

The lobby of the Lodge had been completely cleared now, so Jamie could get some idea of the layout of the ground floor. Eden was equipped with pen and paper to scribble down her ideas for the interior décor. Jamie began to feel the same excitement he usually did when he saw a project coming together. The builders had secured the staircases now, so they were able to get up to the fifth floor. Jamie had decided on creating only four luxury bedroom suites on the top floor, all of them with outstanding views over the sea and the Mull. The view at the back of the hotel was not particularly good, so they would keep the staff rooms at the back.

He went up to the top floor to inspect the progress of dismantling the walls between rooms. There was a rubble chute set up next to one of the empty window frames, although the builders had already cleared a lot out of the debris from this floor. Jamie was impressed at their level of workmanship, also amazed at how far along they had already come. He heard Eden calling him from somewhere below, so he walked back to the staircase.

"What was that?" he called down to her.

"I'm on the third floor! How many rooms are there going to be here? I think I should start sourcing fabric outlets for curtain material," Eden shouted back up.

"Wait a minute, I can't remember straight off, I'll come down," Jamie replied, his eyes suddenly drawn to a figure standing out on the road. He walked to the window and saw the same tall, thin man with the large rimmed black hat that he had seen on his first visit. The man was staring up at the Lodge, though Jamie couldn't make out his face. There was something very unpleasant about him.

Jamie turned and went back down to join Eden on the third floor. "You look like you've seen a ghost," she said when she saw him. "Oh no, you haven't, had you?"

"I'm not sure," said Jamie. "Come to the window, do you see a man in a black hat?"

Eden walked over to join him but there was no one out on the road at all. They scanned the surrounding area but there was no one about. Jamie was suddenly aware that the room began to feel really cold and he spun around, then jumped backwards in fright. Eden screamed as materialising in front of them was the man in the black hat.

"The Preacher!" whispered Eden.

The Preacher just stood staring at them. His apparition kept rippling, and it was hard to get a proper visual look at him. His grotesquely rotten teeth were bared in his sunken jaw as he stood snarling at them like a rabid dog. Jamie could hear Eden's breathing getting more erratic and laboured, and he pulled her over to him, placing her behind him, away from the Preacher. He was not sure what to do next, the room was getting ice cold and the Preacher's eyes gleamed with satisfaction.

"What do you want?" demanded Jamie.

The Preacher raised one arm slowly and pointed straight at them.

"Get out of my hotel!" Jamie yelled at him, then heard Eden fall to the floor behind him. He turned and saw his sister gasping for air. She seemed to be choking.

"Leave her alone!" he shouted, but the Preacher stood motionless, still pointing at them.

Just then, a stiff breeze brushed past where Eden was lying and a blue mist engulfed the Preacher, making him drop his arm. The Preacher's face distorted as he opened his mouth in what looked like a scream, but there was no sound, then a second later, he and the mist had vanished.

Eden was semi-conscious, but her breathing was coming back to normal, Jamie tried to revive her gently, but she did not seem to be responding. He took off his jacket and wrapped her in it, then carefully picked her up and started to carry her down the stairs. They just reached the bottom when a young man and woman came running into the Lodge.

"Is she all right?" asked the young woman. "We came as soon as we heard what was happening. I hoped we would not be too late."

Jamie stared at them. "Too late for what?" he asked, somewhat bewildered.

"Here, put her down here," said the young woman. "I can help her. I'm Moire, your father's sister, and this is Dand," she said, nodding towards the dark-haired young man standing quietly in the doorway.

Eden was getting heavy as it was, so Jamie put her down gently, with her head propped up against the wall. He reluctantly allowed Moire to kneel beside Eden, then watched as she cupped his sister's face in her hands. Moire started to mutter some words that were beyond Jamie's understanding and a few seconds later, Eden's eyes blinked open, both wide and alert.

"Moire, you're here! What happened?" Eden asked, looking around nervously.

"So, you two have met?" asked Jamie. "Funny, I don't remember you telling me that."

"It was only last night, Jamie, I promised them I would keep it secret for now," groaned Eden as she got to her feet. "Has the Preacher gone? What happened? I couldn't get my breath and the next minute, I woke up here."

"I think he was choking you somehow, but then a strange mist came and seemed to attack him. The next thing, he had vanished, along with the mist," Jamie explained.

"That was Colkitto, he sensed the Preacher and he came to warn us before he went to find you. We knew he would have stopped him, but we don't know for how long. This spirit is very dangerous and very powerful. You have to leave this place," said Dand.

"I think we have established that for ourselves. This whole thing is getting ridiculous and now I have a seal boy telling me what I should do!" said Jamie, his anger getting the better of him.

"Jamie, we're not going anywhere," said Eden, looking apologetically over at Dand, who remained silent. "We are going to get rid of him somehow and the other ghosts around here."

Dand shook his head with frustration, but Moire simply nodded, "If anyone can do it, I'm sure you can."

"I need to rethink this. It's too much. I'm going for some air," said Jamie. He needed some space, he just wanted to punch something or someone, and figured it would probably be best if he left.

"Well, I'm staying to do what I came to do," said Eden stubbornly. "He is not going to win, Jamie, and I have all these rooms to go over. I'm not going to let him stop me from planning."

"We'll stay with you for now," said Dand. "Just in case."

Jamie sighed, feeling defeated. "You knock yourself out. I'm going to get some air."

"I don't think you…" Moire started to protest. Eden grabbed her arm to stop her. She could tell Jamie had had enough of it all just now. It was probably best if he took himself off, if anywhere could calm him down, it was the Mull of Kintyre.

***

Colla Ciotach and the Preacher both materialised in the Great Cave. "Colkitto!" roared the Preacher, his face contorted in fury.

"I told ye, Reverend Neave, yer nae gonnae dae harm tae my kin. If I have tae chase ye tae hell and back, then I will," Said Colkitto, raising his claymore and pointing it at the Preacher. He flew at him, swinging his sword, but it fell through empty air as his quarry vanished.

Too late, Colkitto sensed the Preacher behind him and then found himself trapped in a dark spell. He struggled against the magic but it held him tight. He would have to wait, it would wear off, the Preacher could do little harm to him now.

"And I told ye that I would murder every one of yer kinfolk who dare tae set foot here," the Preacher hissed at him.

"Yer spell is nae gonnae hold me fir long, Preacher, ye ken that. I will finish ye," Colkitto snarled.

"I dinnae think so, by the time yer free, yer kin will be haunting these cliffs with the rest of yer clan," sneered the Preacher.

***

Jamie drove to the light house carpark at the end of the Mull of Kintyre. He parked up, then climbed up a small grassy hill to some large, flat rocks that looked out over the cliffs towards Ireland. The mist was beginning to clear and Jamie could see blue sky in the distance. The wind was so strong, it was hard to stand upright, but it wasn't too cold and it blew away the cobwebs. Jamie took a moment to breathe in the fresh ocean air and clear his mind.

He wasn't sure what to do next. He had been so overwhelmed during these last few months that he really had just gone with the flow, so to speak. Finding out that he had sisters, then inheriting the Lodge had put him on a roller coaster of a ride, but now he really wanted to get off, things were getting too dark. Jamie had never been one to listen to ghost stories, and in his line of work, he came across many. But to actually see a ghost and be threatened by it was a whole different kettle of fish.

And then there was the Selkies. What sane individual would believe they were seal people swimming in the ocean? If he hadn't seen it with his own eyes, he would have thought it hysterical. God, how he wished he just had his old easy life back in Brighton.

No, that wasn't true, there was Kate. He had known the first time he saw her working at that bar in Edinburgh all these years ago that their paths would be crossed. It was unrequited love at first sight back then, but to see her again and for her to feel the same way was an answer to all his dreams.

Jamie knew in the short time they had been together that Kate was the love of his life, of this he was sure. He could never walk away from her, and the truth be told, he loved this part of the world. Was Eden right in saying that they should fight to keep it? How could they fight something they couldn't see or touch? Of course Eden was right, this was the most exciting project he had ever undertaken, was he going to let a ghost scare him away?

Jamie jumped down from the rocks and started to hike back up the hill, through the heather that still had a purple hue even at this time of year. He thought about Kate back at her house. She would be going through the notes in the briefcase today with a fine tooth comb, maybe there would be some idea there of what they could do.

If the Riley sisters had managed to keep the Preacher away from the Lodge for all these years, maybe they wrote down somewhere how they did it. They could try to do what the sisters did and keep away as many MacDonald residents as they could without arousing suspicion.

No, that was a ridiculous idea, they would have to get rid of the ghost, period. They couldn't turn people away in this day and age.

Jamie's mind then wandered to Moire and Dand. Moire was his father's sister, so he guessed that made her his aunt. It all felt too weird, he wondered why Eden had not mentioned meeting them before. Why would she hide that from him?

Eden had promised not to go near the water, and he was sure she hadn't. So where had she met them then? He would ask her when he got back, which he should be thinking about doing right now. Jamie checked his watch and saw it was well after lunchtime. He had been gone a good couple of hours, it was time to head back. He looked out across the Atlantic Ocean and had a sudden longing to see Kate and get some clarity on the situation, she always looked at things calmly and thoughtfully.

Jamie turned and jumped off the rock he was standing on. He started to walk down the hillside when he saw something out the corner of his eye. He thought it was a sheep at first, but as he looked around, he couldn't see any near him.

Then there was a movement again and Jamie spotted a huge black dog standing in a deep dell just below him. Jamie looked around for its owner but couldn't see anyone and there were no other cars up here. It was a difficult and hazardous walk up to the Mull, even for the hardiest of climbers. Jamie started making his way down towards the animal.

He tried calling the dog over to him, but it just stood still, watching him. Jamie slid his way down the steep slope into the dell to where the dog was. The dog didn't seem to be paying him any attention whatsoever, it was a big black creature of an undistinguishable breed, with course black hair that hung in untidy, mottled wisps over its body. He couldn't, in all conscience, leave the animal to fend for itself, they were miles away from anywhere and the weather could turn at any moment. He clambered over a rock to get down to where the dog was, but as soon as he landed, he looked up to find the dog had gone. In its place stood the Preacher.

Chapter Twenty-Four

Kate had gone back to bed after Jamie and Eden left in the morning. She protested weakly about going with them, but in all honesty, she was still shaken from her encounter with Colkitto yesterday. It really had knocked her for six, but when she thought about it, the funny thing was, she never felt frightened at any time with his presence. He was, by all accounts, a ghost of some sort, but he had seemed so solid and real. If she had been able to withstand his close presence further, she would have bombarded him with questions. It wasn't often you would get the opportunity to question someone about the past who had actually lived in it.

Kate finally got up around noon and made herself some coffee. After a quick shower, she felt much more like her old self, so she took Gizmo down to the beach to get some air. Kate's writing computer had sat untouched for a few weeks, and she was very aware that she was beginning to let her work slide. She had been so wrapped up with Jamie and the Lodge, that it had taken all her focus, even though she had her own deadlines to meet. It wouldn't be long before her publisher would be on the phone, asking for her next chapters. Kate took her coffee into her office and turned on her laptop and sat looking at the screen. She then switched it off again, who was she kidding? There was no way she could concentrate on anything else just now, not until they got to the bottom of this haunting. It had been like living in a surreal world these last few weeks, what with ghosts, Selkies and Jamie.

Just then, her office phone rang, it was Ronan.

"Hallo, Katie, I hope I havnae interrupted ye, but I remembered where the key tae that old coal cellar wis last night," said the old man.

"What coal cellar?" asked Kate, a bit confused.

"Did I nae tell ye aboot the coal cellar? I must have forgotten; these old brains are useless sometimes. The old coal cellar is up behind the tennis courts. It's underground, which is why we didnae use it, tae much like hard work carrying coal up and doon. But when the Lodge wis a hospital, they used it as a bomb shelter. I wis never supposed tae gae doon there as the hatch wis always locked and the sisters wudnae gie me the key. I never asked why, but I wis curious when Isla and her wee laddie arrived. Isla and the sisters would go doon there quite often and I wondered if they were doing their spells doon there. Ye ken, tae keep the spirits away," Ronan explained.

"So where is the key, Ronan?" Kate asked.

"They used tae keep it under a loose flat slate, behind the third tennis court. Ye ken, the one facing old Keil Hoose. I wis a bit nosy and would watch them from the Lodge. I did go doon there once when the sisters were oot, but I didnae stay fir long. I won't forget what happened, but that's another story fir later. The key should still be there."

"Well, I, for one, am glad you were so nosy, Ronan. Thank you for this. Let's hope I can find it and maybe find some answers to these ghosts down there," said Kate, already grabbing her coat and keys.

"Aye, well, ye be careful. Dinnae be going doon there on yer own," said Ronan.

Kate put Gizmo in the car and set off to the Lodge. She didn't bother to phone Jamie as she knew he would talk her out of coming, then insist on exploring the coal cellar himself. Forty minutes later, Kate was driving up towards the Lodge, but she couldn't see any sign of Jamie's car and wondered if they had perhaps gone for lunch. She parked up, letting Gizmo out the back, watching as he ran off towards the beach to let the gulls know he had arrived. Kate let herself into the Lodge. "Hallo, is anyone here?" she called out. There was no answer. Kate figured they must have gone for a late lunch and was about to head out to the tennis courts when she heard something. It was very faint but seemed to be coming from the bar area.

"Hallo?" Kate shouted again.

"Help us," came a faint male voice she didn't recognise.

Kate rushed into the bar and immediately saw on the floor by the windows a strange young man and woman lying there. The woman was unconscious but the man was moving slightly. "Help us," he said again.

"Oh, my God, what happened?" Kate said, kneeling next to him. The man turned towards her and she gasped as she recognised his Selkie features. He whispered weakly, "It's a spell, he's taken Eden."

"Who's taken Eden?" cried Kate, then kicked herself for being so stupid. "You mean the Preacher has her again? Where is Jamie? Who are you?"

"Jamie's gone… in danger… The Preacher… he took us by surprise."

"Look, I'll phone an ambulance, just stay there," said Kate.

"NO, no ambulance, We're Selkies!" said the man who was now trying to sit up. The girl lying next to him was starting to stir also. "It's a holding spell, it's beginning to wear off."

"What happened?" asked Kate.

Dand shook his head to try to clear it. "Jamie and Eden encountered the Preacher this morning but Colkitto chased him off after warning us. We arrived just after, but Jamie was really furious about the whole encounter, and I don't think we helped appearing out of the blue. He took himself off towards the Mull in his car, said he needed some air, but I could tell he was angry. We stayed with Eden to protect her, but the Preacher was too strong. He caught us off guard and froze us with a holding spell before we had time to protect ourselves. That's the last thing I remember, he must have taken Eden."

"We have to go after her," said Moire, who had also sat up, rubbing her head.

"We can check the caves again," said Kate.

"I think you should go tell your mother," said Dand to Moire.

"Your mother?" asked Kate.

"My mother is Isla, you met her the other day. I'm Moire, and this is my friend Dand. We were watching the Lodge to try to stop this from happening. My mother will want to know, if she doesn't know already," said Moire.

"Okay, you two get yourself together, I'm going to the caves just to check them out. I'll phone Jamie; hopefully, there is some signal at the Mull," said Kate, getting to her feet.

Gizmo came running over as Kate stepped out of the Lodge. Jamie's phone went straight to voicemail, so she gave up after a couple of tries. She jogged down the hill towards the caves and then climbed up the slope leading to the entrance of the Great Cave. Gizmo ran in before her but Kate knew somehow that Eden wasn't here. Climbing through the new entrance to the caverns at the back, Kate suddenly felt a familiar chill.

"Stop where ye are, lassie, I dinnae want tae harm ye again," came the deep, rich voice of Colla Ciotach.

Kate recognised the voice and stopped moving, trying to get her eyes adjusted to the dark. She could hear Gizmo growling but all she could make out was dark shadows. "Colla, is Eden with you?" she asked.

"Nae, lassie, that God forsaken Preacher has her. He's trapped me in here, fool that I am, I cannae help her the noo," growled the old ghost. "Find Isla, she'll be able tae free me, then I'll be able tae find them."

Kate started to back off towards the entrance. The cold was beginning to affect her again and she couldn't risk it if she was to find Eden and Jamie. "I'll get Isla," she promised as she headed back out.

Dand was walking up towards her. "Moire has gone for Isla. Any luck in the caves?"

"Colkitto is trapped there by a spell, he said that Isla could free him and he would find Eden," explained Kate.

"We may not have time to wait," said Dand anxiously. "I'm so sorry I let him take her. I promised I would watch her."

"Have you met Eden before?" asked Kate, suddenly suspicious that there was more to his emotions than he had first let on.

"Aye, we met last night. She has been hearing the ocean calling to her, I was going to help her find her fins so to speak," Dand told her.

"I see, well, we need to find her first, and there is a mist coming in," said Kate, looking out over the water. Great clouds of thick white mist were travelling inland and it wouldn't be long before they were engulfed. Kate suddenly remembered the key and the coal cellar. "I have something else to check out that may or may not help. Do you want to come?"

"Let's go, anything is better than nothing," said Dand.

They raced back up to the Lodge and out towards the tennis courts. "He said it was the third tennis court by Keil House. Look for a flat slate stone, there should be a key under it," Kate shouted as she ran around the courts.

The trouble was there was a lot of old slate lying around, they were virtually on their hands and knees, lifting stone after stone, looking for the key. The mist was almost on them and Gizmo started to bark as he watched it roll in.

"I've found it!" cried Dand.

"Great, now we have to find the cellar entrance. It should be around here somewhere," said Kate, looking frantically as the mist began to swirl around her ankles. In a matter of minutes, it became impossible to see, the mist had engulfed her. "Dand, I can't see you anymore, we are not going to be able to find anything in this."

"I'm over here, follow my voice carefully, try not to fall," said Dand from the left of her. She started to walk carefully over the slate stones and clumps of grass. The mist was white like steam, and she could feel something threatening and aggrieved oozing from it, watching her as she moved.

"Over here," said Dand. "Keep coming, then I can lead us back to the Lodge."

Kate took another few steps, then heard a hollow clunk beneath her feet. She stopped dead and tapped the ground with her foot. Sure enough, she was standing on something wooden, could it be the cellar door? She dropped down and started feeling around blindly with her hands. Gizmo, who had stayed at her ankles, started to lick her face. She felt a latch and a handle and then she could feel a padlock. "Dand, I've found the cellar door," she cried.

"Stay there, I'll find you," Dand shouted back.

Within a couple of minutes, Dand dropped down next to her, as he did so, the mist seemed to part to allow him space, and Kate could see him again. He had the key in his hand and, soon, managed to unlock the padlock.

They tried to heave the old doors open but it was overgrown, so they had to tear away huge clumps of grass before they could get it to budge. Eventually, it started to shift, Dand gave it one huge tug and the door finally swung open. The mist immediately cleared from the entrance as if afraid to go near it. Kate shone her small torch down on the stone steps that led down to the cellar.

"After you," she said, trying to lighten the mood.

Dand started to walk down the steps. "Hey, you'll need my torch," Kate called after him.

"No, we Selkies can see pretty well in the dark. You keep your torch," he called back.

Kate followed him down the steps. She counted each step for no reason other than to keep the fear at bay. There were 20 steps down to the ground where Dand stood there waiting for her. They looked around, surprised by what they found.

If this was supposed to be a coal cellar, there was no coal. Instead, it was a large natural tunnel that led downwards. There were a couple of chairs just standing there by the steps, but nothing else.

"Shall we?" said Dand, pointing towards the tunnel. Kate nodded and the pair of them started walking down the passage. The ground was smooth and the tunnel was fairly wide, it was certainly high enough for Dand to stand upright.

They walked on with Gizmo, who was walking nervously behind them, he didn't like it down there and had become very quiet, with his tail between his legs. The tunnel started to level out as they went on, then turned a tight bend and the ground became sandy under their feet.

"We must be getting near the sea," whispered Kate, unsure why she was whispering.

As if she had willed it, they began to hear the sounds of waves coming from up ahead somewhere. The tunnel continued around another bend, leading them unexpectedly into a large roomy cavern. The room was lit slightly from another tunnel leading in the opposite direction that Kate was sure led out to the beach. Looking around, they could see lots of book cases filled with old ancient-looking books. In the centre of the room stood a huge wooden table surrounded with wooden chairs, there were two old sofas against one wall and there was a storage unit filled with blankets and old gas masks.

"This must have been the bomb shelter," said Kate. "They would have been safe in here."

Dand was leafing through some of the books lying on the table. "I can't read your writing, but I recognise some of these symbols. They are Selkie markings for protection."

Kate went over to look and saw they were handwritten journals. "I think I should read these," she said. "They may help, and we can't go anywhere with this mist outside."

Kate pulled up one of the old wooden chairs and sat at the table. The journals were written by the sisters, although Isla had added to them. They dated back to when the sisters were first here as nurses during the war. They wrote about the patients and the bombings at first, but then Kate saw an entry mentioning ghosts that Janette had spotted from the windows of the Lodge.

The sisters had done their own thorough investigations, writing about the Dunaverty Massacre and the plague victims. They couldn't understand why the ghosts had been unable to move on. The sisters had attempted to call upon the ghosts in a séance they created down here in the coal cellar, but they suspected that there was some dark entity that had stopped the spirits being able to get through.

Kate then found herself reading about Ross MacDonald and the sisters' first meeting with Isla, the Selkie. They knew of the Selkie Folk from Ireland and had recognised her immediately. What they had not realised until it was too late was that something much worse arrived when Ross MacDonald was admitted to the hospital. Betty had sensed it before Janette, but they both soon realised the young soldier was in danger.

Isla helped them set up wards around the hospital to keep the spirits out of the hospital. Selkie magic was powerful enough for that, but not enough to get rid of the dark entity that had arrived on the Mull. By the time the sisters had discovered the identity of the Preacher, and of his curse on all those who bore the name MacDonald, it was too late. Janette and Betty were both devastated when Ross disappeared, leaving Isla, who was overwhelmed with guilt about not meeting him that day, pregnant with his child.

Kate read on and discovered that on Isla's recommendation, the Selkie council came to the coal cellar to meet with the sisters. They came through the secret tunnel from the rocks on the beach, far enough out to sea for it not to be discovered. The Selkies had created these tunnels hundreds of years before. The council decided to give the sisters enough gold to buy the Lodge three times over, and in return, the sisters swore to protect the family MacDonald from the Preacher's curse.

The journals gave little information about what happened over the next few years. The Preacher was no longer mentioned, not until the arrival of Isla with her son, Ewan. The Selkies had shrouded Ewan with a very old magical ward that left him undetected by the Preacher. But the sisters were always on guard, working on ways to destroy the Preacher once and for all.

Kate flicked through the pages, which were filled with stories of Ewan and his exploits as a boy, but there was nothing that would be of any help. Not until the last entry that was written by Betty after Janette had died.

To whomever finds this entry,

I'm leaving the Lodge now as I have done all I can. I miss my darling sister and fear I no longer have the strength to face that dreaded Preacher on my own. Ronan has offered to help, but I cannot, in all good conscience, allow him to put himself in such danger. He has a young family now who need him and I would not be able to live with the guilt. Should anyone find this journal, I pray it is someone who will finally put this evil to rest.

I have discovered how to destroy the Preacher once and for all, but I am unable to carry it out, as my age and health will not permit it. It is essential that the whereabouts of the Preacher's bones must be discovered. I believe he was murdered in one of the caves, but I have never discovered bones there and suspect there may be another cave that we have been unable to find.

Once you (whoever you are) are in possession of his bones, take them to the place of his most heinous crime, to Dunaverty. Lay his remains on the sight of the slaughter, then call for Colkitto and his clan to have their revenge. Set his bones alight and leave them to burn, as they are the source of his power. The Preacher will be vulnerable out in the open amongst the spirits of the damned souls here. He has no power on Dunaverty, but his murdered victims have. They will destroy the Preacher and, in doing so, will release their own trapped spirits.

I pray that this will fall into the right hands and I wish you every success. Lives depend on it.

Betty Riley.

Kate breathed out heavily as she read out the entry to Dand. "We can get rid of him," she said. "I know where the bones are."

Chapter Twenty-Five

Jamie awoke in the dark. He had no idea where he was, he could hear running water and he soaked through. But worse than that, his left arm was in agony, so much so, he was sure it was broken. He pulled himself up, a sharp pain shooting through his arm to his shoulder. It hung useless at his side as he felt his way along what seemed to be a passage way. His feet hit something soft below him and he heard someone groan. He knelt down and as he felt around, his hand discovered a warm body.

"Get away from me," groaned Eden as she started to awaken.

"Eden, it's me," said Jamie. "Are you all right?"

"Jamie, yes, I'm fine I think. Did the Preacher take you also?" Eden asked, allowing Jamie to help pull her to her feet.

"How the hell did he get you? I thought those damn Selkies were supposed to be watching you," said Jamie anger washing over him. "Some use they were, have you any idea where we are? I can hear water but it's so dark, I can't work out whether we are back at the caves or somewhere else."

"I don't know, Jamie, he attacked us, put some sort of spell on Moire and Dand, then I blacked out as soon as he touched me. God, those eyes of his, it's like looking straight into the soul of Satan himself," said Eden. "How are we going to get out of here? And more to the point, why hasn't he killed us yet?"

"Yea, well, I guess we're lucky on that last one. Look, I think we should follow the sound of the water. It makes sense that it's running somewhere; hopefully, it will be to a way out of here," replied Jamie.

Eden went to grab his arm and he yelled out in pain. "I forgot to mention my arm is broken."

"Oh, shit, Jamie, I'm sorry. Look, let me take the lead, my eyes are used to the dark now and I can make out the passageway," said Eden, taking his other hand and pulling him gently forward. Jamie could still only see darkness, but he followed on without argument.

They were stumbling along for about ten minutes or so, with Jamie trying to ignore the pain in his arm. The sound of the water was getting closer and Jamie thought he could also hear the waves of the ocean. Eden seemed to be able to focus on where they were going better than he could, so he was glad she was leading the way. He had a horrible nagging feeling they were being watched and he wondered why the Preacher had gone and left them.

"Jamie, I think there is someone ahead of us," Eden whispered and Jamie noticed the fear in her voice. She suddenly stopped dead.

"Yer nae leaving me so soon," came the sneering voice Jamie was dreading. "We havnae even got started yet."

"Leave us alone, Preacher, we know who and what you are. We're not scared of you," yelled Jamie, still unable to see.

The tunnel filled with an angry roar, followed by hysterical laughter as the air around them suddenly got cold.

"I admit yer a hardy pair, my touch alone should have made ye lose yer senses long before now. I'm thinking there's more than just filthy MacDonald blood in ye. I can smell some fish blood there also. Dae ye really think yer Selkie magic can protect ye frae me? I am stronger than I've ever been and I will have my vengeance," the Preacher hissed at them, his voice echoing all around them.

Eden grabbed Jamie's hand, "Come on, let's go!" and she pulled him along the tunnel towards the water. She had only taken a few steps when the Preacher's face appeared in front of them, even Jamie could see it in the dark. Eden, undeterred, punched the face, but her hand went straight through it and it vanished. "Not much use if we can walk right through you, are you!" Eden shouted.

A furious roar filled the air around them. "Ye think I can't harm ye, girl? Ye have already felt my power," the Preacher screamed.

Eden ignored him and carried on pulling Jamie through the tunnel as fast as she could go. Her vision was clear now, but she was aware that Jamie was still blinded in the darkness. Up ahead, she saw a huge pool of water in a cavern. There were waterfalls running into it and by the way, the edges were splashing around, she could see it was tidal, so it had to be connected to the outside ocean.

The Preacher's laughter still echoed around them. "Where tae noo? This is the end of the line and ye are trapped," said the Preacher as he appeared standing next to the tidal pool.

Jamie could see him clearly now, a tall, spindly and gaunt man, with hideous, watery eyes and a vicious scar running down the left side of his face. He wore a satisfied sneer, displaying a set of rotten teeth. He pointed at a pile of driftwood washed up by the tides and they burst into flame, lighting up the whole cavern. He then pointed to another pile and it also caught fire. Again and again, he did this until the entire cavern was alight. The Preacher stood in the centre of the flames, laughing at them. "Now you!" he said, pointing at Eden. Jamie watched in horror as his sister burst into flames, but an instant later, he saw her throw herself into the water. He felt his own clothes catching fire and heard Eden scream at him to follow her. He threw himself in the pool, almost passing out with the pain in his arm. At least the flames were out, but the cavern was filling with smoke and it was becoming impossible to breathe.

"Jamie, we have to go," cried Eden.

"Go where?" Jamie shouted back as the sea buffeted him. "We either burn or drown!"

"Trust me please, take a deep breath and hold onto my jumper," begged his sister. Jamie took a deep breath and the last thing he heard in the cavern was the Preacher's laughter as he felt Eden pull him downwards into the pool.

As they got deeper Jamie began to feel energised. He kicked out with his legs and the pain in his arm subsided. He found he could open his eyes and see clearly in the water, even in this darkness. His lungs seemed to be comfortable and he was not in need of air. They swam under the rocks, then up again as daylight flooded through the water. They reached the surface, clear of the rocks, and looked at each other.

"How did you know?" asked Jamie.

"I just did, I knew the water would save us," replied Eden.

"My arm feels better, I think I can swim with it now," Jamie said, stretching out his arm. "Where are we exactly?"

"We're at the Mull; look, there's the lighthouse. We could swim for that, but it looks pretty dangerous over on these rocks. We could just swim around to the beach at Southend, it's a couple of miles, I think I can manage it," suggested Eden.

"I'll race you," said Jamie, splashing off. Eden followed him close behind, feeling stronger with every stroke, the fear she felt in the cave long behind her now.

As they rounded the Mull, Jamie stopped swimming and looked towards the Lodge far in the distance. It was shrouded in a mist, which was weird as the mist was nowhere else, just over the Lodge and its grounds. "What do you think that's about?" he asked Eden, who was treading water next to him.

"I'm not sure, but the first time I saw that mist, we were with Ronan in the cave and I felt it was strange then. Like it's carrying the dead souls of all the murdered people of Kintyre," replied Eden.

There was a splash next to them and a grey speckled seal raised its head out of the water just next to Eden. It looked at her with its intense brown eyes. Another huge white seal rose to the surface next to them, then another smaller brown seal. Eden looked at Jamie. "They're Selkies," she said.

The grey seal swam around Eden and offered her its fin. She took hold gently, then let go, jumping back in shock.

"What is it?" said Jamie, swimming to her side. The Selkie remained where it was, looking at them.

"It's our father," said Eden. "As soon as I touched him, I could hear him talking to me. I was just shocked, that's all. Jamie, this is our father!" She grabbed Jamie's hand and pulled him towards the seal and they both touched the fin together.

As soon as Jamie felt the skin of the seal, he could hear his father in his head. "You're both in terrible danger. Selkie magic will only work for so long. It is the only reason you are able to swim in these currents and not feel the cold. But if you do not get to shore soon, I don't know if we'll be able to help you. Fionnlagh and Moire are with us, you must keep swimming," his father urged them on.

Jamie felt no weakness at all in the water. The pain in his arm had completely vanished and he felt he could swim forever. He carried on, holding onto the seal, his father, who led him towards the shore.

"I'm glad we can finally talk. I never would have abandoned you, but I knew your mother was a good woman. I never had to worry about you, but I always kept track of what you were doing. I didn't want to complicate your life. Please forgive me for leaving you the Lodge like this. You must believe that I didn't know about the Preacher until it was too late. I would never have put you in danger otherwise," explained Ewan.

"We know that, we have spoken with our grandmother and she explained it all. It's so strange for me to meet you this way," said Jamie.

"I'm glad we spotted you, everyone is looking for you. Moire came to tell us you'd been taken. Kate and Dand are looking for you, but they are trapped by that spirit mist just now. Your grandmother has gone to help them, we must get you back to shore. How are you feeling at the moment?" asked Ewan.

"I feel great," said Eden. "I'm not cold or tired at all, I feel I could swim forever."

"Yes, well, that won't last, not if you stay in land-dweller form. The ocean has recognised your Selkie blood and energised you, but it will only last for a short while. This part of the coastline is treacherous and you have been lucky so far. As soon as the ocean magic wears off, you will feel exhausted and very cold. We must get moving," said Ewan.

Both Jamie and Eden picked up their speed, they still felt energised, not noticing the strong undercurrents as they ploughed through the water. The Selkies swam with them, egging them on and soon enough, they began to see the beach clearly. About that time, Eden began to flag and a wave of exhaustion washed over her in an instant. She realised she was numb with cold and could no longer move her arms or legs. She sank under the water, but her father swam under her and lifted her back to the surface.

"Try to hold on, Eden, I'll get you to shore," Ewan told her.

Jamie saw Eden slide under the waves, but he was soon suffering himself. His body was frozen and he had no strength left to swim against the current, but worse, the pain in his arm came back with a jolt, he cried out in agony. The currents were sucking him under and he splashed helplessly as Fionnlagh slid underneath him and carried him forward.

Once Fionnlagh touched him, Jamie could hear his thoughts, and the great white seal encouraged him to hold on. Jamie just wanted to go to sleep, he was so cold and tired, but Fionnlagh kept nudging him awake and sped towards the shore.

The Selkies took Eden and Jamie as close to the shallows as possible. Ewan had to stay in the ocean, but Moire and Fionnlagh transformed immediately and pulled the exhausted, frozen pair out of the water. Fionnlagh looked over to the Lodge, the mist was beginning to clear.

"Isla must be there now, she is clearing the mist," he said to Moire. "We need to get these two warm and quickly. They won't survive for long out here."

Moire left Fionnlagh watching over them, she needed to get Isla to them as quickly as possible. She found her mother walking by the graveyard. "Mother, we need you. We've found them, but they need your help. They're on the beach!"

Isla followed her daughter back down towards the water. The Selkie queen had managed to disperse the spirit mist, but not without difficulty. The spirits were angry, they knew the Preacher had risen and they were seeking him out.

Isla found her grandchildren half-frozen on the shore and knelt next to them. She placed her one hand over each of their foreheads and muttered a few strange sounds. A faint yellow light spread from her hands and slowly engulfed their bodies. Their faces began to change from a deathly white to a healthy pink as the light warmed them through. Eden sat up first, gasping for air and looking bewildered. Jamie opened his eyes and stared up at the sky, trying to remember where he was. He turned his head and saw Isla, Moire and a giant of a man with a huge naked chest and long white hair staring down at him. It all started to come back, he sat up with a start, then sighed with relief when he saw Eden sitting there.

"I thought my days were numbered," said Jamie.

"With any luck, the Preacher will think that too and leave us alone now," groaned Eden, rubbing her head.

"I'm afraid you won't be that lucky," said Isla grimly. "He may think you're dead now but he will soon be able to sense that you're alive still. We are going to have to be more careful, you must never be alone."

"I wasn't alone, Moire and Dand were with me in the Lodge. Where is Dand?" asked Eden.

"The Preacher caught us by surprise and imprisoned us in a holding spell. Kate rescued us, then she and Dand went off to search for you while I went to get mother," explained Moire.

"So now we've lost Kate," said Jamie, standing and wincing in pain as he did so. "Well, we had better find her."

"You need to get that arm seen to," scolded Eden.

"When I've found Kate," said Jamie firmly.

Chapter Twenty-Six

Ronan pulled his ancient Ford Capris out of the shed behind his house. He loved this old car, he'd had it since 1985, and he had kept it pristine, although he didn't drive much anymore. Ronan's eyesight was not what it used to be and his space awareness had let him down on a few occasions, so Ronan left the driving to his wife, who had a small modern car. With some relief, the car started the first time, the deep roar of the engine reminding him of his boy racer days around Campbeltown, although he hadn't really been a boy then. He couldn't remember the last time he had it out on the road, he wasn't even sure if he had tax or insurance for that matter, but need's must and he had to get to Kate. The road around Arran was a fairly easy route to drive, Ronan told himself that once he got the hang of it again, he would be fine.

He pulled out onto the road and put the car in second gear as it started to roar at him. Soon, he was in third, but that was quite high enough for Ronan, he would take it easy, especially around the bends. Frustrated cars sped past him from time to time, but Ronan took no notice, he was determined to get to the Lodge, as he hadn't been able to get Jamie or Kate on the phone. When he got to the ferry port, old Angus, the boat captain, offered to put his car on the boat for him. Angus knew Ronan and was more than surprised to see him driving. The captain was not going to take any chances with his boat and couldn't risk Ronan trying to manoeuvre his car with a ridiculously long bonnet onto the ferry. He had his other customers to think about.

Once aboard, Ronan sat in his car and reflected on what he had done. He was regretting telling Kate about the key as he hadn't been completely honest with her and the more he thought about it, the guiltier he felt.

It was many years ago that Ronan used to watch the sisters going down into the coal bunker. They visited the old bomb shelter regularly and Ronan was eaten up with curiosity about what could be down there. He was a young man, not yet married and full of mischief, so one day, when the sisters went into town for supplies, he decided to take the key and explore the bunker. He crept down the steps as if expecting someone to jump out, then, when he arrived at the bottom, he found the lanterns, so he lit one, then walked on through the tunnel. He came out in a cave that had been made into a comfortable shelter. He suspected this was where the sisters came, but there was nothing that gave any clues to what they were doing down there. He was about to leave when he noticed the journal on the table. It was lying open, so Ronan convinced himself it wouldn't be wrong to read the open page.

The sisters had written about a ghost that was haunting the Lodge. The spirit of some Bloody Preacher who had destroyed the MacDonalds at Dunaverty hundreds of years before. They also mentioned his own clan name, MacDougall, who had aided the MacDonalds, only to be slaughtered themselves.

Ronan was puzzled as in his previous conversations with Janette and Betty, they had completely poo-pooed the idea of ghosts on the Mull. But here, black and white was evidence to the contrary, the sisters were obviously very concerned about this spirit.

They had tried to conjure up a trap to keep the Preacher at bay, but had only managed to keep him from the Lodge and the nearby grounds. As Ronan was reading, the cave grew icy cold, it didn't take him long to he realise he was not alone.

Ronan had seen many ghosts around the Lodge and the churchyard but had never encountered one in close proximity. A pale blue mist floated into the cavern, then started to manifest into the shape of a man. Soon he could make out in front of him the image of a great highland warrior, and Ronan knew he was looking on the ghost of Colkitto. Ronan started to shiver as the ghost spoke to him.

"Honoured by my clan and murdered by oor foe, your forefathers remained true tae oor cause. Ronan MacDougall, ye are nae safe, ye must be gone and dinnae come back doon here. Yer blood will awaken the Preacher, for ye are tainted with the blood of the damned MacDougalls that walk here, unable tae find their way tae everlasting peace. Trapped by the Preacher in death, as they were murdered by him in life," the ghost of Colkitto told him before it vanished into a mist and drifted away.

Ronan was shaking with cold and frozen to the spot. He collapsed onto a chair, trying to calm his breathing down, but his teeth were chattering uncontrollably.

The air around him started to crackle and the cold was becoming unbearable. Then a hideous voice started to laugh and the distorted image of a grotesque looking man appeared. Ronan was paralysed with fear as the creature came towards him. Then there was a roar and Colkitto appeared again and threw himself at the dark spirit. They both vanished in an instant.

"Ronan, what on earth are you doing down here?" Janette's voice came ringing through the cavern.

Ronan tried to answer but couldn't get his words out. Betty arrived a second later. "Janette, he's come in contact with a spirit. Get the tonic the Selkies gave us."

Janette went to a small cabinet sitting on the floor, opening it to reveal rows of bottles filled with strange-looking liquids. Janette pulled out a dark green bottle and poured a little of the same coloured liquid onto a glass, then handed it to Betty. Betty immediately tilted Ronan's head backwards and poured the liquid in his mouth. Ronan spluttered a little at the foul taste, but the heat from it spread throughout his body very quickly and within a few seconds, he had stopped shaking and could speak again.

"Now, young man, I'll repeat the question. What are you doing down here?" asked Janette sternly.

"I wis just curious aboot what wis doon here. I didnae mean any harm, I didnae ken the ghosts were here," Ronan garbled, more terrified of Janette than he had been of Colkitto or the dark entity.

"Who did you see?" Janette asked.

"It wis Colkitto, he came tae warn me tae stay away," answered Ronan not wanting to mention the monster he had seen.

"Laddie, are you going to take heed of him?" Janette demanded.

"Aye, I'll nae come doon here again," promised Ronan.

"Well, you're lucky we came when we did. These ghosts do not realise the damage they can do to mortals. Now your job is to mind the Lodge, Ronan MacDougall, you leave the ghosts to us," said Betty with a gentler tone than Janette.

Ronan had run out of there like his tail was on fire, he never went back down, but now he had foolishly sent Kate down there. What if she went down there on her own and came across one of the ghosts, she had no potion to rescue her and no one would know where she was. It would be his fault.

The ferry captain banged on his window as the ferry sailed into the port. Ronan got out of his car and the captain slid in his seat, drove his car off the ferry for him, then handed him back his keys. "Ye be careful the noo, I dinnae want yer wife after me, Ronan," the captain eyed him suspiciously.

Ronan drove his car down the one-lane road towards Carradale, though by the time he reached the small town, four frustrated vehicles were stuck behind him. The road widened and the cars were able to pass, some glaring in at him as he sat looking dead ahead, his hands gripped tightly on the steering wheel. Some of the steep bends were quite tricky and Ronan went off the road a couple of times, but he managed to straighten out. He promised himself this would be the last time he ever drove, praying he would reach the Lodge in one piece. It was mid-morning by the time he reached Campbeltown, which was thankfully very quiet, allowing Ronan to manoeuvre his way through the streets without too much trouble. Another 40 minutes later, his car bumped over the cattle grid at the entrance of the Lodge and he drove slowly up the hill, it was with a huge sigh of relief when he finally switched off the engine.

Ronan grabbed his walking stick from the passenger's seat and climbed slowly out of the car. He had stiffened up, so he stood for a minute, allowing his circulation to get going again. Ronan could see Kate's car, but the place seemed deserted, so he limped slowly towards the entrance, perhaps if he waited inside, Kate would find him. He pushed his way through the door and looked around, a wave of emotion washed over him when he saw how much the old place had been cleared. It was beginning to look more like he remembered it all those years ago.

About 20 minutes later, voices began to drift in from outside, then Jamie walked through the door, but walking next to him was someone Ronan had not seen for over 50 years. Isla was every bit as young and beautiful now as she had been back then.

"Ronan, how did you get here?" said Jamie surprised.

"Ronan, is that you?" said Isla. She moved towards him, giving him one of her rare smiles, then leaned over and hugged the old man. "It is so good to see you again."

"Ye havnae aged a day, lassie, I'd recognise ye anywhere," he said with tears glistening in his eyes.

"Ronan, is that your Capris out the front? Did you drive that thing here?" asked Jamie looking horrified, holding his arm tight to his body.

"Aye, I did, but dinnae ask me tae dae it again. I havnae driven for years and I think I terrified the locals. What have ye done to yer arm, laddie? Ye need it seeing tae," Ronan replied.

"Not until we find Kate, I take it she's not here?" asked Jamie.

"Nae one's here, laddie, but I think I might ken where she is. I spoke tae her this morning aboot the old coal bunker," said Ronan.

"I'd forgotten about that place," said Isla. "Of course, the sisters and I spent a lot of time there trying to find ways to protect the Lodge. I never went back after I left, but if Kate's down there with Dand, she should be safe. The Preacher won't go near her."

"Aye, safe as long as nae other ghosts decide tae pay them a visit. I once came across Colkitto there and the experience nearly killed me. The sisters found me and managed tae gie me some of that Selkie potion ye had made them. It straightened me oot pretty fast. If it's still doon there, it may be worth bringing it back with ye. I have a feeling ye could be needing it in the next wee while," suggested Ronan.

Isla led Jamie over to the entrance of the bunker while Ronan waited by his car. The ground was too uneven for him to try to follow, so he said he would wait for Eden to tell her where they were. He lit his pipe and leaned against his old Ford Capris, its gold paint shining in the morning sun. He saw Eden and another young woman climbing down to the road from the caves. They must have been searching for Kate there and, clearly, hadn't found her.

Ronan sucked on his pipe but his eyes were drawn to a strange low mist snaking around the gravestones in the churchyard as if it were waiting for something. And then he saw Colkitto standing still at the entrance of the St Columba's chapel tomb, watching over Eden as he promised he would. Ronan had a strong sensation that things were about to get very complicated. The spirits seemed rattled and on edge, Ronan could sense the tension in the air. The Preacher was close, and Ronan began to feel afraid.

Chapter Twenty-Seven

Jamie heard Kate's voice echoing through the tunnel before he saw her. She and Dand were still pouring over the journals they had found. Kate looked up when she heard them coming. "Jamie, thank God, I thought the Preacher had you," she cried, grabbing hold of him, then letting go immediately when he cried out in pain.

"He did for a while, but we got away, but I think I've broken my arm," said Jamie, bending down to kiss her on her head. "What is this place?" he asked, looking around.

"It's an ancient tunnel that we Selkies created so we could come ashore unseen. It was then found and used by smugglers from Ireland for a couple of hundred years before the owners of the Lodge said they turned it into a coal bunker for their use. Of course, it was never used as a coal bunker, it would hardly be efficient dragging coal all the way from here, and smugglers still used it up until the war. That was when it was used as a bomb shelter, then after the war, it became forgotten. I think the sisters and I were probably the last ones down here," Isla explained.

"I think you're right, look what we found, Jamie. I think we may be able to get rid of this Preacher," said Kate, handing him the journal with the last entry Betty had written.

Jamie read the entry out loud for the benefit of the others. When he finished, he looked at Kate. "And we know where the bones are," he said.

"What bones?" Eden had arrived with Moire in tow. "Ronan told us where you were. What are you talking about?"

Jamie showed her the journal and her face lit up. "I told you to leave them where they were," she said. "Well, what are we standing here for, let's go and get them."

"I think we had better come up with a plan first," said Kate. "If you or Jamie go anywhere near these bones, he will know what we are trying to do. I think I had better be the one to retrieve them, the Preacher doesn't seem to care that I exist. And now is not the time.

Jamie needs his arm set, and you look like you could do with a rest after your experience," Kate continued, taking control of the situation.

The cavern was suddenly thrown into darkness as the candles inside the lanterns blew out all at once. Gizmo started to bark frantically as the temperature dropped dramatically and the air around them began to crackle.

"It's the Preacher," cried Eden.

"Get behind me," yelled Isla as she started to pull on her magic. They crowded behind her just as the Preacher came shrieking into the cavern. His face was full of raw contempt as he floated into the middle of the room, his skinny body glowing in the darkness.

"Your Selkie magic won't stop me," he hissed. "I am too powerful now."

Isla was still mumbling strange sounds and words and the room started to glow with a pale blue light. The Preacher shrieked again, then flew at Eden, ploughing into her torso, knocking her screaming to the ground, clutching at her chest and gasping for air. The Preacher reappeared behind them, still shrieking, as Kate had dropped to the floor next to Eden.

Jamie ran across to the other side of the cavern. "You want me, come and get me!" he yelled at the entity.

The Preacher turned but Isla finished her spell and a pale blue orb sprang up around them. Jamie was still at the other side of the cavern. "Get in the light," cried Isla and Jamie ran towards them.

The Preacher flew at him, with arms outstretched and face contorted with rage. Kate screamed with terror as Jamie threw himself towards them. The Preacher grabbed at him but only managed to touch Jamie's shoulder before he blasted into the orb. The Preacher was thrown backwards, vanishing instantly. Jamie lay breathing heavily. Kate was kneeling over him, he could not move his shoulder and his broken arm was now in agony.

"How's Eden?" he asked, unable to get up.

"She's still breathing," said Moire, who had Eden's head in her lap. "But she's not conscious. I don't know what he's done to her. Kate, are you all right?" she asked as she noticed Kate shaking.

"I'm j–j–j–just s–s–s–so c–c–c–cold," stammered Kate.

"It's ghost magic, it affects land-dwellers badly. I have some potion for that," said Isla, running to the small cabinet of the floor. She pulled out a small green bottle, returning to Kate with it and pouring some of the contents gently into her mouth. Within a few seconds, Kate stopped shivering and felt the warmth spread through her body.

"Here," said Isla, giving Kate the bottle. "You had better keep this on you for now."

"Can you help Eden now?" Kate asked.

"If she were a land-dweller, she would be dead," said Isla. "Her Selkie blood has saved her, but even I don't know how to waken her. We need to destroy the Preacher, it's the only way we can get rid of his curse."

"I think we should get out of here," said Dand. "It's not safe for them. I can carry Eden, can you help Jamie up?"

Kate and Isla helped Jamie to his feet. Kate could see the pain etched all over his face. "You're going to the hospital now."

Kate had her arm around Jamie as they walked through the tunnel, she wasn't sure how she was going to explain all this to the staff at the hospital. Dand carried Eden with no problem at all, but Jamie was really struggling to walk and it took them some time to get him out of the bunker. It was getting dark when they finally stepped out in the open. Dand had already put Eden in Kate's car, he came back to help with Jamie. Ronan was waiting for them as Jamie collapsed in the passenger's seat of Kate's car. He climbed in the back of the car with Eden while Kate put Gizmo in the back. The Selkies stood watching them quietly.

"I'll be back first thing in the morning, I need to come back for these bones," Kate told them. "We have to see this through."

"Look for us when you come, we'll be watching," said Dand. "You must not do this alone."

Kate got in the car. Jamie was silent, she could see he was struggling to stay awake. The pain and exhaustion had finally got to him. She drove to the small hospital at Campbeltown, and when they arrived, Kate concocted some story about a boating accident. The team at the hospital were very professional and soon had Eden in a bed, on a drip. They tried to get Jamie to stay, but once his arm was set and plastered, he was determined to leave with Kate and Ronan.

They all drove back to Kate's house, she heated some canned soup for them all. Jamie ate a little, he was still quiet, and his face was grey. Kate went over and kissed his cheek gently. "Jamie, go to bed. We can talk in the morning."

"What are ye going tae do 'hen? I recognise that look on yer face," Ronan asked her when they were sitting alone in the conservatory. Kate had poured them both a large scotch and she twirled the amber liquid around in her glass as she thought.

"I'm going to destroy the Preacher before he destroys anyone else," she replied firmly.

"Aye, and I'm coming with ye. I may be old, but I have my own score tae settle with that devil," said Ronan. "It's my ancestors that walk aroond the Mull, trapped there until that monster is finally laid to rest. Wherever hell that may be. We need tae come up wi a plan, Katie."

They sat for another hour talking about the Preacher and how they would retrieve his bones. Kate was sure that if she went alone, the Preacher would not sense her, then she would be able to sneak into the cave and get the bones without the Preacher knowing what she was doing.

Ronan was too connected to the MacDonalds, so there was a strong chance he would be detected by the ghost. They couldn't risk Ronan's presence alerting the Preacher before they got his remains out of the cave. They decided that Ronan would wait for Kate at Dunaverty Rock, where the Preacher's powers were limited. Providing Kate could get the Preacher's bones there without being detected, then they had a good chance of getting rid of him for good.

Ronan suggested they leave Jamie behind and Kate agreed. His presence would alert the Preacher, but Kate knew Jamie wouldn't go for it. So, they planned to leave the house at dawn without him knowing. He would be angry, but at least he would be safe and he couldn't drive with his broken arm.

Kate slid in bed next to Jamie, she knew she wouldn't sleep much, and it seemed to take hours before her silent alarm started to buzz under her pillow. She looked over at Jamie, he had had a fitful night trying to get comfortable sleeping with an arm in plaster. He seemed to be out for the count now, so she crawled quietly out of bed and slipped out of the room. She had left clothes in the other bathroom, so she got dressed, brushed her teeth, then put a brush through her hair. She opened the door quietly but jumped back with a start.

"So, when are we leaving?" said Jamie, standing there fully dressed. "Did you think I didn't see you take your clothes and toothbrush out last night? I'm not letting you go alone."

"Jamie, I have to get his remains by myself. If the Preacher senses you in the caves, he will stop us. I can get in, and out, without him knowing," said Kate.

"I agree, I'm not arguing, but I need to be nearby in case you get into trouble. I'm not letting you go alone," said Jamie.

"Well, she wudnae be alone. I'm gonnae gae wi her," said Ronan, appearing from the kitchen.

"We'll all go, no argument. My arm feels a lot better, if you try to go without me, I will drive after you," said Jamie stubbornly.

"Okay, okay, but you have to stay at Dunaverty with Ronan while I go and get the bones," said Kate reluctantly.

Ten minutes later, they were all driving towards the Mull.

Chapter Twenty-Eight

Eden awoke in her hospital bed around 3 in the morning. Her mouth was dry as parchment and her throat felt like she had swallowed glass. She sat up, fumbling around for the tumbler sitting next to a jug of water by her bedside. She poured some water, and gulped it down, it was lukewarm but eased her throat. Looking around, she could see there were four beds in the room, lit up by the street lamp outside. Only two of the beds were occupied, hers being one of them. She went to reach for her phone but remembered that it was probably at the bottom of the sea after her encounter with the Preacher, so she lay back down again.

The last thing she remembered was the Preacher flying straight at her, then a sharp pain rip through her body. Her chest was so tight, she couldn't get any air, so Eden guessed she must have passed out. But what about the others? Had they made it out unharmed? Someone must have brought her here, so surely, they were safe. She was wide awake now, there was no way she could get back to sleep. She could feel a strange sensation wash over her, as if something or someone was trying to reach her.

Eden reached over to the little cupboard at the side of her bed and found her clothes tucked inside.

She got dressed quickly, then snuck quietly past the other occupied bed in the ward. When she got to the doorway, she peered out towards the nurse's station. There was a dim light on and Eden could see the nurse sitting at the desk, watching an iPad screen. Eden had to pass her to go out, so she prepared herself for the argument that would probably ensue, but as she got closer, she could see that the nurse was asleep in the chair.

She crept past and was out of the door and into the corridor without being noticed. Five minutes later, Eden was out on the dark street, looking for the police station, perhaps they would contact Jamie or Kate for her.

The sky was clear and sparkling with stars as Eden walked through the empty streets of Campbeltown. She walked down towards the harbour, there was more life down at the docks as the local fishing boats were getting ready to go fishing and to check their lobster pots.

"Do ye want some tea, hen?" a large, burly man by the boatshed asked her. "Ye look like ye need it."

Eden sighed, she had no money, no phone and a cup of tea sounded just about perfect now. "Yes, please, I could do with one," she said, surprised by how hoarse her voice sounded.

The man introduced himself as Angus, a local salmon fisherman. He had salmon nets set up at different parts of the coast and he liked to get to them just before daybreak. The tea was hot and way too sweet, but it soothed her sore throat. She was grateful Angus didn't ask too many question about what she was doing there at this time in the morning.

He chatted away like they were old friends telling her about basking sharks ruining his nets and the state of the fishing industry that was falling apart in these waters, Eden pretended to listen, though her mind kept drifting off to the Preacher. She had to get home.

"Eden, I've been looking for you," a voice she recognised interrupted Angus. She turned to see Dand standing there. She took a minute, it was odd to see him dressed in jeans and a sweater, but it was Dand.

"Oh, thank goodness, I thought I'd lost you all," she said, relief washing over her.

Angus frowned at Dand for a minute, then looked harder at Eden with sudden recognition. "Well, ye'll be all right the noo. I'll get back tae work."

"Thanks so much, Angus, you were a life saver," said Eden, waving goodbye before taking Dand's arm and leading him off to walk around the harbour basin.

"What are you doing here?" Eden asked when they were out of earshot.

"I went to the hospital, but you were gone. I sensed you had come down to the harbour, so I followed my instincts. Did you hear me calling out to you?" said Dand.

"That was you? I don't know what I heard, I just knew I had to get out of that hospital," said Eden. "Now tell me what happened after I passed out."

Dand went on to explain what had happened with the Preacher in the bunker. He had been worried when he saw the colour of Eden's face, so he carried her to Kate's car, then decided to swim around to Campbeltown harbour to keep an eye on her. Moire had followed Kate and Jamie back to the house at Carradale. Jamie had been treated at the hospital, then gone home with Kate and Ronan.

"I need to get back to them, Dand, but I've no phone and no money. I don't suppose…" asked Eden.

Dand shook his head. "It's not something we Selkies carry unless we are prepared beforehand. We could swim?"

"Are you crazy, I'm a good swimmer but I couldn't swim that far," said Eden.

"You could if you transformed, you could become a full Selkie," he said, turning her to face him. "I know the call of the ocean is within you, Eden. You've felt it, it's crying out to you, or you wouldn't have heard me calling you. You are connected to us, much more than your brother is. Don't you want to feel what it's like under the waves?"

"Of course I want to, I just wouldn't know how," said Eden, trembling. She could feel the desire rise within her as he spoke.

"Do you trust me?" Dand bent his head down towards hers. He kissed her lightly on the lips, then led her gently to the water's edge.

"I trust you, but I don't know if I'm ready for this," said Eden.

"The choice must be yours, but I will be at your side every moment. You belong in the ocean, Eden, I know you feel it calling you," said Dand, watching her closely.

Eden stared down at the clear water lapping against the harbour wall. She longed to submerge in its depths, the feeling had got stronger since her connection with Moire that day on Sanda Island. It couldn't be a bad idea, could it? Her father had chosen to go back to the water after all his years living as a human. Eden knew that all her life she had never really fitted in anywhere, she just felt unconnected to the world around her. Perhaps this was what she was looking for all along. She looked over at Dand, with his dark, sincere eyes promising to protect her, what could go wrong? After all, it would be possible for her to return to her human life if she wished.

"Okay, I'll give it a go," she said more to herself than to Dand.

The two of them walked around the bay until they reached a small jetty tucked behind some rocks. The sky was beginning to give off an orange hue as dawn approached. Dand looked around to check they were still alone. The fishermen's jetty was deserted now as the boats had already left, and the streets were still deserted. Dand started to walk down the jetty and into the water, holding his hand out for Eden to follow him.

"Don't we have to take our clothes off or something," she asked nervously.

Dand laughed, then pulled her to him. "No, we don't. Don't be scared, my love. Just tell the ocean this is your choice, your own decision to join us, and the magic of the deep will do the rest."

Eden allowed Dand to lead her gently down the little jetty and soon she was knee-deep in the water. "Now close your eyes and wish for your Selkie blood to transform you. Wish to become a Selkie," said Dand as he pulled her in deeper. Eden squeezed her eyes shut and imagined becoming a Selkie. It was easier than she had anticipated, almost as if she was being guided. She could feel Dand's hand in hers, leading her forward slowly, then she felt the cold water lap around her waist, her clothes feeling heavy as they stuck uncomfortably to her skin.

In an instant, Eden slipped under the surface, no longer aware of the cold water pulling at her water-logged clothes. She opened her eyes and stared in disbelief at the vision before her. Dand was now a chocolate brown seal, beckoning her to follow him. She looked at her own sleek form and found she could move with accuracy and speed through the water. She swam up to the surface and looked out over the lights of the harbour, Dand's head appeared next to her.

"How do you feel?" he asked her through telepathy.

"I feel wonderful," said Eden. "Lead the way."

They both dived under the surface as the sun rose upon the water. The sky was clear and the sun shone down through the waves. The speed they swam at was breathtaking, Eden found herself dodging all manners of sea creatures as they made their way out of the bay and into the open waters. The fish were larger here and they scattered as the Selkies swam through them. Eden was elated and leapt out of the water to take in some air before diving back down to swim around Dand.

"Show off," he laughed at her.

"I love it," Eden cried and swam faster through the seaweed forests on the sea bed.

"Slow down!" yelled Dand. "Selkies get tired too. I think I can hear Moire. Stop and listen with your mind."

The pair of them rose to the surface and floated on their backs as they listened. Moire's voice appeared in Eden's head.

The Selkie had followed Kate and Jamie back to Carradale. Moire told them that Jamie, Kate and Ronan had left the house and were heading back towards the Mull. Moire was on her way there and she would meet them at Southend.

"I see Dand convinced you to join us," said Moire.

"I feel wonderful, like I belong here," replied Eden, she felt like she could swim forever.

"I'm not sure your brother will feel the same way, but I think we have more to worry about now," said Moire. "I will be with you soon."

With a jolt, Eden suddenly remembered the Preacher and it was a sobering thought. She wondered what Jamie would say when he knew what she had done; after all, she had promised him. But that was before the circumstances changed everything, she was sure he would understand. Eden knew now that she would be remaining in the ocean, it was where she was supposed to be.

Chapter Twenty-Nine

Kate pulled up at Dunaverty Golf Clubhouse carpark. It was early, but the clubhouse was open for breakfast, feeding the hard-core golfers before they set off on their first game. Jamie suggested that they ate first as none of them had eaten much in the last couple of days, so they ordered tea and bacon sandwiches from the kitchen. They sat by the window with a good view of the Lodge and the dramatic Mull coastline with the sun shining down on the sparkling water. It was hard to believe that there was so much darkness existing there and Kate gave an involuntary shiver when she thought of the Preacher.

"I don't like the thought of you going to the cave alone," said Jamie.

Kate raised her eyebrows. "We talked about this, Jamie. You can't go, you'll bring him right to us."

"Yes, well, I was thinking about that in the car," said Jamie and Kate rolled her eyes in frustration. "If you go into the cave, who is to know he's not there already, I mean, his remains are there, so it stands to reason that's where he'll be residing."

"Well, I'll just have to take that chance," said Kate. "Perhaps Colkitto will be there to help me if that's the case. He said he would be watching."

"What if I go to the Lodge?" said Jamie. "The chances are the Preacher will sense me there and it will draw him out to attack me. If we call on Isla and the Selkies, then perhaps they could protect me while you're getting his bones. That way, you will go undetected and I will feel a lot better about you going there alone."

Kate went to argue but Ronan spoke first. "Aye, laddie, that's a good plan. I didnae like the idea of the wee lassie going intae that cave, but if the Preacher is busy, he'll nae ken that she's there."

"Well, only if we find Isla, you're too vulnerable on your own, Jamie, and your injured," said Kate, knowing she was beaten.

Kate and Jamie finished their breakfast, then headed out to the car while Ronan ordered himself another pot of tea. Kate gave him an old mobile she had, explaining with some degree of effort how it worked. She told him that when it rang, he was to go out to the rock and get ready to burn the bones. Kate then drove Jamie down towards the Lodge, pulling the car up beside the entrance gates. They got out and walked down to the beach, looking for the seals. Sure enough, a grey speckled seal watched them, Jamie was sure it was his father. A few minutes later, Isla was walking along the beach towards them. Kate breathed a sigh of relief when she saw Jamie's grandmother.

"I'm surprised to see you here, Jamie," said Isla. "I take it you have some sort of plan?"

"I think it's time we ended this," replied Kate. "We think we know how, but we'll need your help."

"Of course, you have it. What do you need me to do?" said Isla.

The three of them strolled back to the car while Jamie explained their plan to Isla. Isla nodded thoughtfully as she listened and seemed to be impressed. Kate drove them all up the hill to the Lodge and they all let themselves inside. The builders would be starting soon, Jamie thought he would be safer when they arrived.

"Just promise me you'll stay with him," said Kate to Isla.

"Of course, be safe, Kate, remember to take that potion I gave you before you go into the cave, it will protect you from any spirits that wander in there," said Isla.

Kate kissed Jamie long and hard before she left. She could tell he was fighting back his desire to stop her going. "I'll be okay," she promised.

Gizmo was waiting in the car, so Kate let him out and pulled out a large bag from the back of her car, as she would need something to carry the bones in. She made her way down and across the churchyard, towards the caves. It was a clear, fine day and there was no mist to be seen, perhaps this was going to be easier than she thought. Kate jumped over the wall and started to climb up towards the caves. She remembered the potion Isla had given her and slipped it out of her pocket. She pulled off the top, then took a big slug of the green liquid. She hadn't remembered the taste from the last time she took it, which was probably a good thing, as it was foul.

She was still choking from the taste when Gizmo started barking. She was entering the cave, but the little dog refused to follow her. "Okay, stay here," she said as she carried on into the darkness.

"What are ye doing here, lassie?" said Colkitto as he materialised at the back of the cave. "It's nae safe fir ye."

"I'll be all right," replied Kate. "I have a potion now, it protects me from the ghosts, Isla gave it to me. We think we know how to stop the Preacher."

"Do ye now? Can I assist ye in any way?" asked Colla's ghost.

"Just keep the Preacher off me if you can. I've got to collect his bones," said Kate, shivering only slightly as she walked past Colkitto.

She climbed through into the next cavern, then found her way around to the cave behind that. The bones from the bottom half of the Preacher were lying on the ground, but the top half of him was still hanging from the cave roof. Kate picked up the bones on the ground, putting them into her bag. Then she looked up, she hadn't thought this through. How was she going to climb up to get the rest of them, perhaps Colla could help her?

"Colla, are you still here?" she called to the darkness.

"Aye, I'm here. What can I dae for ye?" said Colkitto.

"I need to get his bones, but I can't reach them," said Kate, pointing to where the Preacher's skull, ribcage and one of his arms hung.

"I cannae touch his bones, lassie, his curse prevents any MacDonald from taking them. But I can touch the ropes that hold him. It may take a wee while, but I'll get that bastard doon fir ye," said Colla, vanishing into a mist that curled its way upwards towards the ropes.

Kate stood watching as the bones of the Preacher started to swing gently. Colkitto's spirit mist remained spinning on the bindings and she could see the ropes weakening. Just then, the bones of his remaining arm came crashing down and the rest of the skeleton jerked suddenly downwards before it stopped again just out of her reach. Kate picked up the bones of the Preacher's arm, putting them in her bag, it shouldn't be long now before she had the rest of them.

***

Jamie and Isla stood at the large bar window, looking out towards the caves. Jamie was sick to his stomach that Kate was in there alone and it took all his will not to run down and join her. He looked at his watch, it was coming on for eight o'clock. He wasn't sure what time the builders started but he imagined it would be soon.

"I'm sure she will be fine, Jamie," said Isla, who had seen him look at his watch.

"I thought she would be out of there by now," he replied just as his eyes were drawn out to sea. There was a mist forming, he was sure of it. It wasn't as bright as it had been a few minutes ago.

The air around them started to crackle and a bucket flew across the room, just missing them as it crashed into the wall. The workmen's tools started flying off in different directions, they ran for cover behind the bar to avoid getting hit. Isla started her protection spell, and soon, a pale blue orb of light engulfed them, just as the Preacher manifested.

The Preacher stood staring at them, his hooded eyes narrowed as he pondered. "Ye are foolish tae return, but I wonder why so soon. Are ye trying to trap me, witch?"

"We just want to be left alone. I thought I could talk with you," said Jamie.

"Ye lie, boy! Ye think I cannae see through ye," said the Preacher, floating closer, then stopping just before the orb.

Jamie could see every detail of him clearly now, the Preacher's sunken, pale watery eyes staring from grey and black greasy strands of hair that covered his white, withered face. His skin was almost translucent as it was pulled so tight, and his thin lips were set in a contemptuous sneer, revealing what was left of his rotten brown teeth.

The Preacher was tall, but spindly and he wore a long black coat that was tight around his skinny frame. He still wore his large rimmed black hat, and his fingers twitched erratically as he floated close to the orb, staring maliciously at Jamie.

"Why are ye lying?" hissed the Preacher and Jamie took a step back.

"Be gone, Preacher, leave him alone," warned Isla.

"I wasn't addressing ye, sea hag! Why have ye come here, boy?" The air crackled with power and Jamie could see Isla was struggling to hold on to her spell.

The Preacher moved away from them, looking slowly around in all directions, as if expecting someone to jump out from behind him. His eyes were dark with anger as he turned to stare directly at Jamie. They stood silent for what seemed an eternity and Jamie could see the suspicion on the Preacher's face.

Then suddenly, the Preacher moved away, his face frozen in horror. "NOOOO, what is she doing!" he shrieked, then the air crackled again as the Preacher vanished from the room.

Isla collapsed against the wall, breathing hard as she let go her spell. "I think he knows," she said weakly.

"God! Kate!" cried Jamie and ran out of the Lodge and straight into a wall of thick mist.

**

The remaining bones and the Preacher's skull crashed to the ground as the rope snapped. Kate picked them up with a disgusted shiver, then put them in her bag. She was mindful to get every piece of him as she didn't want to leave anything to chance.

Colkitto materialised again in front of her. "Ye have tae get oot of here, lassie, the Preacher kens ye have his bones. He's coming."

Kate didn't need telling twice, but as she spun around to find the way out, the Preacher was already standing at the exit. She screamed in terror, backing herself against the cave wall.

"Run, lassie!" shouted Colkitto as he suddenly sailed past her, straight into the Preacher. They both vanished in a mist, but she could hear them battling and raging.

Kate sprinted through to the next cavern and then into the Great Cave. She ran for the daylight, but her relief from escaping the caves diminished when she saw the mist lingering at the exit. Where had it come from, the day had been so clear.

She couldn't stay in the cave, it was too dangerous, she didn't know how long Colla could keep the Preacher at bay. She started to climb blindly down from the entrance, sliding down on her backside, dragging the bag with her, feeling for the rocks with her feet as she couldn't risk falling. Gizmo was whimpering next to her, but he followed on.

She was unaware she had almost reached the road when she heard a voice calling her in the distance. It sounded so far away, but it was hard to tell in the mist. It sounded like Eden, but wasn't Eden still in hospital?

"I'm over here," she yelled at the top of her lungs swallowing some of the mist and gagging, it was so thick, it almost had substance to it.

"Stay where you are, Kate," Eden shouted. "I will come to you."

Kate wondered how Eden was going to find her, so she kept moving slowly downwards until her feet eventually hit the stone wall. She realised, with relief, that she must be at the road and she gingerly climbed over the wall, pulling the bag and lifting Gizmo over with her. The mist grabbed at her, then out of nowhere, an enraged face formed in front of her. It started to roar and raced towards her, knocking her backwards onto the ground before it vanished from sight.

"Kate, where are you?" Eden's voice sounded closer.

"I'm here, I'm on the road by the wall," she shouted back.

"Don't move, it's too dangerous. I will find you," Eden told her again.

This time, Kate obeyed and stayed where she was. This was no normal mist, it seemed to be attacking her. Then she heard another voice ring out through the fog.

"GIRL! Bring what ye've taken back to me!" roared the Preacher and Kate froze, terrified, to the spot. She didn't dare move or make a sound, expecting the Preacher to be on her at any moment.

Suddenly, someone grabbed her. "Sshhh," whispered Eden. "It's me, we've got you."

"How are you here?" Kate whispered back, relief washing over her.

"We don't have time for that now," whispered Eden. "Dand is here with me, we can get you through the mist. We will get you to the Lodge."

"No, not the Lodge," whispered Kate. "We must go to Dunaverty Rock, we have to burn the bones. Ronan is waiting there for us."

"It's too far in this mist," Eden argued.

"I don't care, if we go back to the Lodge, the Preacher will find us. His power is strong there, we need to get these bones to Dunaverty," insisted Kate.

"It's okay, I can get us there," said Dand. "But we need to get moving before the Preacher finds us."

Eden grabbed Kate's hand and led her slowly through the mist. The white clouds seemed to part for them as they moved through it, Kate realised she could see Eden's face clearly.

Her friend looked different somehow much more confident, but Kate couldn't figure why. The mist had soaked Kate to the skin and she should have been freezing, the Selkie potion was definitely doing its job at keeping her warm. Eden kept hold of her hand and continued to pull her forward; hopefully, they would get to the rock before the Preacher got to them.

Chapter Thirty

Isla was exhausted, the spell she had to cast to protect Jamie had taken almost all of her energy, she needed to get back in the ocean. The Preacher's strength had been much more than she had anticipated. She hadn't the energy to stop Jamie from leaving when he realised Kate was in trouble. And now the mist was here and Isla could tell the spirits within it were angry.

The Preacher had been among them too long now, and as his strength grew, so did theirs. They sought him out, wanting to destroy him so they could be released from their endless wandering. They cared little if they harmed anyone else, for all they could see was his spirit mocking their existence. Isla could usually calm the spirits, dispersing the mist, but she had no strength left to do this. She tried calling after Jamie but didn't know if he could hear her.

Jamie was disoriented, unable to see his hand in front of him and no idea which direction to go in. He knew he shouldn't have let Kate do this on her own, if anything happened to her, he would never forgive himself. He could hear Isla calling after him, but her voice sounded so distant, it was hard to tell where she was as the mist was so thick. He was beginning to feel helpless when the mist began to ripple in front of him and Jamie knew what was coming next.

The mist cleared almost reluctantly around a tall, dark figure, the Preacher stood there, glaring at him. Jamie could feel a deep rage build in the mist around him as it seemed to try to attack the Preacher but could not touch him. The Preacher reached towards him and Jamie felt himself being pulled forward like a rag, his feet no longer on the ground. He wanted to pass out but he struggled to stay conscious, somehow succeeding, though the dark energy flowing through him was overwhelming.

The next thing Jamie knew was that he was out of the mist, lying in a small graveyard surrounded by four walls covered in ivy. He couldn't see the Preacher, but he could feel his presence, so he struggled to his feet. He recognised the tombstones from Eden's description, the skull and crossbones etched into the stone. He was in St Columba's chapel, or the old pirates' graveyard as the locals called it, but why the hell did the Preacher bring him here? He could see the mist hovering overhead like it was watching him but unable to come any closer. Then he heard a loud scraping noise like metal on stone.

Jamie turned to see the huge metal gate of an enclosed crypt swing open. The Preacher stood at the gate and Jamie felt himself being pulled forward.

"Where are my bones?" the Preacher hissed at him.

Jamie didn't answer, he was relieved that Kate had got away. All he had to do now was keep the Preacher busy while she escaped. Jamie was flung hard against the stone tomb with the mark of the Knights Templar carved into it. Winded and gasping for air, he tried to stand, but as he did, the lid of the tomb began to slide slowly open.

"Where are my bones?" the Preacher demanded again.

Jamie again didn't reply, he looked into the tomb, afraid of what he might see. There was a skull protruding from under a metal helmet, complete with a suit of armour, ancient and discoloured. An old sword lay in its hands, again old and discoloured, but Jamie grabbed for it anyway. He grasped hold of its hilt, lifting it out of the tomb. It was much heavier than he anticipated, he nearly dropped it, but he hung on and managed to swing it around to point it at the Preacher.

The Preacher's smile was hideous as he stood gazing at him, almost challenging Jamie to attack. Jamie was right-handed, but because of his broken arm, he held the sword in his left hand, which made him a little off balance. He swung the sword at the Preacher's head, but the Preacher vanished as Jamie was almost pulled over by the force of his swing.

The Preacher reappeared, but this time, his face was filled with anger. "Where are my bones?" he demanded.

Jamie tried to lift the sword again, but it suddenly flew out of his hand, striking the ivy wall, where it lodged deep into the stone. Jamie blinked with surprise, but before he could pull himself together, he was lifted in the air, then slammed down inside the tomb, on top of the ancient remains of the knight that rested there. Jamie was winded again as he tried to move, gasping for air, the lid of the tomb slid shut over him, leaving him in blackness.

***

Ronan had his eyes focused on the Lodge while he sat in the clubhouse. He had no idea how long it would take them, and he prayed to himself that the Preacher would not find them. Then he saw the mist start to appear, forming on the sea just off the beach, then rolling quickly into shore. In a matter of minutes, the Lodge, the caves and the churchyard were engulfed.

"Strange mists around here, aren't they," said the waitress who was clearing his table.

"Aye, they are that," replied Ronan, frowning. He knew the Preacher did not control these mists, and he hoped Isla would be able to clear it. Kate would never get the bones to him if she was stuck in the mist and the longer it was there, the more likely it was that the Preacher would find her.

Ronan cursed himself for not dealing with the Preacher himself when he was a younger man. He was very fond of Kate and the other two, but seeing Isla again had brought back so many memories he had long buried. Betty confided in him after Janette had died and told him that the bones were the key to destroying the Preacher. Perhaps he should have looked for them then, but Betty was leaving and the new owners didn't seem to care, nor wanted, to know about spirits.

His family was young, so leaving the Lodge seemed the easier option, he knew he would never be able to work for the new owners. Perhaps if the sisters had told him more about the Preacher back then, he would have done more to find them, but he had only just learnt his forefathers were part of the massacre.

His MacDougall blood was spilt alongside the MacDonalds here at Dunaverty, which explained why he was always able to see and hear the ghosts. His ancestors roamed these shores, along with all the other lost spirits that fell victim to that Bloody Preacher. They had to end it now.

***

Colla Ciotach walked through the mist of his clansmen and women. "Be patient," he told them. "Oor time has come."

The Preacher was waiting for him at St Columba's tomb, Colkitto could feel the venomous dark soul simmering there, unsure and perhaps for the first time, afraid. Colkitto emerged through the ivy thicket, his claymore in his hand, he turned and faced the Preacher.

"Are ye ready for the end, John Neave?" Colkitto asked.

The Preacher sniggered. "It will never end, MacDonald, ye and yer kin are tainted fir all time."

He lifted his huge sword and charged towards the Preacher, who vanished from sight.

"Stand and fight, ye coward!" Colkitto cried to the sky. "Ye cannae keep running for ever!"

He looked over at the crypt and saw the door was open. "So ye've taken to desecrating oor ancestors' graves noo, ye shameless devil."

He went over to the tomb, looking down on the stone lid. Something was wrong here, he could feel it in his bones, it was then he noticed the old sword lodged in the ivy. Someone had been fighting the Preacher before he got there, and the lid of this tomb had been moved. Someone was in there. He slid the stone lid across to find Jamie lying there. He was still breathing but only just.

"NOOO!" the Preacher's voice shrieked somewhere overhead, but he was nowhere to be seen.

"Laddie, wake up," Colkitto shook him.

Jamie's eyes blinked open as he sat up, suddenly gasping for air.

"Yer all right noo," said Colkitto. "That coward has gone for noo."

Jamie crawled out of the tomb and onto his feet. He was pretty battered, his arm throbbed painfully. "I thought I was a goner," he said. "I just hope we've given Kate enough time to get the bones to Ronan. He doesn't know where she is, he kept asking me where his bones were."

"She's a brave lass, she's wi the Selkie Folk, they're taking her tae Dunaverty. The mist has slowed them doon, the spirits of the deed are following them tae the rock. They ken she has the Preacher bones and they want their vengeance," said Colla.

"Can't you tell them to let her through?" Jamie asked.

"I cannae make them understand, they only see their foe, noo within their grasp," said Colla sadly.

Jamie got himself steady on his feet, then searched around to find his way out of the tiny graveyard. Colkitto took the knight's sword from the ivy and returned it to the crypt. He nodded with respect at the knight that lay there, then closed over the stone tomb and left the crypt, shutting the metal door to protect it once again.

He joined Jamie outside on the churchyard, the mist had moved away from them and was heading towards Dunaverty Rock.

"It's following Kate," said Jamie. "She's got his remains, it looks like she hasn't far to go. Come on, you want to finish this as much as I do."

As they walked towards the road, Jamie turned and saw Isla coming towards them with Fionnlagh and Moire helping her. She looked very pale and ill.

"Isla, I'm sorry I left you, I was worried about Kate," said Jamie, trying to avoid the hard glare he was receiving from Fionnlagh. "I didn't realise you were so weakened."

"I know you were thinking of Kate, you didn't know. Did you find her?" Isla asked weakly.

"She has the bones, she is on her way to the rock," said Jamie.

"Eden and Dand are with her," said Moire.

"Eden's here? How on earth did she get here?" asked Jamie.

Moire didn't answer and seemed to avoid making eye contact with a slight guilty expression on her face.

"You can worry about that another time," said Fionnlagh. "You should be going to help them. I need to get Isla back to the sea."

"Yes of course, I'm sorry, I didn't realise she was unwell," said Jamie, feeling guilty he had left her without checking.

Jamie watched as the Selkies went back into the water. Colkitto had vanished, leaving him on his own, so Jamie turned and started to follow the cloud of white mist that was heading towards Dunaverty.

Chapter Thirty-One

Ronan watched the spirit mist come closer, he picked up his walking stick as he pulled himself out of his chair. He lifted his old, battered satchel over his shoulder, leaning hard on his stick while he hobbled slowly out of the clubhouse. His old joints had stiffened with sitting so long.

"Cheerio," said the young waitress. "Ye be careful now in that fog."

Ronan tipped his cap to her and went outside. It would be a steep climb up the rock, but he didn't need to reach the top. He only needed to get close to where the castle once was, then lay the kindling. He started to walk up the grassy bank, taking one step at a time, watching carefully for animal burrows and holes as he couldn't afford to fall over. The climb wasn't as bad as he had anticipated, though he would struggle getting down again.

He walked to the edge of the rock to check how far he had come, he was relieved to find he had climbed high enough to be looking down onto the rocky coastline. He was on the site of the castle so opened his satchel and emptied out the dry kindling wood they had collected from the beach. He laid it out in a round circle, ready to douse with the lighter fluid he carried also. He turned around to watch the mist crawling across the bay towards the rock. He pulled out his pipe and filled it with tobacco, then struck a match and drew on his pipe heavily until the tobacco was lit.

Colkitto appeared at the top of Dunaverty Rock and called down to Ronan, "The Preacher is coming, are ye ready fir him, old man?"

"Aye, I'm ready this time," said Ronan, sucking on his pipe.

"Yer forefathers are here, Ronan MacDougall, and they will aid ye. The battle at Dunaverty isnae finished yet," said Colkitto.

Ronan didn't reply, he just stood watching the mist rolling in, it wouldn't be long now.

***

Jamie was following on foot along the road. The mist had turned out towards the coast, but he dared not go into it. He knew it would be useless to get caught up in these clouds again, so he had to remain patient until it reached the rock. Colkitto hadn't come back, but Jamie was in no doubt that he would be seeing him again before the day was through.

As he carried on along the road, he spotted Stuart Aiken and his team of builders driving towards him in their vans. Stuart slowed his van down to a stop next to him. "Are ye oot for a stroll?" he asked with a grin on his face that soon disappeared when he saw the state of Jamie. "What's happened to ye? Have ye had an accident, nae at the Lodge, I hope?"

"Aye, I had a bit of a nightmare. I'm sorry, Stuart, but I can't explain just now. It might be a bit of a mess up there, but I'll be back later," said Jamie, knowing it wasn't much of an explanation.

"Dae ye need a lift?" Stuart asked with a puzzled expression.

"No, no, I'm fine, I'll see you later," Jamie replied and waved Stuart off. He would have to buy the man a pint to explain all this. He carried on up the road towards the lane to Dunaverty Golf Club and the Rock. The mist was hovering near to the rock now just out at the sea edge, so Jamie turned up the lane and quickened his pace.

***

The mist around Kate had not lessened any and she was beginning to feel the cold. She unzipped her pocket, pulling out the Selkie potion and took another swig. It couldn't do her any harm just to make sure, and almost immediately, the cold disappeared from her body. They hadn't spoken much as they travelled, they were afraid the Preacher might hear them. He was looking frantically for them, but the mist was hampering his efforts. Every now and then, they could hear him shriek close by, but he never discovered them.

Dand was concentrating on which direction they were taking while Eden had her arm linked through Kate's, pulling her onwards as if she could see where she was going. When they reached the lane that led to the rock, the mist veered off towards the sea, leaving them blinking once again in the bright sunlight. It was like stepping out into a different world, they had been trapped in the mist for so long.

"Look, there's Ronan," said Eden, pointing up towards the rock.

They made their way up the slope and onto the rock. It almost seemed too easy, the mist was still hanging along the coastline, but there was no sign of the Preacher. Ronan waved at them as they continued their climb upwards, before long, Kate could make out a victorious smile on his face.

"Ye did it, lassie, it's a proud moment tae be here wi ye," said the old man.

The air started to crackle. "I think we may have incoming!" cried Eden. "We'd better hurry."

The sky around them went dark and the seagulls took to the sky, screeching in panic. Kate was suddenly knocked to the ground hard without warning. She pulled herself up to see the same had happened to Eden and Dand. The Preacher stood between them and Ronan, the rage pouring from the entity as he raised his hands and pointed towards them. Kate watched in horror as dark entities spilled out from him, like an army of giant bats flying towards them. Their faces were hideously deformed, their mouths too large for their heads as they shrieked down on her and her friends. Kate was sent flying, too close to the cliff edge. Kate could hear Eden screaming something, but she couldn't make out the words. The dark beasts were all around her, tearing at her and dragging her towards the edge, as she fought and kicked out at them, to prevent her certain death on the rocks below.

Then there was a deafening roar and, suddenly, Kate found she was free. She looked up to see Colkitto descend on the Preacher, his claymore in hand. The dark entities flew at him, but he fought as if he were fighting a hundred warriors at once.

The mist rushed in from the sea, as it hit the rock, it transformed into a ghostly army of Highlanders, weapons in hand as they charged at the Preacher's evil army. The battle noise was deafening, and it was hard to make out what was happening around her. Kate staggered to her feet, she saw Dand with his arm protectively around Eden, who had another gash on her head.

The fighting was all around them, but Kate couldn't see the Preacher anywhere. Colkitto was still in the midst of the entities, striking blow after blow with his sword. The beasts that were struck screamed in agony, then vanished, only to be replaced by more in their place.

"Kate!" she heard Jamie's voice from below, she turned to see him scrambling up the side of the rock. He reached her, breathing hard. "Have you got the bones?"

"Yes, we have to get them to Ronan," said Kate, then realised she hadn't seen the old man since the battle started.

Jamie grabbed her arm, pulling her up through the ghostly battle that ensued around them. Dark entities were surrounding the Highlander spirits, outnumbering Colkitto and his army ten to one. Every swing of the giant Highlander's claymore sent his enemy scattering, and he kept calling out for the Preacher to face him, but the Preacher was nowhere in sight.

"Avoid the dark beasts!" called Dand. "They can harm you if they touch you."

Jamie and Kate kept moving forward, ducking and running from the entities that flew all around them. Kate looked up to see Ronan beckoning them forward, his face looked hurt and he had lost his glasses, but he was on his feet. They were moving as fast as they could towards him and were almost there when the Preacher was suddenly standing in their way.

"Ye have something that doesnae belong tae ye," he said, raising his hands towards them.

Ronan threw more lighter fluid over the kindling and struck a match, the flames roared upwards. Quick as a flash, Jamie grabbed Kate's bag and threw it at Ronan, who caught it in mid-air. But as the old man turned to empty its contents on the flames, the Preacher flew at him. Ronan fell backward, dropping the bag as he rolled over the edge of Dunaverty Rock.

"Noooo," Kate screamed as she threw herself in his direction, trying to catch him, but he was gone. The Preacher's laughter filled the air around them, he was standing by the bag that held his remains. "I told ye that ye will never be rid of me. The house of MacDonald shall suffer fir all time," the Preacher roared at them.

Then out of nowhere, Colkitto was on top of the Preacher. "Ye forsaken devil, ye think ye can defeat us again. Jamie, get the bones!" shouted the old warrior.

Jamie ran to the bag whilst Colkitto and the Preacher fought. He turned and saw the dark entities flying down towards him, and he threw himself towards the fire, throwing open the bag and emptying the bones out onto the flames.

Jamie fell to the ground as the entities struck out at him, all the sky turned black and he could hear an agonised screaming. He pulled himself up and looked over at the fire. The Preacher stood in the centre of the flames while the dark entities flew back into him, shrieking. The Preacher's face was filled with horror and then it crumbled into a pile of ash.

The silence was deafening, no one moved as the darkness slowly vanished and the sky turned blue. Then the sunlight came and Dunaverty Rock stood standing peacefully as it had done for thousands of years, looking over to the Mull of Kintyre.

Kate looked around at the hundreds of people in old highland garb standing on and around the rock. They were all fading fast, but looking upwards as they did so. Within seconds, they had all transformed into hundreds of twinkling lights that shot to the sky like a swarm of fireflies.

"Ronan!" cried Kate as she and Jamie rushed to the cliff's edge and looked over. Ronan was nowhere to be seen. "Oh, no!" cried Kate. "This is my fault."

"I dinnae think so, lassie, I kent what I wis doing," said Ronan, who was standing leaning on his stick behind them.

Kate gave a loud sob as she and Eden both ran over to throw their arms around him, almost knocking him over again. "We saw you fall over the edge. We thought you'd been killed," cried Kate, still bubbling.

"Nae maer MacDougall's blood will be spilt on this bloody rock," said Colkitto from above them. He was standing once again on the top of Dunaverty Rock, this giant of a man, dressed in the MacDonald tartan, his white hair and beard blowing in some invisible breeze. His bright blue eyes shone through the deeply etched wrinkles around his eyes as he looked down on them. "My kinfolk are finally at rest. Goodbye, Kate MacPhee, yer braver than yer namesake back in the day. And as fir ye, Jamie MacDonald, I'm proud to ken ye are my kin. Look after that, lassie," he said, then vanished into a mist that headed out towards the Mull.

"Colkitto saved you?" said Kate.

"Aye, he put me safe on a ledge so I wudnae fall. Then he came back fir me when the battle ended. There's nae many people who can say that old Colkitto saved their lives," said Ronan with a twinkle in his eye. "Noo, my wife is gonnae kill me!"

Epilogue

Opening day at Seal Lodge was finally here. There had been a few hiccups along the way and although they were opening six months after they originally planned, the place looked spectacular. Jamie and Kate decided that they would keep the original colour of the building so with its new coat of white paint, the Lodge could be spotted miles away.

The new window frames were a deep mahogany, which was a nice contrast to the stark white building, giving it a warmer feel. The bedrooms were magnificent, each one walled with beech wood panelling, which showed off the green, blue and red of the MacDonald tartan that hung as drapes and covered the soft furnishings. Jamie had decided to use the MacDonald tartan as a theme throughout the Lodge and was thrilled with the end results. The reception area had many paintings of the Mull of Kintyre on the wall, some of them done by local artists. However, on the wall leading from the reception to the bar and restaurant was the most impressive picture of them all. Kate had commissioned an artist to paint a large full-length portrait of Colkitto. She had provided the description and the artist had manged to capture the essence of the old hero after many sittings with Kate. There the great man stood, his claymore in his hands, with a twinkle of humour dancing in these pale blue eyes of his.

The bar area was just an extension of the reception, except for the view that looked over the water to Ireland. There had been quite a few chefs who had applied to take over the kitchen, but they had eventually gone with a young man from Arran named Will. He knew the local produce well and presented some stunning dishes at his trials. Everything had come together, even though it had all seemed last minute.

Eden had a difficult time explaining to Jamie about her transformation. After the battle on the rock, Eden had to return to the ocean if she wished to remain a Selkie. Jamie lost his temper with

Dand, blaming him for not allowing Eden to think it through clearly. Eden tried to explain that it was her choice and it was where she felt most comfortable. Eventually, Kate intervened, telling Jamie that Eden could come and visit with them as often as she wanted. His sister looked glowing and happy, so perhaps he should just try to understand her decision. Eden told him that the ocean had been calling her, she had just not recognised it. Now she was happier than she had ever been. Jamie relented, though he still glared at Dand when they left.

As the months went by, Jamie wasn't sure how he could explain Eden's absence to their sister, but Eden promised that she would tell Carly everything at the opening day. Until then, Eden would visit the Lodge often, making sure to phone her sister each time. It was unlikely that Carly would be able to visit them at the Lodge easily, anyway, with her busy life in Edinburgh.

Isla and Moire had agreed to come to the Lodge opening, along with Eden and Dand. Fionnlagh thought it would be better if he stayed away. He was an unusual, huge white seal, but also a strange-looking giant of a land-dweller. He would definitely raise many an eyebrow, it would draw less attention to the Selkies if he remained in the ocean.

In an ironic turn of events, the Duke of Argyll had come over to see how the rebuild of the Lodge was going, one day when he was golfing at Dunaverty. He offered to come and officially open the Lodge for them. It was an offer Jamie couldn't turn down, but he wondered what old Colkitto would think if he knew that Jamie had allowed the Campbell chieftain to come to the Lodge.

Kate's parents and Jamie's father and his brothers, along with their families, had arrived a couple of days before, which was a blessing. They had rolled up their sleeves and got stuck into whatever needed doing before the big day. They were all really excited about the place and Jamie's young nephews and nieces had a ball exploring the grounds, the beach, the pirates' graveyard and the caves.

Ross MacDonald's remains had been retrieved from the cave and he was given a proper burial by the navy. He had no living family now, but some of the Selkies had attended the ceremony at Campbeltown and Isla had laid a small wreath made of coral on his coffin. There had been a small investigation into what had happened to Ross, but it was left as unexplained. The caves were deemed safe, people came and explored the new caverns that had been found, and, of course, in true traditional Scottish style, old stories started to be created about the gruesome discovery of Ross' bones in the cave. Jamie and Kate laughed it off, it would only bring more curious visitors to the Lodge. There was not a mention of the Preacher's remains.

What was really strange to them was that no one had admitted to seeing anything on the day they were fighting the Preacher on Dunaverty Rock. The sudden darkness that befell them and the ghostly entities went unseen by the golfers, who had carried on with their games, unaware of the battle that ensued around them. Mist was so common on the Mull, that no one had given it a second thought. This made life a lot easier, as they would have found it difficult to explain what they were actually doing up there on Dunaverty. It had taken some doing getting Ronan back down the rock, the old man was shattered, he also had a black eye and had lost his glasses, in spite of his good spirits. Ronan's wife, Sheena, was livid when she heard he had driven his Ford Capris all the way over to Kintyre. She arrived at Kate's later in the day to collect him, and even his black eye (he told her he had a fall) didn't stop her telling him off all the way to her car and, no doubt, all the way back to Arran.

Ronan and Sheena were the first guests to stay in one of the luxury suites at the Lodge. They had arrived yesterday, and a very emotional Ronan had tears streaming down his face when he saw the place. Sheena was overwhelmed with their room, she had bought two new outfits on a trip to Glasgow with her daughters before she came. Last night, Ronan had them up until the wee small hours, listening to him regaling his old stories of the Lodge when the sisters ran it. He held quite the captive audience. Jamie wished he could hire him as a permanent entertainer.

The guests started to arrive around three o'clock, and it was thankfully a beautiful warm sunny day. They were welcomed by a champagne reception and canopies on the newly laid terrace, and, eventually, the Duke arrived, declaring Seal Lodge open. The doors were opened and the guests went in to explore the new hotel.

Jamie looked down at his wife, putting his arm around her shoulders. He and Kate had married a year before in a small ceremony at the Campbeltown registry office. Neither of them wanted a big wedding.

Kate was now expecting their first child, which was due in three months. They decided to move into the Lodge, although they kept Kate's house in case they had a change of heart after the baby came.

Jamie had hired a manager to run the Lodge, leaving him free to look at other local projects. Kate continued with her writing, she had not yet written a story around what happened at the Lodge. It had been her intention, but somehow, it was still too fresh, and she would never be able to write about the Selkies, who would believe that anyway?

"Come on, let's get some air," Jamie whispered in her ear.

"What about the guests?" she asked.

"There are plenty of staff to take care of them, and Ronan will keep them entertained," he laughed.

They walked over to the tennis courts, which had been resurfaced and modernised. Gizmo appeared, sniffing around the old ruin of Keil School House, which still stood looking over to the Lodge, and Kate and Jamie strolled over to it.

"Are you happy, Kate?" Jamie asked.

"Blissfully," she replied and reached up and kissed him.

***

Colkitto stood atop Beinn Na Lice looking out to Ireland, the land of his birth, but not his home. His home had been on Colonsay, it had been on the Hebridean Islands, and it had been here on the Mull of Kintyre, he was a Highlander and would remain so forever.

His last battle had been fought and he had avenged his clan. They lay in peace now, and Colla Ciotach was free to wander his beloved Scotland.

Notes from the Author

Southend and the Mull of Kintyre coastline were and remain some of my favourite places in all the world. When I was a child we would come on holiday to the Mull and stay at the spectacular Keil Hotel. I have so many memories of the place and the sisters who ran it. My brother and I would explore the caves and the beaches and walk the brutally steep road down to the Mull of Kintyre lighthouse, watching Golden Eagles sore overhead. A couple of strange incidents happened, that to this day I cannot explain and would not try to. On a recent trip to Southend with my daughter, she tried to take pictures of me in Keil Caves with her phone. My face was blurred on every one of these shots, for no reason we could fathom. This ghost story is completely from my imagination, but it has a great location with the caves, the pirates' graveyard and all the brutal history.

Seal Lodge is a name I came up with for the old Keil Hotel which is now sadly a ruin. It's huge white walls still stand overlooking the horse shoe bay at Southend. I was told by the lovely lady who owns the Muneroy Tearoom there, that a local fisherman has bought the old ruin and is slowly trying to restore it. I wish him every success as the place holds so many magical memories for me. I would like to thank the locals for some of the stories I learnt on my recent visits there.

The character 'Colkitto' is a Scottish legend. As soon as I heard his name my imagination was set on fire. The facts behind the Dunaverty Massacre and Colkitto's legendary status are straight out of the history books. I bought a book by Kevin Byrne, named *Colkitto! A celebration of Clan Donald of Colonsay 1570-1647*. It was a wonderful book, leaving much to think about, as different historians had different versions of events. I think it is safe to say that back in the 17th and 18th century the Campbells and the authorities would have been happy if the name of 'Colkitto' was wiped from the history books. But that was not to be, and the great highland warrior legend still continues.

The Reverend John Neave (Nave or Nevoy) was indeed blamed for the brutal murders at Dunaverty and was known as 'The Bloody Preacher'. Apart from the fact that he was a Chaplain for the Covenanter cause, I could not discover much more about him. The story I created around him, and certainly his meeting with Colkitto is straight out of my imagination. Although Colkitto was imprisoned and finally executed at Dunstaffnage Castle near Oban, I have no idea if the Reverend John Neave was there.

The Selkies come from the seals who live on the coastline around the Mull. My brother and I used to watch them for hours when we were children and imagined them to be actual Selkies.

I hope you enjoy the story as much as I have writing it. The Mull of Kintyre is a special place.